The *Last* ONE

A NOVEL

TAWDRA KANDLE

The Last One
Copyright © 2014 Tawdra Kandle

Formatting by Champagne Formats

Champagne
Formats

Dedication

To Haley, daughter number two, middle child extraordinaire ... this book would not be here without you. We'll always remember the summer of 2014 as our time of limbo, but your humor, your constancy and your resolve made it not only survivable, but actually fun. I love our book events and beach walks ... and I love you, sweet girl! Remember ... the one you're waiting for is the last one you'll expect.

ONE

Meghan

THE WHITE BRICK BUILDING looked a little dingy in the waning sunlight, but after the three-hour drive I'd just made, I was ready to kiss the cracked sidewalk that led to the door. I pulled my trusty blue Honda into the small parking lot and turned off the ignition. For a minute, I sat in the silent car, resting my forehead on the steering wheel.

A loud bang on the roof made me jump, and I looked out the window at a familiar grinning face.

Owen. Lovely.

I opened the car door and swung my legs to the ground as Owen stepped aside, still resting his hand on the top of my car so that he stood over me. I tamped down my annoyance as his eyes swept down my body in an all too-intimate way.

"Hey, beautiful. Is this good timing, or what? I was just coming by to see if you were back yet."

"And here I am." I stood up, forcing him to step back. "And yeah, it's perfect timing because you can carry my bag." I closed the door and looped my purse strap over my head. "It's in the backseat."

Owen reached for the handle of the backseat door and pulled out my bright pink rolling suitcase. "Just the one? Weren't you there for a week?"

"Five days." I clicked the lock on my key fob. "And I travel light."

"Yeah." He extended the handle and started for the front of the building. "Don't you want to know why I'm here?"

I shrugged. "Not really."

In front of me, Owen's back stiffened just enough for me to notice. He swiped back the long black hair that always seemed to hang in his eyes, and I caught the look on his face. I swallowed a sigh. He was annoying as hell, but he was still a friend, and he didn't deserve to take the brunt of my mood.

"Sorry. I'm tired. It was a long drive up from Florida." I forced a smile as Owen held the door for me. "Tell me why you're here."

Luckily Owen was the kind of guy who bounced back fast from a slight. "I came over to take you to the biggest party of the year. Oswald, Lloyd and Ziggy are throwing a kegger at their new place. Everyone's going. You have an hour to get ready."

The wheels on my bag squeaked as he trailed it behind him across the small lobby. Out of habit, we ignored the slow-as-molasses-elevator in favor of the staircase. I gripped the banister and pulled myself up the steps.

"I don't know, Owen. I told you, I'm tired."

"Aw, c'mon, Megs. You'll feel better once we get there."

I didn't answer, and we climbed the rest of the way in silence broken only by our footsteps echoing against the cavernous walls. I opened the door at the top of the steps, holding it for Owen this time. My apartment was the second one to the left down the hall.

The doorknob turned in my hand, and I shook my head. No matter how many times I warned her, Laura always forgot to lock the door. She was sitting on our hand-me-down couch, a sketch pad on her lap. Her blonde hair was piled high in a messy knot, and she bit her lip in concentration as her pencil moved across the paper. "Knock, knock, I'm an intruder. Thanks for leaving your door unlocked for me, lady." I made my voice deep and tried to sound threatening.

"Meghan!" She tossed her drawing aside and jumped to hug me. "You're home. How was the drive?"

"Long and monotonous, like it always is." I lifted my purse over my head and hung it on the back of a kitchen chair. "How are things here?"

"The same." She glanced over my shoulder, and her left eyebrow rose. "Hey, Owen. Are you pulling bellhop duty tonight?"

He propped my suitcase against the back of the sofa and dropped down into the fuzzy blue recliner. "Right place, right time. I'm trying to talk Megs into going to Oswald's party tonight."

"Ah." Laura met my eyes. "I heard about that. Dani and Ash are going." That didn't surprise me. They were neighbors and classmates of ours, but they'd never met a party they didn't like.

I sank down onto the sofa and let my head fall against the cushion. "No offense, Owen, but I don't want to go to some party where everyone's going to be screaming and drunk. And there're going to be so many people, no one'll be able to move."

"But everyone's going to be there. It'll be epic." He was trying to look confident and convincing, but I caught the hopeful pleading behind the bravado. It irritated the crap out of me.

"Will there be dancing? 'Cause that's what I want to do. I want to dance. If I'm going to get my ass in gear to dress up and go out, it won't be to get pawed by drunk boys and have beer spilled all over me. It'll be to hit a decent dance floor. And I doubt that's going to happen at Oswald's party." I opened one eye and fastened it on Owen.

He shrugged. "Probably not, but hey, we could make it happen. They have a sound system, and we'll plug in and clear a space." He leaned forward, his blue eyes going soft and suggestive. "And I bet we could find a dark corner for some slow dancing. Some special slow dancing." He winked.

I thought I might gag. "God, Owen, is that all you think about? This—" I pointed at him and then at myself. "It happened once. Get over it. No repeat performances."

"Geez, Meghan, can't you take a joke?" He huffed out what was supposed to pass for laughter. "I was just saying, it's going to be a party you don't want to miss. Everyone's going to be talking about it for weeks."

Laura tucked her bare feet beneath her, curling up in the corner of the couch. "Actually, the girl who does my hair was telling me about this place that just opened in her hometown. It's in ... ummm ... God, what was the name of the town?" She rolled her eyes up, thinking. "Burton. She said it's like forty-five minutes southwest, and this bar that opened has a huge dance floor and some killer local bands. The guy who owns it used to be in the music biz, so he gets all the best acts."

I brought my hand down onto my knee with a loud smack. "Sold! We're going to—what was it? Burton? And we're dancing."

Owen fell back in the recliner. "Seriously? You're driving an hour to some podunk town to hang with locals just because they have dancing?"

"Yep." I smiled at him. "You know me, Owen. Unpredictable."

He sighed, long and loud. "Well, I guess I can do that. I can't believe I'm going to miss the biggest party of the year—"

"Oh, no, my friend. This is a girls-only night. You go to Oswald's and get wasted. I wouldn't want to be responsible for you missing a fun time like that."

Owen frowned, and for the space of a breath, I thought I saw a flash of hurt in his eyes. But he recovered fast and shook his head. "Whatever." He stood up and pulled keys from his pocket. "I'm gonna bounce. Later."

I watched until the door closed behind him, and then I let out a long breath. "Crap on a cracker, that boy wears me out. I'm not trying to be mean, you know? But he doesn't seem to get subtle."

"Meghan Hawthorne, leaving broken hearts in her wake as usual." Laura leaned over and bumped her shoulder against mine. "Owen's a big boy. He'll get over it." She stretched her arms over her head. "So were you serious about going out tonight? Or was that just to get Owen off your ass?"

"Of course. I never kid around about dancing, you know that." I shot her a look. "Why, you didn't make up the whole thing about the bar, right?"

Laura held up one hand. "Nope. Scout's honor, Natalie told me."

"Okay. I need about an hour to get myself together." I nudged her with my foot. "Get ready, bitch. Taking no prisoners tonight. We're gonna dance the cowboys off the floor."

"Oh, joy." She reached for her drawing pad and flipped it closed. "Bring 'em on."

"I'LL BE DESIGNATED DRIVER. From the look on your face when you got home, I think you need to let loose tonight." Laura stepped out of our building's front door, concentrating on her high-heels as she navigated the uneven sidewalk.

I twirled car keys on my index finger. "Thanks, that sounds good. Want to take the Honda? Might be a little more dependable."

She tossed me a glance of mock indignation. "Are you insinuating that my car couldn't make this trip?"

"Not insinuating. Saying it loud. I love the Bug, but let's

face it, that car spends more time up on the mechanic's lift than down on the road."

Laura sighed. "Sad but true. Okay, we'll take your *dependable* car, and you can drive us out there, since I'll be getting us home."

"It's a deal." I unlocked the Honda and wiggled into the driver's seat.

We maneuvered our way through the neat squares that made up so much of Savannah, out of the city and onto a two-lane country road. Laura had mapped directions on her phone.

"So we stay on here for about twenty miles, and then we should see the place on the ... it looks like the right."

"What's it called again?" I set the cruise control, frowning a little at the hesitation I felt in the engine.

"The Road Block. Where do they come up with these names?"

"Who knows? If it's serving up liquor and hot music, I don't really care what it's called. I need loud music and enough of a buzz that I don't have to think about anything." I caught Laura's wince out of the corner of my eye.

"What happened this week? In the Cove?"

I grimaced. "Nothing happened. It's all sunshine and roses. Joseph and Lindsay love running the Rip Tide, and Mom seems to be accepting that. She and Uncle Logan are ..." I lifted one shoulder. "You know. Sickeningly in love. She's remodeling the kitchen at Uncle Logan's house. Well, I guess it's her house now, too."

"What about your house? I mean, where you lived before."

"There're strangers living there now. Mom rented it out."

"Well ..." Laura's voice was tentative. "At least she didn't sell it. Didn't you say she wanted to keep it in the family? That's something."

"Yeah." I rolled my eyes. "Not for me, though. It's for Joseph and Lindsay, so one day when they have more kids, they'll have a place to live." I sniffed a little. I loved my brother, no question about that, and my new sister-in-law was great. But still, being at home in Crystal Cove, Florida made me feel like a fifth wheel lately. I was the only one in the family who hadn't had a major life upheaval in the last six months, the only one still on the same boring path. It made me feel both a little self-righteous and left out all at once.

"You know if you told your mom you wanted the house, she'd make sure you had it. Or at least she'd work it out between you and Joseph. I'm not taking sides." She laid her hand on my arm, probably sensing that I was starting to bristle. "I'm just saying, if you look at it rationally, it makes sense. Joseph and Lindsay have the baby, and they're married. It's not unlikely that they'll have another kid at some point, right? So it would make sense for them to need a bigger place to live sooner than you."

"Because I'm the loser without a husband. Or a fiancé. Or even a boyfriend."

"That's bullshit, Meggie." Laura and I had been friends for almost four years, and she was one of the few people who could get away with calling me on my crap. "You don't want that. Or at least that's what you say all the time. You could have any guy at SCAD. I mean, Owen would probably propose if you so much as smiled at him."

"Owen," I scoffed. "Yeah, because that's who I want to spend my life with. A rich pretty-boy who's only worried about the next party, the next good time."

"You're not being fair to him. Owen's a decent guy. He's just not the right one for you."

"I'm starting to think the right one doesn't exist." I rubbed my thumbs over the rubber of the steering wheel. "Not that I'm looking. I don't need permanent. I just need right now."

"That's okay, because the right one is going to be the last one you're looking for. Trust me."

"Whatever you say." I knew it wasn't any use to argue with Laura, who steadfastly believed in soul mates and true love. And why shouldn't she? She'd been with her one-and-only since they were both fourteen years old.

"Did anything else happen while you were home? Seems like something's bothering you."

I shook my head. "I don't know. It just feels like ... everyone has a plan. You know? Mom and Logan are buying a house in Siesta Bay—that's the next town down the coast from the Cove—and they're going to refurbish it and open another bed-and-breakfast. Mom's still partly running the restaurant, and she and Uncle Logan are planning this month-long trip to Europe in the fall. Joseph and Lindsay are both in school and taking care of the baby and doing everything Mom isn't at the Tide. It feels like I'm the only one still in limbo."

"Oh, Meggie, you're not in limbo. You've still got another year of college. You're not supposed to have all the answers yet."

"Yeah? Well, you're the same age as me. But you've got a plan, too."

A faint pink tinged Laura's cheeks. "I have an idea, yes. But I don't have all the details ironed out."

"Bull, Laura." I said it with a great deal of love in my voice. "You know as soon as Brian gets home, that engagement's going to be official, and then you're going to be the best damned Marine wife around. I know you have it worked out to do graphic art online from wherever he's stationed. So don't tell me you don't have a plan."

"Nothing's definite," she mumbled, but she glanced away, out the window, and I knew I was right on target.

"I made a decision about the summer." I hadn't intended to tell anyone, but it seemed right. "About what I'm going to do, I mean."

"I thought you were going back to the Cove and working at the Tide. Doing some private lessons on the side."

"That was before everything changed. I was only going back down there because I thought Mom would need me. She doesn't anymore, not really. Uncle Logan tried to talk me into signing on to volunteer at the art museum in Jacksonville, but I don't feel like spending the summer walking bored tourists around, pointing out the same shit to people who couldn't care less. Plus if I spend the summer in the Cove, I'd end up sleeping with Drew again, and I don't want to go back down that road." My high school boyfriend had never left our hometown, and it was all too easy to fall into old habits when I was there for any length of time.

"So what're you going to do? Are you staying in Savannah?"

"No. I don't know where I'm going to be, exactly. I signed up to work with ArtCorps."

Laura frowned. "I've heard that name, but what is it, exactly?"

"Like the Peace Corps, sort of, but with art. Volunteers teach in areas where all the fine arts programs have been cut or lost funding. ArtCorps assigns art students to summer programs and schools, and we get to work with underprivileged kids."

She raised her eyebrows. "I thought you weren't sure you wanted to teach."

I nodded. "I'm not, but I thought, what better way to figure out if I do? I mean, this is not going to be a cushy job, I know that. But if I can do it, and if I enjoy it, I can be pretty certain about teaching anywhere."

"Yeah, that sounds like a great idea. I'm proud of you, Meghan." She smiled at me. "Do you know where you'll be?"

"Not yet. I put in for the Southwest, because I've never gotten to spend any time in that part of the country. There's a lot of need in the area. And being far away from everyone and everything familiar just feels right, you know?" I glanced at Laura. "I can reinvent myself for the summer. I can go without wearing makeup, dress in old jeans and stuff ... and I'm going to make it a male-free summer. No dating. No hook ups. Nothing. I'm going to enjoy just being me and figure out what I want next."

"Hmm." She stared straight ahead, but I caught a hint of

9

smile playing about her lips.

"What?" I demanded.

"Oh, nothing. Just that most of the time, when a girl says that, she ends up meeting The One."

I stuck out my tongue at her. "Give it up, girlfriend. The whole true love deal isn't happening for me. Not this summer anyway. And look here, saved by the bell. Or at least the Road Block." I smirked at her and turned into a parking lot that was full of cars and pick-up trucks. At the back of the huge gravel lot rose a tall building made of rough-hewn boards, with the name of the bar spelled out in uneven neon letters on the side.

I maneuvered the Honda around random clumps of people who were either loitering outside or making their way to the door. We found a spot in back, far from the entrance. Laura looked around us, worry on her face.

"It's not too bad now, but coming out in the dark is going to be a different story. I'm not sure about this."

"Oh, come on, Lo." I teased her with the nickname that was the only one she tolerated. "We're in the middle of the country. It's a small town. We'll be fine."

She didn't look convinced, but she followed me toward the door behind a small group of girls.

Inside, the place was dark and loud. There were people everywhere, sitting at the bar, around small tables and standing around the dance floor, which I was glad to see was as big as advertised.

"What now?" Laura yelled into my ear.

"Drink, then dance!" I answered, taking her hand and leading her to where the bartenders were trying to keep up with the orders. We stood waiting for a few minutes before one of them got to us.

"What'll it be, ladies?" He grinned, taking us in with an expression that was appreciative without being creepy.

"Rum and Coke for me, just plain Coke for my DD, please."

"Designated drivers drink free." He pulled up the soda hose

and filled a glass, set it on a napkin and slid it across to Laura. "Captain, darlin'?"

"Please." I watched him splash in the rum and then fill the glass with cola. I sipped and nodded, eyes closed. "Perfect. Can we run a tab without a credit card?"

He hesitated. "We usually only do that for locals. But ..." He winked. "I think you two look trustworthy."

"Here." I fished my credit card out of my purse and handed it to him. "Just use this."

He waved it away. "Nah, really. It's cool."

I leaned onto the bar, pressing my arms to the sides of my chest so that my boobs popped out, accented by my v-neck shirt. "I appreciate you being nice, but by the end of the night, I might not be able to think straight enough to give this to you. So let's do us both a favor and just take my card."

He skimmed his eyes down me, raking over my deep auburn curls, tight black shirt and short denim skirt. He shook his head. "Whatever makes you happy, darlin'. But listen, you be careful out there. Nice folks around here, but lots of out-of-towners here tonight. Stick close to your friend here." He nodded at Laura.

"Thanks. Will do." I turned in my seat and took a long drink, scanning the crowd. There was a wide variety of people, with some guys in cowboys hats and others in khakis and polo shirts. Girls in skirts as short as mine hung on men or chatted with friends. Up on a small stage, a group of musicians in jeans and flannel were unpacking instruments and setting up mics.

Across the room, a guy sitting at a table with three of his friends caught my eye. He wore jeans and a gray t-shirt with his ancient-looking boots. He was drinking a long-neck, and a slow smile spread across his face as he looked me up and down. I kept my gaze on him as I brought my glass to my lips.

"See that guy over there?" I spoke to Laura without looking at her, maintaining the eye-lock with Mr. Sexy Cowboy. "Once the music starts, he's going to be over here, asking me to dance.

Want to lay a bet on it?"

"Nah." She shook her head. "No way. There's smolder in those eyes, baby. I think you caught yourself a live one. So what are you planning to do with him?"

I smiled, sipped my drink and pulled my shirt a little tighter. "Anything I want."

Chapter TWO

Sam

THE ROADS BETWEEN KENNY'S Diner and my house were dark and empty. I didn't drive them this late if I could help it, but I never missed a Burton Guild meeting, either. The talk tonight had run long, not because we had any exciting new business to discuss, but because old men liked to spin yarns. And even though all of them were at least twenty years older than me, I had enough respect to sit and listen until Kenny shooed us out so he could close up.

I kept one hand tight on the wheel and clicked on my cell phone, hitting speaker button since Georgia had a strict law about using cell phones while driving, and Ali was even more of a stickler about it.

Her phone rang on without an answer. It didn't surprise me; she was probably still trying to get Bridget to sleep. Either that, or she'd laid down after reading to her, and they'd both fallen asleep. Bridge was seven and the smartest little girl I'd ever known, but she'd always had an issue with her sleep. The pediatrician called it delayed sleep onset disorder or something like that. He said she'd outgrow it, but meanwhile, Ali kept experimenting with different home remedies. The latest was reading her daughter the driest, most boring books we could find. Only problem was, the books put Ali to sleep faster than they did Bridget.

I left a brief message on her voice mail and then tossed the phone back onto the seat next to me. Rounding the curve just before Nelson Road, the headlights of the truck swept over a small blue car, pulled precariously onto the shoulder. I slammed on my brakes, startled.

"Shit." The back of the truck fishtailed as I swerved, just missing the rear of the other car. I maneuvered off the road, pulling about ten feet in front of it. Turning in my seat, I could just make out the silhouette of a girl leaning of the hood on the car, her head bent.

Cursing old men who like to talk too much, thus putting me in the position of having to help some idiotic female who didn't know how to deal with an automobile, I flipped on my hazards, jumped out of the cab of the truck and slammed the door.

The girl glanced up as I approached, and I saw she was holding a cell phone. When I got close enough, she held it up.

"I've called for help. People know where I am. The police are on their way." There was a quiver in her voice, and I realized that she was scared of me. Well, yeah. Here we were on a lonely back road, and I come at her like I'm loaded for bear. I swallowed my irritation and tried to think how I would feel if it were Ali in this position.

Only she wouldn't be, because I keep her car in good shape and she knows better than to drive deserted roads at midnight.

"Okay." I held up both hands. "I'm only here to help. I promise, I'm not going to hurt you."

She made a sound of derision, somewhere between "Yeah, sure" and "Pbbbt." "Because the murderer-rapist is always kind enough to announce his intentions."

She had a point. "All right. Well, here's the deal. I don't know who you called, but no one in Burton is going to be coming out here tonight. If you got in touch with your auto service, they might make it before dawn. Maybe. But there's only one mechanic around here, and he's closed, for sure. So why don't you let me take a look at it for you? If it makes you feel better, you can get back into the car and lock the door before I get any closer. And keep your cell handy, of course."

She eyed me suspiciously. I could see caution battling with a sense of self-preservation—the part of her that didn't want to spend the night alone on the side of this road—and that part won.

"Okay. Come look at it. Please." She didn't move to get back in the car, and I had to give her points for gumption.

"Can you pop the hood for me? And what happened? Did it make it noise or just quit running?"

"It made some kind of weird whining sound, and then all the warning lights came on and started flashing, and then it just kind of ... died." She opened the driver's side door and leaned in to find the hood latch.

"Hey, listen, turn on your flashers while you're there, too, okay? I don't expect anyone else to be coming this way, but you never know. And you're right on the bad side of the curve."

She complied, and soon we were both bathed in intermittent yellow light. I leaned under the hood, holding my phone's flashlight down to see what was happening.

"Do you live around here?" The girl was thawing out a little, though I noticed she still kept her phone clenched in her hand. Smart.

"Yeah, about fifteen minutes down the road. I had a meeting in town tonight, though, which is why I happened to be coming past here." I lifted my head to take a closer look at her. She was wearing those tight legging things Ali sometimes wore to exercise, and over them, a bright red dress. It didn't go very far down, but still, she didn't look trashy. She was short, with long blonde hair that was piled on top of her head, making her look like one of the pixies Bridge loved to watch on TV.

"I'm thinking you're not from this area, are you? What were you doing out here, if you don't mind me asking?" I lifted an eyebrow.

She sighed, long and loud. "My friend and I came down to go to the new bar that just opened outside town. We're both students in Savannah."

I frowned at her as I stood up. "What happened to your friend? Did she—or he—ditch you at the bar?"

"No." She made the single syllable emphatic. "*She* is sitting right there in the car." She pointed through the windshield.

I stepped to the left, and sure enough, I could see a body slumped in the passenger seat. "Is she okay?"

The blonde girl sighed and ran a hand through her hair. "Yeah, she's just sleeping it off. Too much rum. She knew she had a designated driver, and so she might have gone just a little overboard."

"I'll say," I muttered. "So what you're looking at here is a bad serpentine belt. Needs to be replaced before you can drive it."

"Oh, that's just peachy." Frustration filled her voice. "What the hell am I supposed to do about that?"

I leaned my hip against the car, my hand on the top of the raised hood. "Well, the mechanic in town is a good guy. He can get you fixed up."

"But how am I supposed to get it there?" She twisted her fingers, and for the first time, I saw the glint of a ring on her left hand.

"I can help you with that part." I disengaged the hood prop and let it slam. "I have a winch and chain on my truck. I'll take it into town."

Hope blossomed on her face. "I can't ask you to do that. I don't even know your name."

I stuck out my hand. "Sam Reynolds. And you didn't ask, I

offered."

She took my hand in a firm grip and shook it. "Laura Swanson. Thanks. I don't know what we would have done if you hadn't come along."

I glanced at the figure in the car. "Is there someone you can call to come get you once we drop off the car?"

"Yeah, there's—shit. No. All our friends went to this big party in town tonight. I doubt any of them are sober enough to drive." She chewed on her lip. "Is there some place we can stay? A hotel?"

"Not in town. Closest is going to be at least half an hour away."

"Great. Just perfect."

I mulled over the situation. I figured I was a pretty good judge of character, and it seemed like this girl was on the level. I thought of Ali again and spoke.

"Boomer—he's the mechanic—he's got a few loaners that he lets us use when he's working on our cars. Nothing fancy, but it'll get you back to the city."

Laura seemed to sag in relief. "Okay. And you're sure it would be okay for us to borrow it? I can leave a credit card or some cash—" She glanced into the car, thinking about her handbag, I guessed.

"Nah, you don't have to do that. I'll vouch for you." I pointed at my truck. "I'm going to back up closer, so you might want to get in the car for the time being. Wouldn't want to hit you by mistake."

She nodded, and I jogged over to climb into the cab. Turning around to watch behind me, I eased back until the tail of the truck was a few feet away from the Honda. When I got out and began retrieving the chains, Laura joined me again. She watched in silence as I worked.

"You must live pretty far out in the country."

I looked up at her, sitting on the edge of the bumper, her arms crossed. "Yeah." I attached the chain to the chassis of the car. "Got a farm down the road."

"Hmm." She was twisting her ring again. "Is the serpent belt—"

"Serpentine," I corrected.

"Okay, is that going to cost a lot?"

I shrugged, struggling to my feet. "Shouldn't be bad." "Meghan's usually good about taking care of her car. She's going to be pissed."

"This is her car?" I jerked my chin toward the front seat.

"Yeah. Mine is much older. It's my boyfriend's, actually, but he's overseas." She smiled, and through the pride I saw a little wobble of strain. "He's a Marine."

I was never sure how to respond when someone told me that. "*Hoo*-ah!" seemed a little weird, seeing as I'd never been in the military. Sometimes I fell into the lame "Thank you for your service." But now, seeing the hint of worry in Laura's eyes, I didn't have to stop and think. "That must be hard on you."

"Yeah." She held out her hand in front of her, looking down at the ring. "It is, but it's part of the package, you know? Brian always wanted to be in the Corps, so it wasn't a shock. It's part of who he is, and I wouldn't change that." Even in the dark, with only the blinking lights on her face, I could see the love in her eyes. It almost made me feel like I was missing something. I shook it off and finished tightening up the connection.

"Okay, I think we're set here. You'll have to ride in the truck with me. And we'll need to get your friend in there, too."

"That ought to be interesting." Laura stood up and opened the passenger door. I watched her lean in and shake the sleeping girl's shoulder. She finally stirred, and I saw her twist to look up.

"Meghan, come on. The car broke down, and this nice guy is helping us out. You've got to ride in the truck."

I moved closer, thinking they might need a hand. The dome light from the ceiling illuminated a pale face, bleary green eyes and dark red hair that looked like it might have been pulled back at some point tonight. Now it was messed up, hanging over one shoulder.

"What?" The girl blinked at her friend.

"The car needs a new belt. We broke down. You need to stand up and let me help you to the truck." Laura bent further over and unlatched the seat belt.

Meghan was trying to pull her legs out of the car, but she was moving slowly, as though stuck in quicksand. Laura helped her to her feet, where she swayed for a minute, making me wonder if she was about to pass out. I grabbed one arm while Laura looped the other over her own shoulder. Together we stumbled our way to the truck.

I tried to keep my eyes from straying to Meghan's chest, where the deep V of her neckline was riding low and tight over a really nice set of breasts. Her black shirt was hiked up around her stomach, revealing a strip of skin above her short denim skirt. She was taller than her friend, for sure; the top of her head reached my chin. Or would have, if it weren't bobbing around at the moment.

I boosted her into the truck, careful to keep my hands at her waist over fabric, not touching skin or her ass. Laura climbed into the other side and settled her in the middle seat, fastening the seat belt and then going around to sit on the passenger side. I went back to tighten the winch and put the Honda into neutral. When I got into the driver's seat of the truck and started up the engine, Meghan's head lolled to the side, resting against Laura.

I pulled out onto the road, watching the towed car to make sure everything was holding. I was glad Boomer's wasn't too far away, since towing the car made me nervous. I thought I'd made the right connections and tightened the chains, but since I didn't do this often, I wasn't positive.

The tight quarters in the cab didn't make it any easier. The redhead next to me was breathing loudly, and her leg was pressed against mine. I could feel the heat of her skin through my jeans. Her hand was flopped palm-up on her thigh, fingers twitching in her sleep.

"Does she do this often? Get smashed?" I kept my eyes on the road and tried to keep the judgment out of my voice. "No." Laura shook her head. "She had a rough week. Actually a rough year. Her dad died almost two years ago, and last fall, her mom got re-married, to one of their best friends. Meghan likes him, but you know ... it's still difficult. This week would have been her dad's birthday, and we had a school break, so she went home. She got back this afternoon. I think that's why she wanted to just forget everything tonight."

I nodded. If there was one thing I understood, it was grief and wanting to escape from it, any way I could. My preferred method had been hard work and avoidance, but I remembered my fair share of drunken nights, too.

We turned onto Central Street. A few blocks in, I slowed and eased the truck into Boomer's parking lot. I pulled the keys from the ignition and opened the door. "Stay here until I get the car unhitched. I'll get you set up in the loaner in a minute."

It didn't take me long to disconnect the chains and push the small blue car into a spot alongside the chain link fence. I retrieved the keys and locked it up, hesitating a minute before I went back to my truck.

Laura had opened her door and was watching me. I pointed to the small office on the side of the garage.

"So listen. I don't want to offend you, but I need to say this. Boomer's a trusting guy. Everyone in town knows where he keeps his keys and how to get into the office, but we don't talk about it to outsiders. I think you're okay, which is why I'm taking a chance on letting you use the car. But don't tell anyone about this. You might think it's funny and all, but one of your frat boy friends gets drunk and decides it'd be funny to come down here and take advantage of Boomer by trashing his office or stealing his cars ... that's not cool."

Laura frowned. "I won't say anything. I get it. Believe me, I'm just grateful for what you're doing."

I nodded and went back to the office door, reaching high

to find the key along the top of the molding. The door opened easily, and I stepped into the cluttered office. Dropping the keys to the Honda onto the desk, I found a small piece of paper and wrote, "Honda. Needs new serpentine. Laura—"

I leaned out the door, calling through the dark. "Hey, I'm sorry, what was your last name again? And your phone number? I want to leave Boomer all the information."

"Swanson." She rattled off the number and I noted it, tucking the paper beneath the keys. The set that belonged to an ancient Chevette were hanging on a nearby hook, and I grabbed them before locking the door behind me again.

"Okay, let's get you on your way." I stood in the open driver's side door. "Why don't you shove her a little more my way, and I'll just carry her to the car?"

"You sure?" Laura's eyebrow rose.

"Yep, it'll be easier all around. Here." I handed her the Chevette keys. "Go open it up, and I'll bring her over."

I slid my left hand beneath Meghan's knees and at the same time wrapped my right arm around her back and tugged her toward me. She moaned as I lifted her off the seat, settling her against my chest.

Wide green eyes, clouded with confusion, stared up at me. She struggled to free her arm where it was pinned between her side and my stomach. When she could move it, she reached up and touched my face.

I couldn't jerk back, even though the feel of her fingers on my jaw, coupled with the tantalizing view of cleavage I was getting from this vantage point, sent unsettling feelings down my body.

"It's you," she murmured, and the whisper only added to my arousal. Her lips curved into a smile before her eyes shut again.

I stood rooted to the ground for a minute. I couldn't remember where I was supposed to go or what I was supposed to be doing.

"Hey, are you all right?" Laura had opened the passenger

side of the Chevette, but now she walked over to me. "She's okay, isn't she?"

I swallowed hard. "Yeah, I was just making sure I had a grip so I didn't drop her." I strode over to the car and eased Meghan onto the seat. She made a small sound, almost like a kitten, and her hand trailed down my chest on its way to settle in her lap. The jean skirt had hitched up until I could almost see her—

"Thanks, I'll get her buckled in."

I jumped as Laura spoke from behind me. Gritting my teeth, I stepped back and let her through.

"Let me have your cell phone." I held out my hand after she'd shut the passenger door. "I'll put in my number, just in case. I think the Chevette'll get you back to Savannah without a problem, but better safe, right?"

"Yeah." She was quiet as I punched in the numbers. "And someone will call me when the car's ready?"

"Boomer'll probably get in touch Monday. Garage is closed tomorrow, of course, but he'll give you a call, let you know how much it'll be with parts and labor. And then you can just trade out the cars when it's fixed."

"That works." She took back her phone from me, tucking it in her pocket, and then stuck out her hand. "Thanks again, Sam. I don't know what we would have done if you hadn't been driving down that road. You're a lifesaver."

"No problem." I shook her hand and focused on not looking into the car, where Meghan was stirring in the seat. "Drive safely going back."

"Will do." Laura smiled and climbed into the Chevette. I watched while she started it up and pulled out of the lot before I returned to my truck.

Images of green eyes and tousled red hair flashed in my brain as I headed home—again—but I ignored them. It had been a long time since I'd been tempted by a girl, and this one, I knew for sure, wasn't for me. A college girl, one who came with baggage and apparently partied a little too hard sometimes ... nope.

I shook my head to clear it.

I'd go home, have a bracing cold shower, and then I'd forget all about her. After all, it wasn't like I'd ever see her again.

Chapter THREE

Meghan

"PLEASE TELL ME THERE'S coffee. And maybe something to chop off my head. Oh my God, make the pain stop." I stumbled into the living room, one hand over my eyes to hide from the light pouring in through our large windows and the other reaching out for anything that might help me stay upright.

"Good morning, sleeping beauty." Laura's voice held laughter and way too much peppiness for this time of day.

"Fuck the morning. Coffee, if you love me at all."

I heard the clink of the glass pot as I pulled myself onto a stool and dropped my head onto the breakfast bar, covering it with my arms.

"Since of course I love you, here it is. Hot and strong. Just like that dude you brought home last night."

I straightened up so fast the room spun, panic gripping my heart. "God, are you freaking kidding me? Where is he? You're joking, right?"

Laura collapsed against the counter opposite me, holding her middle. "Oh, you should have seen your face. Priceless. Absolutely priceless. Drink your coffee before you knock it over." I reached for the mug and glared at her. "You're a bitch, you know that? A mean, lying bitch. God, you almost gave me a heart attack."

"It wasn't that far-fetched. You wanted to take Mr. Sexy Cowboy home, don't you remember? You tried to talk me into it. Hell, he tried to talk me into it."

"Mr. Sexy Cowboy?" I frowned, trying to remember. The guy who'd been sending me smolders across the room had asked me to dance, as I had predicted. He'd bought me a drink ... maybe two ... and then we'd danced some more. There was a slow song, and I'd felt his fingers at the waistband of my skirt, slipping down over my ass. I didn't remember anything after that.

"Yeah, he was, um, motivated. I had to tell him that you and I were both nuns, and that we'd run away from the convent for one last night of forbidden fun before we took our vows, but that now we had to go back or God would smite us. And him, if he didn't just let you go."

I sipped the coffee, almost moaning in appreciation. "Damn, this is good. So he bought that? He actually believed you?"

One side of her mouth lifted in a half-smile. "I was very convincing. I almost cried. Plus, the guy might have been Mr. Sexy Cowboy, but he wasn't Mr. Smart Cowboy. He had more brawn than brain cells."

"Nice, Lo." I took another drink and hummed. "Well, thanks for getting me out of there and making sure I got home safely. I'm sorry if I was a pain in the ass."

Laura raised her eyebrows. "So you don't remember the rest of the evening at all? The part where your car died in the middle of a very dark, very lonely stretch of country road, and the auto service couldn't send anyone out to us? And where we were rescued by a really nice guy, who towed your car to the nearest garage and then arranged for us to have another car so we could get home?"

My brows knit together. There was a vague familiarity about what she was saying. I could almost remember her leaning over me, saying something about a belt, and then walking along the side of a road and getting jettisoned into a truck. Then the rest of her words registered.

"My car? Where's my car?" I slid out of the seat and ran over to the window. Or I sort of ran; I fast-walked, because my head still wasn't quite sure it was going to stay on my shoulders, and I didn't want to risk it falling off.

In the spot assigned to the sweet little blue Honda my dad had bought me before I started college sat an old ugly brown car. I turned back around. "What did you do with it?"

"Weren't you listening to me? It's at a garage in Burton. That's the loaner. Calm down, Sam said it shouldn't be too long. Boomer's going to call me on Monday."

"Who the hell is Sam? And what's a Boomer?" I was hungover and my car was stuck in some stupid little town in the middle of nowhere. I was entitled to be a little irritable.

"Sam is the wonderful man who stopped to help us last night. Boomer is apparently the owner of the garage, and the mechanic who's going to make your precious car like new."

"Hmm." I turned back and flopped onto the couch. "Do we trust a man named after an explosive?"

"Since he was our one and only choice, we trust him implicitly. And we will thank him for his kindness when we go back to get the car this week. Or rather, you will. Since I had the fun of getting through last night while you were passed out in the front seat, you get to handle car retrieval."

"Awesome. I can hardly wait." I paused as another image flashed across my mind. "This Sam ... what did he look like?"

Laura shrugged. "I don't know. It was dark out there, you know. Um, I think his hair was light brown, maybe almost blond? He was kind of tall. But then everyone looks tall to me. Pretty built, I guess. Why?"

"I think I sort of remember him." But in my memory, I was looking up into the deepest brown eyes I'd ever seen, watching my own hand stroke the side of his face. With a pang, I recalled touching his skin, how the soft stubble had felt beneath my fingertips. Which was ridiculous, because if I couldn't remember leaving the bar last night, let alone the car breaking down, how on earth could I still picture those eyes?

"Well, that doesn't surprise me. He helped get you to the truck and then carried you to the Chevette. You were semi-awake then."

I bit the side of my lip. "His name is Sam, you said?"

"Yeah. Why?" I heard her curiosity.

"No reason. I just want to know who has my car."

"No, that would be Boomer, remember? Sam just drove us there. I don't think you'll see him again."

I closed my eyes against the remainder of the headache still pinging under my forehead and stomped down the feeling of disappointment. Why would I care about not seeing a man I'd been nearly too drunk to remember? What did it matter if it felt like those brown eyes had seen deep into me, maybe the first guy ever to look beyond the surface? It meant nothing. He was just another male, one more in a world full of men I didn't need.

I BEGAN TO FEEL more alive around two that afternoon. When Laura suggested that we log some studio time, I put on some yoga pants and a T-shirt and walked the few blocks to a tall brick building that used to be a department store but now housed classrooms and practice rooms. We had access to the art studios twenty-four hours a day, seven days a week, but the weekends were still the busiest times. I was surprised to see the day's sign-in list was virtually untouched when Laura and I arrived.

"Geez, are we the only losers who care about their craft

today?" I printed my name on the line and handed the pen to Laura.

"Or maybe we're among the few who didn't hit the party of the year last night. Could be the rest of campus is still sleeping it off." She smiled and handed the pen back to the security attendant. I followed her down the hall and into a nearly empty room. The studios were divided between the different disciplines. Laura's major was drawing, with a concentration in pen and ink. Mine was painting. Those two disciplines shared a room, although Laura didn't come down here as often as I did. She could draw virtually any place, and most of her homework and projects could be finished in our living room as well as anywhere else. I, on the other hand, had to be in the studio at least three to four times a week. I was pretty sure she'd suggested us coming down today as a distraction for me, to take my mind off my hangover, but that was all right; I was willing to play along if it gave me some time on the easel.

The room was a study in chaos. There were canvases in the process of drying propped against the walls, half-finished three-dimensional sculptures scattered on tables and windowsills, and boxes of paints and brushes piled here and there. I felt perfectly at home.

"Meghan! Hey!"

I turned my head to glance down the haphazard row of easels, where a tall, skinny boy in chino shorts and a paint-splattered T-shirt was waving his brush at me. Forcing a smile, I returned the wave and clenched Laura's arm. "Don't leave me alone."

"Why?" She followed my gaze. "Oh, shit." As he approached us, her phony grin matched mine. "Hey, Preston. How are you?"

"I'm awesome, just like always." He slung an arm over my neck, pulling me close. I stood perfectly still, trying not to stiffen my body. "What're you ladies doing down here? Gettin' your paint on?" He laughed at his own lame joke.

"Yeah, just putting in some time down here before it gets too intense." Laura slid her eyes to mine. "You know, with finals and everything coming up."

"I hear you. So Meghan ..." He bent his arm, forcing me to look up at him. "I looked for you last night at Oswald's. Where were you hiding, girl?"

I clamped down my lips to hold back a wince. Some guys could pull off calling me 'girl'. Preston couldn't.

"We didn't go. I just got back from Florida last night, and I was tired." It was the truth. He didn't need to know about our adventure into the wilds of Georgia.

"Florida, huh? Rockin' a little spring break action? Wet T-shirt contests? Niiiice."

I ducked from beneath his arm and took a step back. "No, actually, I went home because it would have been my dad's birthday. I wanted to be with my mom and my brother. The closest I got to a wet shirt was when my nephew spilled his juice down his onesie."

Preston had the good grace to look abashed. "Oh ... yeah. Sorry. I forgot that's where you're from." He gave me all of thirty seconds to absorb that apology before he plunged ahead. "So listen, want to go out with me tonight? I thought we could head back to that coffee shop you liked, down on Broughton. Get a cappuccino, and then you know ..." He trailed one finger down my arm, from shoulder to elbow. "See where things go."

"Thanks, but no." I was suddenly nauseated again. "I'm staying in tonight."

"Aw, c'mon, sugar." Preston closed his hand around my upper arm. "We had a good time last fall."

"Sure we did." I pried his fingers off me. "That was then. I'm not interested now. Thanks." I walked away, looking for an open easel, preferably far away from wherever Preston was working.

I picked up a blank canvas on my way and set it up in a quiet section near the windows. The light was good, and I could keep my back to the rest of the room, making it easier to ignore assholes like Preston Riker.

"Meghan." He was behind me, and I closed my eyes, counting to ten.

"Preston, I'm sorry, I really am, but I'm here to work, not to socialize. I don't mean to be rude, but I said no, and I meant no. I'm not interested in going out with you again."

"Don't be a bitch." His tone lost some of its honey. "I like playing the game as much as anyone, but you don't want to mess with me too long. I might get ..." He leaned to speak into my ear. "Impatient."

"I hope you're not threatening me." I unrolled my brush kit. "I'd hate to have to turn you in for sexual harassment, Pres. Though I'm pretty sure I'd find some corroborating witnesses."

"It's not harassment when you want it, too." He slid an arm around my ribs, snugging me against his body. His thumb brushed against the lower swell of my breast.

"What the fuck do you think you're doing?" I grabbed his hand, squeezing it tight and moving it away from me. I pivoted to face him and, keeping him off-balance, I twisted his arm behind his back. "I don't want to make a scene here. But if you don't step away now, you're going to be curled up on the floor, clutching at your dick and crying like a little baby. Get the message. I'm not going out with you. I don't want to see you now or ever. Now go away." I released his hand and pushed him away.

"Fucking ice bitch." Rubbing his elbow, Preston snarled the words, but he stepped away from me and stalked across the room and out the door.

I turned back to my easel and concentrated on taking out my paints and other supplies. My hands didn't shake, but my jaw was tight and my teeth clenched.

"You okay?" There was a hint of sympathy in Laura's voice.

"Yeah." I set the paint tray and brushes on a nearby table. "He's just ..." I shook my head. "You know. Preston. He's harmless."

"Just another of your conquests." This time there wasn't as much sympathy as there was resignation.

I glared at her over my shoulder. "That's not it. I went out with him a few times, and it was fun, but he wanted more than I did. Same old, same old." I picked up a glass tumbler. "I'm going to get some water and start working. Just let me know when you're finished."

Once I was set up with brushes, palette and water, I put on my ear buds and plugged them into my phone. A few seconds later, Bastille flooded through my head, and for the next three hours, nothing existed except music and paint.

LAURA LEFT THE STUDIO before I did, and by the time I got outside, it was dark. Tourists and residents were still wandering the streets of Savannah, and as always, I felt safe as I made my way back to our apartment. I stopped on a corner to give a couple of older ladies directions to The Pirates House restaurant, and I smiled at a group of teenage girls sitting at a sidewalk table.

We ordered in salads from the deli around the corner for dinner and watched our favorite black and white movies, this time making our theme for the evening Claudette Colbert. I went to bed early, slept hard and woke up in time for my eight-thirty Narrative Painting course.

All of my morning classes were within walking distance, but in the afternoon, I had to drive to the other side of town for Conceptual Art Practices. I made a face at the ugly Chevette as I opened it and slid in, but I had to admit that it got me where I needed to go. I just hoped no one saw me behind the wheel.

My phone buzzed after class as I walked toward the parking lot. It was a text message from Laura.

Your car is ready. Sending you address to go get it.

I sighed. I wanted my Honda back, but the idea of driving

31

all the way to that backwater town was not appealing. *Want to ride out with me? I can pick you up.*

I opened up the Chevette and climbed into the driver's seat, waiting for Laura's reply.

Nice try, Megs. You're on your own.

I typed in one last message before I started up the car. *Can't blame a girl for trying. I'll call on my way back. If I don't get kidnapped by the rednecks.*

I plugged the address Laura had texted into my phone's map program and aimed the car out of town. It was a pretty afternoon; only a hint of intense heat that would hit in a month or so floated on the breeze. The old Chevy didn't have air conditioning, so I rolled down all four windows, blasted the rock station and made the most of the ride.

The majority of the landscape on the way to Burton consisted of grassy swampland, dotted by small copses of trees now and then. It looked a little different in the daylight than it had on Saturday when Laura and I had driven to the bar, which I passed a few miles before I turned onto the main street of the town. In the late afternoon sunshine, empty, it looked less exciting than it had under neon and moonlight with a parking lot full of cowboys.

I found Boomer's without any trouble, even though the sign that hung near the curb was faded and rusting. An old tow truck sat in front of the garage, and a rag-tag assortment of vehicles surrounded the building. I pulled in and found an empty spot to leave the Chevette. I didn't see the Honda anywhere, but surely there could only be one Boomer's in a town this small.

Slamming the car door, I walked toward the building. There was an entrance with the word OFFICE stenciled on the window. I didn't see anyone inside, but I could hear music and the sound of machines coming from the garage. I gave the door an experimental push, and it opened with a loud squeak and a ringing bell.

A chest-high counter took up most of the room. There were

a few worn paper signs advertising products and services that were foreign to me. I stepped closer and saw a desk below the counter, covered with piles of papers, some of them edged with grease stains. An old rotary telephone was parked off to the side next to an equally ancient adding machine. Pushed under the desk was a rolling office chair that had been patched in spots with duct tape.

Another door led into the garage itself, and I spied a few men in coveralls bent over an open hood. A piece of notebook paper had been torn out and taped up on the window. It read, *Employees Only. No Admittance.*

I rapped on the glass, hoping to catch the attention of one of the men. But they were running some kind of loud drill, and neither of them even glanced my way. I looked over the counter, in case I'd missed a hidden bell or button. Nothing. I glanced around the room, at a loss. It looked like I was going to have to wait for Boomer to find me.

Tucked back in a corner on the far side of a counter was a cracked brown leather couch. A wooden coffee table showcased a number of what I was sure were the finest in automobile magazines. I maneuvered my way between the two and perched on the edge of the sofa. Taking out my phone, I was about to blast Laura with a text about leaving my car in the middle of nowhere when I heard the squeak and bell of the door again.

I stood up fast, smiling in expectation. When I saw the man in the threshold, my heart thudded against my ribs.

I remembered those brown eyes, though in my memory, they were softer and full of warmth. Now they were wide in surprise.

"You—" I cleared my throat. "Are you—Boomer?"

"No." His voice was deep and sounded vaguely insulted. "Where is he?"

I shrugged, pulling my jacket tighter around me. "How would I know? I thought you were him, so clearly I have no idea."

The man shoved a hand through his hair, his lips pressing together into a thin line. "If he's not in the garage, he'll probably be here in a minute."

"Yeah, that's what I figured. I was just ..." I pointed at the couch. "Waiting."

He nodded, and those gorgeous eyes darted around the room, as though he was anxious to look anywhere but at me. "Here to get your car?"

"Yes. They called earlier." I toyed with the silver ring on my right hand. "So, um, you're the guy who helped us out the other night, aren't you?"

His eyebrows rose once again. "Yeah, I am. I'm surprised you'd remember."

I smiled, this time for real. "I must have woken up just enough to see you. Your eyes—I remember them." I stuck out my hand, though it seemed ludicrous when this man had carried me in his arms only a few nights before. "I'm Meghan Hawthorne. You're Sam, right?"

He stared at my hand before taking his own out of his jeans pocket and putting it in mine, just long enough to grip and then pull back. It was as though he were afraid to touch me. "Yep. Sam Reynolds."

I frowned, looking down at my hand, wondering why he'd seemed reluctant to shake it. "Well, thanks. For saving us, I mean. Laura said she didn't know what she would have done if you hadn't come along."

"I hope you'll think about that before you go out and get wasted again. Do you know how irresponsible that was?"

My mouth dropped open. "What are you talking about?"

Sam pointed at me. "You. Getting so drunk that your friend had to drag you out of a bar and then when your car broke down—*your* car, that she was driving—you were passed out in the front seat and couldn't do a damn thing to help her. Yeah, I call that irresponsible. And being a bad friend, too."

Anger began to kindle down in my stomach. "First of all,

you know nothing about me. Or Laura. You met us at a very low point for me on one night out of our lives. You have no idea how many times I've dragged her drunken ass out of bars or parties, driven her home and put her to bed. Because she's my friend. And regardless of what you might think, I'm actually a very good friend."

He held up his hands like he was pushing me back, though he wasn't standing anywhere near me. "Whoa. I'm just saying what I saw, and that was a girl who was desperate to figure out how she was going to get home or take care of the car, when her best friend was too drunk to even help her figure it out. We had to carry you into the loaner because we couldn't wake you up."

"She was the designated driver. That's how it works." I threw up my hands. "Why am I even arguing with you about this? It's none of your damn business."

"When I'm the one who has to stop and rescue your ass, yeah, damn right it's my business. You—"

"Hey, now. What's goin' on?"

I jumped, my hand flying to my heart in an admirable impression of my own mother's favorite gesture. The voice came from just behind me. Apparently the door to the garage had neither squeak nor bell.

Sam's face was red as his jaw worked. "Hey, Boomer. I just came down to check on those spark plugs you ordered for me."

I tore my eyes from his face and turned toward the man standing at my shoulder. He was about my own height, rotund and balding. I figured him at about fifty years old. His gaze flickered between Sam and me without surprise or judgment, just interest.

"You must be here for the Honda." Boomer ignored Sam, which won him instant points with me.

"Yes, I am. But please ..." I coated my voice with honey. "Please go ahead and take care of Mr. Reynolds here first. I'd hate to hold him up."

One side of Boomer's mouth tipped up. "Plugs are in, Sam.

Give me a minute here and I'll get 'em for you." He stepped around me to get behind the counter, where he flipped a few papers and then slid one across to me. "Replaced the serpentine belt, took her for a test drive. Looks good." He picked up the invoice and squinted at it. "Comes to $131.48."

"Fine. Thanks." I dug into my handbag. "You take credit cards, right?"

"Yup." He nodded and took my Visa from me when I presented it. "Gotta go in the back to run it. I'll have Vic bring the car around the front. Sam, be right with you." He came back around the counter, and I sidestepped out of his way, trying to keep as far away from Sam as I could at the same time.

Boomer paused with one hand on the door to the garage. "Y'all can keep from yelling again while I'm gone, right?" His eyes cut to Sam again, and then he grinned at me and winked before the door shut behind him.

Sam wheeled around and braced his hand against the frame of the main entrance. I took advantage of the opportunity to study his back, the way the thin cotton of his dark blue T-shirt clung to the tensed muscles. Following the line of his shoulder, I eyed his arms, strong beneath the tanned skin, and tried not to remember the feeling of being held against his firm chest. Even as annoyed as I was with him and his idiotic assumptions about me, being in the same room made my mouth go dry and my heart beat just a little faster. I wanted nothing more than to duck under his arm and run my fingers over the ridges I was certain I'd find on his abs.

I shook my head to clear it. The guy might make me hot and bothered, but it was clear that the feeling wasn't mutual. His expression of distaste was something I couldn't ignore, and the fact that he'd judged me based on one night pissed me off.

"Look, maybe I'm out of line—" he began.

I snorted. "You think?"

He ignored me and continued. "But your friend seems like a nice girl, and I hate to see her get taken advantage of. And getting wasted when you're in a strange place, an hour from home, is a really bad idea. That's the kind of stuff you pull in high school, not when you're an adult."

My eyes narrowed, and a feeling of disappointment along with something akin to jealousy filled my chest. "First of all, you're not my father. You're not even my friend. So I couldn't care less what you think about me or your opinion on what's a bad idea and what isn't. Second, Laura's practically engaged, you know. In case you were thinking you're making points or whatever with her by yelling at me."

Sam jerked his head around to look at me, his forehead wrinkled. "What the hell are you talking about? I know about her boyfriend. She told me about him the other night. This has nothing to do with her, other than she must be a saint to put up with someone like you."

My fists clenched, nails digging into my palms. "Fuck you."

His face went dark again. "You know what? Right back at you. I don't know why I should care. Not like I'm ever going to see you again."

"Not in this lifetime."

The door behind me opened again, and I turned back to the counter, resting my elbows on the edge and bringing my fingertips to my temples so that my hands blocked any view of the jerk on the other side of the room. Boomer slapped my credit card and receipt on the Formica and hunted up a pen.

"Here you go. Vic's got her around front, and she's ready to go. Nice little car there. Looks like you've taken good care of her."

"Thank you." I signed the receipt and pushed it across to Boomer. Keeping my gaze firmly on him, I added, "Taking care of your car is the *responsible* thing to do. I keep up with maintenance and I don't drive like a maniac."

Boomer nodded, though the edges of his eyes crinkled in confusion. "Uhh ... yeah. Well, the keys are in it. If you have any more problems with her, y'all give me a call." He stuck one grease-tinged hand into the front pocket of his navy blue coveralls and came out with a creased white business card. "Numbers on here, and all our work is guaranteed."

"Thanks." I forced a wide smile. "I appreciate it, and you've been great, but I'm not planning on being back here again. Ever."

I picked up my copy of the paperwork and pivoted toward the door. Sam took an exaggerated step back, hands behind his back. I opened the door and then let it slam behind me as I stomped to my car. I slid into the driver's seat and went to jam the key into the ignition before I realized they were already in there ... and what I had in my hand were the keys to the crappy little Chevette.

"Damn, damn and double damn." I blew out a breath and wished I could pound my forehead into the steering wheel without drawing too much attention. Instead I climbed out, and gritting my teeth, went back inside. Sam was leaning over the counter, talking to Boomer, and both men turned in surprise at the sound of the bell over the door.

I marched over and dropped the keys onto the counter. "Sorry. I forgot to return the keys to the loaner. It's parked outside. Thanks again for that."

I felt Sam's eyes drilling into my back as I flung open the door again. I didn't bother to acknowledge Boomer's call of thanks behind me. I got into my car, locked the doors and pointed it toward Savannah.

Chapter FOUR

Sam

I BANGED OPEN THE kitchen door and stamped through it, dropping the paper bag with my spark plugs onto the table. The sack tipped over and hit the salt shaker, spilling small white crystals all over the checked tablecloth.

"Sam! What the hell?" Ali turned around from the stove and glared at me. "Don't put your crap all over the table. Can't you see it's already set for dinner?"

I bit back the smartass reply I wanted to make and instead picked up the bag. "Where am I supposed to put it, then? So much shit all over every surface here. I don't have any place to put anything down before you're griping at me to move it."

She stepped toward me and tugged open a large drawer at the bottom of the built-in roll top desk that flanked the long kitchen table. "Here. Put it in the drawer, and feel free to leave any of your precious junk in there. I promise I won't touch it."

I grunted and tossed the bag inside, feeling just a touch of guilt for taking my lousy mood out on Ali. It wasn't her fault I'd had a run-in with the party girl from Savannah when I'd stopped in town, but she made a handy target. Not that I was going to bother to explain it to her; she wouldn't understand why the pretty redhead with the huge green eyes stepped on my every last nerve. Hell, I wasn't sure I even understood it.

"Go get washed up, okay? The chicken's done, and I'm about to pull out the potatoes. Oh, and will you yell for Bridget, too? She's upstairs doing homework."

Without answering her, I headed for the tiny washroom just off the kitchen. I stopped at the bottom of the staircase that sat to the left of the front door and called.

"Hey, Bridge! Supper."

Before I turned all the way around, I heard the sound of foot-steps running down the hallway. The wooden floors in this house were original, built and put down by my great-great-grandfather, and they were beautiful. But they sure didn't do much to keep the noise level down.

I washed my hands and dried them on the rag Ali kept on a hook at the back of the door. I hated her little frou-frou towels, the ones that hung on the side of the antique wooden wash stand, and she hated trying to get grease or dirt out of them after I used them. So by mutual consent, she made sure I had a rag and I made sure I used it.

Bridget was sitting in her seat at the table when I came back into the kitchen. Her dark hair was tied back in one long braid, and her brown eyes, so much like mine, were sparkling. She held a large sheet of white paper in her hand.

"Hey, Uncle Sam! Lookit what I drew." She held it out to me, and I took the paper, studying it closely.

I squinted at the figure. "Is that Poker?" It was definitely a horse, and by the way she'd drawn it, I could see that it was one that belonged to our neighbor, Fred. The proportions were close to being right, and the setting was definitely our own farm. I made out our barn in the background.

"Wow, squirt, look at this. It's da—dang good. Ali, did you see what your kid drew?"

My sister set a bowl of steaming green beans on the table and leaned to glance over my shoulder. "Nice job, baby. Why's that horse on our land, though? I think your picture puts him right in Uncle Sam's melon patch. Probably not a good idea."

Bridget took the paper from her mother and trotted to the fridge, where she added it to her other masterpieces. "That's what it would look like if Poker came to live at our house." She flashed me a brilliant grin, showing off her missing front tooth.

"Poker would be lonely if he came to live here." Ali scooped potatoes onto her daughter's plate. "He'd miss his friends Rummy, Gin and Solitaire over at Mr. Fred's. You wouldn't want that, would you?"

"Noooo." The little girl shook her head. "But they could visit."

"Sorry, toots. No horses here." I stabbed a slice of white meat and put it on my plate. "Pass the gravy, please."

"But Uncle Sammy, we live on a farm. We don't have any animals. It can't be a real farm if we don't have any animals."

"That's not true, Bridge." Ali reached over to tug her daughter's braid. "We have Loopy and Butler."

"But Mom, they're not real farm animals." Her voice came dangerously close to the whine line, and I watched Ali's eyebrow rise. "They're only a dog and cat. And they have to live outside."

"I'm pretty sure Old McDonald includes those, right? With a woof-woof here and meow-meow there, here a woof, there a meow, everywhere a woof-meow ..." My sister had many fine qualities, but singing in tune wasn't one of them. Bridget and I clapped our hands over our ears.

"Make it stop!" I moaned, and Ali stuck out her tongue at me. Bridget giggled, and another crisis was averted.

"The drawing really is good, sweetie. You should take it in and show it to Mrs. Norcross." Ali sipped her water.

"I drew one for her in school today. She asked me if I was gonna take art lessons." Bridget poked at her green beans.

"Hmmm. Did she?" Ali frowned. "Eat your vegetables, Bridget, don't play with them."

My niece dropped her fork to the plate with a clatter. She clutched at her throat and pretended to gag. "Poison ... beans ... killing ... me ..."

I rolled my eyes. She'd been on an anti-veggie kick for the last month. "Just eat them, Sarah Heartburn. No drama tonight."

She scowled at the four beans and then used her fork to push them into the small mound of mashed potatoes she hadn't eaten yet. Before I could yell at her for trying to hide them, she scooped up the whole deal and put it in her mouth, chewed a few times and swallowed. "Done!"

"Chickens are done, little girls are finished. Go scrape your plate and put it in the dishwasher, please." Ali patted her back as she passed.

I watched her skip over, dump crumbs into the trashcan and then slide her plate onto the bottom rack.

"Do I have a little while before I have to get a bath? I want to draw some more."

Ali nodded. "Fifteen minutes, then I'll be up to run it for you."

We finished eating in silence. Bridget had gone a long way to soothing my mad, but in the quiet, I started thinking about red hair and flashing eyes again.

"So guess what?"

I'd known my sister for twenty-six years, ever since the midwife had plopped her onto my four-year-old lap in our living room about twenty minutes after her birth. I knew that these three words were the opening to something she was nervous to tell me. She'd begun that way the day she'd told me she was marrying that loser, Craig Moss, and again when she was pregnant with Bridget. So the wave of dread that washed over me wasn't an overreaction. I put down my fork and stared at her.

"Just tell me. What did you do?"

Ali rolled her eyes. "Talk about the drama. Why does it have to be something I did? Maybe I just have some gossip.'

"Nah, if that were it, you'd start with, 'Do you know what I heard?'"

"Bite me."

"Nice talk for a mom. C'mon, just tell me whatever it is."

"I don't know if I want to anymore. You came home in a lousy mood, and now you're making fun of me." She pushed her chair back and picked up her plate and the empty potato bowl.

"Yeah, well, I had an annoying afternoon."

Ali glanced back at me, interest etched on her face. "What happened? I thought you just went in to pick up the spark plugs."

"I did. Never mind, I don't want to talk about it."

"Did you and Boomer have a lover's spat?" She grinned, wiggling her eyebrows. My sister liked to tease me that the garage owner and I had a relationship that was closer than just friends, mostly because we could talk about cars for hours on end. Hey, girls had their hairdressers and guys had their mechanics. It all worked out.

"I told you, I don't want to talk about it. Stop trying to stall me. What's happening?" I finished my last bite of chicken and began to clear the rest of the table.

"Well ... it all started when Bridget brought home that painting last month. Remember? The one with all the flowers?"

"Yeah." It had been the most colorful piece of paper I'd ever seen, heavy with paint, but somehow more defined than what I expected from a little girl in first grade.

"I ran into Mrs. Norcross, her teacher, the next day. We started talking about how Bridge has a talent for drawing. And painting. She was saying that it killed her that the kids don't get art in school any more, at least not beyond what she does with them."

"When did they stop having art class? What happened to

..." I wracked my brain. "What was her name? Mrs. Downey?"

"Sam, Mrs. Downey was ancient when you had her, and that's been twenty years. They had an art teacher in the elementary school until two years ago, and then they had to cut the program. Not enough money."

"Huh." I rinsed off my plate and put it in the dishwasher. "That sucks."

"Yeah, it does, especially when you consider none of the sports programs were touched."

"Sports have value, too." I thought about my football coach from high school. Coach Trank had been the first person to show up at the house the morning after my parents had been killed. He'd stayed by my side through all the terrible decisions I'd had to make over the next few days—caskets, burial plots and church services—and even now, though he was retired and lived in Arizona, he called me every few months just to check in.

"Well, sure, but nobody's trying to get rid of them. But they stop funding an entire program and not one of us blinks. That's not cool."

"Isn't there an art teacher in town who could teach Bridget?"

Ali poured powdered soap into the detergent compartment of the dishwasher and closed it up with a click, pushing the start button. "Not that I know of. And even if there were, private lessons aren't in our budget. You know that."

I winced. The family farm and food stand, plus rent for the land we'd leased out to neighboring farms, paid most of the bills and kept us fed, but extra money wasn't something we ever had to worry about. I wished I could've afforded to give my sister and her daughter every advantage, but it wasn't realistic. Not yet.

"But no worries. Because I think I found the solution today." Ali walked over to the desk, slid up the roll top, pulled out a glossy red brochure and handed it to me.

"ArtCorps." I flipped it over. "What is this, some kind of

military school?"

"No, silly." She pointed to a list of bulleted points. "It's a really cool volunteer program. Art students are sent into under-served communities to teach the kids. Right now, it's new, and they're just offering a summer course, but if it ends up taking off, Burton could apply for a year-round teacher."

"Okay." I gave her back the brochure. "So do you have to apply? Or I guess the school does."

"Any member of the community can request a student artist. We had a meeting of the home and school association today, and we voted unanimously to apply." She brought her thumb up to her mouth and bit the side of it, and instantly I was on guard. Biting her thumb was Ali's tell. I didn't have the whole story yet.

"And ... ?" I prompted.

She sighed and then spoke in one long sentence without coming up for a breath. "And the one condition is that room and board has to be covered by the community, meaning that the student artist has to live with someone in town for the summer. And I volunteered us."

I groaned. "Aw, Ali, why us? We don't even live close to the school."

She pulled out one of the chairs from the table and sat down. "For two reasons. One, if someone didn't volunteer, we couldn't send in the application, and no one else was stepping up. Two, and this is key, if the art teacher lives with someone else, Bridget will get to learn in class, with other kids, and that's great. But if the teacher lives here, with us ..." She smiled, wide and wicked. "Then Bridge gets the class *and* she has access to that teacher on off-hours. It's like getting free private lessons."

"But a stranger living with us all summer?" I flipped a chair around and straddled it, leaning my hands on the back. "What if it's someone ... weird?"

"Sam, seriously. Why would you assume that? And the program is world-wide, so we could actually get a student from France or Spain ... wouldn't that be amazing?"

All I could picture was trying to talk some Goth-looking chick who couldn't understand me. "And just how are we suppose to communicate with an art student from France? Neither of us speaks anything but English. Georgia English."

"All the student volunteers are English-speaking. And maybe you'd learn something, too. Imagine that."

I pushed back the chair. "I don't need to learn anything else. I'm fine like I am."

Ali sighed. "Okay, but are you all right with us doing this? I promise, I'll try to make it so you're not bothered. She—or he, you know, it could be a guy—can stay down here in Grandma's room." And then she pulled out the big guns, her lips curving into that huge winning smile that had been twisting me around her finger all our lives. "Think of what a great opportunity it'll be for Bridget."

"Okay, okay." I held out my hands, palms toward her. "Fine. I surrender. Pierre Le Pew can stay here all summer and enlighten the young minds of Burton." I stood up and flicked her nose. "Just don't expect me to wear a beret."

Chapter FIVE

Meghan

I'M A MUTTERER.

Ever since I was a little kid, I muttered. According to my mom, when other toddlers were throwing temper tantrums, I was sitting in the corner, my arms folded over my chest, talking low to myself about the injustices of life. She swore it came from spending too much time with Sadie, the gray-haired dynamo who, along with her husband Mack, had worked in our family restaurant for generations. Sadie had a tendency to walk around wiping down tables, talking to herself. Since I'd hung out with her at the Rip Tide since I was a baby, it wasn't surprising I'd picked up some of her bad habits.

I muttered all the way from Boomer's garage in the middle of Burton, down the empty country roads and into the rush-hour traffic of Savannah. And I was still at it when I stalked into our apartment and slammed the door behind me.

"Hey." Laura glanced over her shoulder from the stove, where she was stir-frying something that smelled delicious.

"You get the car back okay?"

"Hmph." I threw my handbag onto the sofa and flopped down next to it. "Yeah, I got it."

"What's the matter?" She leaned her elbows on the counter and frowned at me. "Was Boomer a creep? Did he over-charge you?"

"No, and no. The price was more than reasonable, and he seemed like a good guy." I scowled and jiggled my leg up and down, all my pent-up frustration waiting to burst out. "I ran into your hero while I was there."

"My hero? Who ... oh, Sam? That's funny, that you ran into him. Isn't he nice?"

"No, nice is not the word I'd use for him. He was a jerk."

Laura's eyes widened. "What do you mean? What did he do?"

"He called me immature and irresponsible. He said I wasn't a good friend to you. What did you tell him about me? I felt like he was ready to string me up and brand me with a scarlet D."

"D?" Her forehead wrinkled.

"Yeah, for drunkard. He said I was an idiot and that I put you in danger and ... I don't know, there was more." I sniffed. Now that my mad was subsiding, the hurt feelings were making themselves known.

"Megs, I promise, I never said anything. I mean, he knew you were wasted because you were passed out in the front seat. But I never said anything else. Just that maybe you'd had a little too much rum. I wasn't upset about it." She rounded the breakfast bar and sat down next to me on the sofa. "C'mon, you know I'd never complain about being your designated driver. You've done it for me enough."

"That's what I said. God, Lo, he was so mean. I've never had anyone who I just met hate me like that."

"Yeah, it usually takes at least a month." Laura elbowed me in the ribs, and I couldn't help a tiny smile.

"Whatever, bitch." I closed my eyes, drew in a long, deep

breath and then let it out in a whoosh. "Okay. I am officially letting it go, forgetting about him. Tell me what you're making over there. It smells yummy."

"Veggie stir-fry. You sit still, I'll bring it over."

I didn't have to be told twice not to move. My temper was legendary among friends and family, but after the worst hit me, I was drained.

"I'd offer you a glass of wine, but we all know what a lush you are. If I give you something to drink, you might go off and be irresponsible and immature again."

"That's me. Don't forget thoughtless. And idiotic."

Laura set down our food on the coffee table, and we ate in silence for a few minutes.

"You're brooding." Laura laid her chopsticks across the plate. "He really got to you, didn't he?"

I lifted one shoulder. "It just took me by surprise, I think. I was kind of happy to see him when he walked in, you know? To say thank you for his help, and then he just jumped all over me."

"Or maybe you wish he had. Jumped you, I mean."

I screwed up my face. "What are you talking about? I don't even know him."

"Yeah, but what he said really bothers you. Meggie, I've heard people say horrible things about you right to your face. Nothing ever fazes you. You blow it off, or you laugh. Or both. But for some reason, what this stranger spouted off got under your skin. Don't you wonder why?"

"Are you saying it stung because there's truth in it? Is this an intervention? Shouldn't there be a sign?"

"Don't be stupid. You're not an alcoholic. I'm just saying maybe it's not so much what he said but that it was Sam saying it."

"Why should it?"

She smiled and raised one eyebrow. "Maybe *he* matters. Maybe you had some kind of ... instant connection. You know, like with Meg Ryan and Tom Hanks in *You've Got Mail.* Even though he was obnoxious, she was drawn to him.'"

I shook my head. "Lo, give it up. This is real life, not a movie, and I wasn't drawn to him. He's the equivalent of a grouchy old man, only he's not old. At least, not that old. And besides ..." I remembered his parting words to me. "It's not like I'm ever going to see him again. You couldn't pay me enough to go back to that dinky little town."

IF I THOUGHT ABOUT Sam Reynolds at all over the next month, it was only a fleeting memory, some little stab of hurt pride as I fell asleep at night. Laura and I were both busy with finals and end-of-the-term projects, and some days we hardly saw each other. Sleep became a scarce commodity as I pulled more than one all-nighter at the studio.

When I did see Laura, I could tell that she was walking around in a state of nerves and excitement. Brian was supposed to come back stateside at the end of May, and they'd planned for Laura to spend the summer living near his new assignment in North Carolina. Brian had to stay in the barracks on base, but Laura was sharing an apartment with one of his buddy's girlfriends who lived there year-around. I knew she was counting the days until his return, even though she was nervous.

"We haven't seen each other in over a year." She was sitting on our living room floor, laying out a chronological drawing project that was due the next day. "What if I'm not the person he expects to see when he gets back? What if we've both grown too far apart?"

"Lo, get real. You talk to him once a week, you email all the time ... and I've never seen anything like the two of you. No, that's not true." I rolled to my side on the sofa, where I'd collapsed after a particularly grueling final exam. "My mom and dad were like that. When my mom came into a room, everything stopped for my dad. He only saw her, and it was the same for her with him. That's going to be you and Brian. Forever."

She looked up at me, and I saw the understanding shining in her eyes. "Oh, sweetie, that's about the most wonderful thing you could say to me. Thank you. I know it's going to be okay. I'm just—" She put her hands to her cheeks. "You know, a bundle of nerves. Once I know Brian's back here, on American soil, I'll feel better. I can't relax until then."

"Then we'll just keep thinking about that. Just a few more weeks, right?" I grinned at her and pushed to sit up. "God almighty, I'm exhausted. That test wiped me out." I reached for the coffee table to pick up my tablet. "I'm going to check my email real quick and then go to bed. I'm beat."

"I'll be up for a while finishing this. Luckily, I can sleep late tomorrow morning."

I opened up my mail program and scanned the inbox. Junk, spam, a picture of my nephew DJ—I opened it fast and smiled at his sweet chubby face. More junk, something from ArtCorps—

"Laura!" I jumped to my feet. "From ArtCorps! It's my assignment for the summer."

She turned to look up at me. "What did you get? Arizona? New Mexico? Ooooh, SoCal?"

"I don't know, I haven't looked yet. I'm almost too scared. I've been so excited about this. What if I get, like, the mid-west? Or Alaska? I don't think I'm cut out to be an Inuit."

"Open it! Come on, inquiring minds want to know."

"Okay." I took a deep breath, pressed my hand to my fluttering heart and touched the message. My eyes skimmed down the page as I read the high points aloud. "Congratulations, happy to have you on board this project ... report June first, transportation ... supplies ..." My voice trailed off as I read the final paragraph.

"No way. No. Fucking. Way."

"What? Tell me. Alaska?"

I fell back onto the couch, dropping the tablet onto the cushion next to me. "Someone hates me. Maybe God. Maybe fate or whatever's out there. I can't fucking believe this."

"Meghan Hawthorne, tell me. Or I'll come up there and smack it out of you."

I lifted my head and stared down at her. "You're not going to believe it even when I tell you. Or maybe you will." I swallowed hard and let my head drop to the sofa cushion. "ArtCorps has assigned me to Burton. Burton, Georgia."

Laura didn't move. Her eyes widened, and her mouth dropped open. "You're kidding, right? You've got to be kidding. There's no way ..."

Without another word, I handed her the tablet and watched her read the email. When she finished, she laid the tablet on the coffee table and gazed at me. "No fucking way. Well ..." She sat back on her heels. "At least you know the town has a decent bar, a place to dance and a trustworthy mechanic."

I flipped her the bird.

"Nice. Can you ask them to change it? Switch you? Maybe they made a mistake."

I shook my head. "I can ask, but it won't happen. When I signed up, I agreed that I'd work wherever they assigned me."

"You have to admit, this is weird. I mean, you've never been to Burton the whole time we've been in school here. Then we just happen to go to a bar, your car just happens to break down there ... and lo and behold, your assignment for the summer is that same town."

"What're you trying to say? The universe is conspiring to screw up my life?"

She rolled her eyes. "No, I think the universe is moving you to the place you need to go. Now it's up to you: are you going to roll with it or fight the tide?"

"No ocean analogies, please." I closed my eyes, trying to settle my mind and think clearly. "I don't know what I should do."

"Look, Megs. You really want to do this program, right? You were so excited about it."

"That's when I thought I was going to be a hippie artist in New Mexico."

"Yeah, I get that. But was it really the setting or what you were going to be doing there?"

I pursed my lips. "Will I sound terribly shallow if I say a little of both?"

"Nope. But remember why you wanted to sign up in the first place. It was to teach kids, to find out if that's what you want to do long-term. Right?"

"Yes." I nodded. "You're right. I just thought I'd go a little further from home to figure it out." I stared down at my hands. "I need to be away from everything. And from everyone. I'm tired of being Meghan Hawthorne from the Rip Tide when I'm at home. Or Meghan Hawthorne who sleeps with lots of boys but can't keep a boyfriend when I'm in Savannah."

"It's not that you can't." Laura rubbed my knee. "You choose not to have a boyfriend. Love 'em and Leave 'em Hawthorne, right? Isn't that what you wanted, never to be tied down to one guy?"

"Sure." I swallowed over the lump in my throat. "I guess. But Lo, it's exhausting. I need a break from being me. I thought that was what this summer would be."

"It still can be that. No one knows you in Burton, except that Boomer dude." She wiggled her eyebrows. "And of course Sam."

"Yeah, that's what I'm afraid of. I'll be walking into a situation where at least one person has already decided I'm a drunken slut."

Laura rolled her eyes and shook her head. "You might be exaggerating a tiny bit. But it's your decision. What're you going to do?"

I ran my finger along the seam of the sofa cushion. "I think I'll call tomorrow and find out if there's any way to change it. But if not, I guess Burton it is."

At nine o'clock sharp the next morning, I was on the phone,

listening to the recorded voice prompting me to press one for help with an application or two for a list of locations where Art-Corps would be sending volunteers this year. I hit zero and waited for a live person.

"Good morning, this is Tina. How can I help you?"

I mustered up my best professional voice, the one I'd perfected over years of waiting tables at the Rip Tide, dealing with rude tourists and testy locals. "Good morning, Tina. I'm Meghan Hawthorne, and I—"

"Oh, Meghan! Hi. I remember your application. Actually, I processed it myself."

"Wow. What are the odds?" I bit the corner of my lip.

She laughed. "Better than you might think. We're pretty small here, since we're just starting out. Everyone pitches in. And I remember you because I was so excited about the location we matched you with. It was a last-minute add, and when I read their needs, I thought about you right away."

"Oh. Really?" I tried to keep the skepticism out of my voice.

"Definitely. They're so excited about you coming. We sent them your portfolio, and the home and school association said you were exactly the kind of teacher they'd hoped to have. I spoke to Mrs. Moss yesterday. She was positively giddy."

"Mrs. Moss?" I searched my memory for the name.

"Yes, she's your host. She's been the driving force behind getting ArtCorps to Burton, and she also agreed to open her home to you while you're in town. She was telling me about where she lives, and I have to tell you, I'm jealous. Apparently it's a farm house that's been in her family for generations."

"I'm sure it's lovely." I hesitated, not wanting to sound unappreciative in the face of Tina's enthusiasm. "I just wanted to check, though, and make sure that there hadn't been a mistake. I read that usually you try to give applicants their first or second choice of locations. I had said either the southwest USA or the west coast."

"Yes, that's true. We do try. But we had a few special circumstances this year. We had a number of people request Arizona or New Mexico. We had intended to place you in northern California, but then one of our volunteer applicants had a family emergency. She's from that area, and her mother is ill. She asked for a special placement, and when the request from Burton came in, everything fell into place. I'm sure you understand."

I did, all too well. I'd had my experience with a sick parent, and if giving up my spot in California let someone else have more time with her mother, I was fine with it. I still wasn't sure about Burton, though.

"So if there's nothing else ..." Tina was ready to wrap up this convo.

"Just so I can be clear, there's no other options for me as far as location? No way for me to ... I don't know, switch with someone?"

"No, we don't allow switching." Tina's voice lost some of its patience. "We're careful about how we make the assignments. We have a process. Your options are either Burton or withdrawing from the program."

I gritted my teeth. "Okay, well, thanks. I'm sure Burton will work out fine. I appreciate your time." I turned off my phone and stuck out my tongue at it. Or rather, at Peppy Tina who'd been on the other end up until a few seconds before. Damn her and her process that was sending me to purgatory in the form of Backwater, Georgia.

"You're up bright and early." Laura shuffled out of her bedroom, blinking at me. "Everything okay?"

"Sure." I rubbed my forehead, where a wicked headache had just begun to blossom. "Guess where I'm spending the summer?"

Chapter SIX

Sam

IN THE MONTHS AFTER my parents died, I had to make way too many hard decisions. Would I be Ali's guardian? That wasn't even a question. She was fourteen, and sending her off to live with our grandparents in Alabama was the last thing either of us needed. Would we keep the farm? That was more complicated. The land where I'd been born, where generations of Reynolds had lived and died, wasn't something I could toss away lightly. But I was eighteen, just about to graduate from high school. I'd been working with my dad as long as I could remember, but helping out was a far cry from running the place.

That was when the Burton Guild had stepped in. Those men walked me through my options, and from the vantage point of twelve years distance, I knew they'd saved our lives. The Guild had helped me decide how much land I could reasonably manage on my own, and then they'd found people to lease the rest of the farm. The idea was that as I gained years and experience,

I would be able to take back parts of the farm that I needed, as I needed. It was a good plan. So far, we'd been able to close out two leases.

I stood now in the late afternoon sun, scanning the acres of rich red Georgia clay. The field that butted the rear property line was my favorite place to stand at the end of the day and survey what I'd accomplished and what still needed to be done. Vidalia onion plants surrounded me, healthy green tops swaying in the breeze. Harvest was underway, but it was a slow and painstaking process that had to be done by hand. We'd hired on a few high school kids to help as we did every year, and the work was coming along. Several truck loads of the bundled onions were already crated in the barn, and we could barely keep up with the demand at our farm stand.

The stand was our main source of income. It was well known in the area and had been since my great-grandparents had sold their first basket of tomatoes back in the thirties. I glanced down at my old beat-up work watch, the one I wore in the fields to keep track of time so I didn't have to risk losing or destroying my cell phone. Ali should be closing up about now, walking back to the house with Bridget. I snagged a bunch of onions, thinking of dinner, and made my way through the half-picked rows.

I passed through the tomato plants, pausing to rub a leaf between my fingers. Something was eating them, and I frowned. I'd have to amp up our organic pest spraying—only natural ingredients, as defined by the state—or risk losing the plentiful white blossoms and tiny baby green fruit. If there was one thing I'd learned over the past decade, if I got lax on any front, the bugs, the critters or the weather would get ahead of me, and I'd lose plants, food and money.

The walk back to the house was quiet, with only the occasional buzz of cicadas to keep me company. At the shed, I stopped, stripped off my sweat-drenched T-shirt and ran water in the old sink. I used the rag hanging on a hook nearby to wash my face, my arms and my chest. I remembered my dad and my granddad making this stop every day during the spring, summer and fall as they returned from fields, and it had become part of my ritual, too. Ali said it saved on the mess in my shower and in the kitchen sink, and anything that kept my sister happy was worth doing.

I climbed the two steps to the kitchen door and opened it, making a mental note to oil the squeak tonight. Or maybe this weekend. I tried to remember where I'd left the WD-40.

"Sam, is that you?" Ali called from the front of the house.

"No, it's your other brother who's been working out in the fields all day and brought you some fresh-picked onions. Who else were you expecting?"

"Could you please come in here and stop yelling?"

I frowned. What was she up to now? I tossed my dirty shirt into a basket in the laundry room and followed the sound of her voice.

"What do you ..." I began speaking as I rounded the corner and then stopped abruptly. All rational thought left my brain, because sitting on my mom's blue love seat was an all-too familiar red-head with big green eyes that mirrored my shock.

Her eyes closed, and I saw her lips press together as her chest rose and fell in a deep breath. Her chest. No, I couldn't go there. I jerked my gaze up and stared at my sister.

"What the hell's going on? What's she doing here?"

Ali's eyes widened. "Sam, language. And what's wrong with you? This is Meghan. Our ArtCorps volunteer. She just got here a little bit ago, and Bridget and I were showing her around." She drilled me with a hard stare that said I was being rude, I was embarrassing her, and if I didn't pull it together, she was going to make me pay.

"I didn't know it was you. I had no idea. I mean, I knew it was the town, but it's not like I chose to come here. I was assigned." Meghan spoke through clenched teeth. "I wasn't supposed to be in Georgia. I signed up for Arizona. Or New Mexico." She stood up. "I'm sorry. I can leave. I can—"

"No." Ali caught her arm. "Just hold on a minute. I'm lost here, but clearly you know my brother. Or at least he knows you. Would one of you care to fill me in?"

Involuntarily I glanced back at Meghan. Her eyes had fastened somewhat south of my face, and I remembered I wasn't wearing a shirt. Her lips parted a little, and I saw the tip of her tongue dart out.

"Any time now, Sam." Ali's arms were folded, and she was wearing her no-nonsense mom face.

I exhaled and rubbed the back of my neck. "Remember a few months back when I stopped on my way home to help the girls whose car had broken down?"

My sister's brows drew together. "Yeah, I think so. From out of town, right?"

"Yeah. Well, Meghan was one of the girls."

"Okay."

I looked down at the floor, studying the intricate design at the edge of the Persian area rug. "Then I ran into her again. At Boomer's, when she was picking up her car."

Ali rolled her hand in a keep-going gesture.

"I may have ... I guess I kind of, uh, gave her a hard time about being drunk that night. When her car broke down. I might have gone a little overboard with it."

Ali opened her mouth, and then she popped it shut. She looked at Meghan, and then at me. "What exactly did you say to her, Sam?"

I flushed. "I don't remember. Um, I guess, that she was irresponsible. And that it was stupid to get so hammered when you're in a strange place."

"And that I wasn't a very good friend to Laura," Meghan added. When both Ali and I turned to look at her, she glanced away. "Sorry."

"Sam, did you lose your mind? Why would you ..." Ali shook her head. "Was she driving drunk?"

She already knew the answer to that question. I'd told her all about it the morning after I'd towed Meghan's car to Boomer's.

"No. Her friend was the designated driver."

"Uh-huh. And just how was this any of your business? What did she say to you at Boomer's that day?"

I swallowed. "She said ... thank you. For helping them."

Ali blinked several times in rapid succession. Shit, she was pissed. I knew the signs. I braced myself, ready for her to explode on me. Instead, she swung her head around to Meghan.

"Meghan, I'm so sorry. My brother is an ass. I have no clue what got into him to say those things to you. Sometimes I think he was raised by wolves. But please, don't let his idiocy ruin this for all of us. I promise you, I'll make sure he behaves while you're staying with us." Ali gripped my forearm, her nails digging into the skin. "Right, Sam? You're going to try to remember how to be a decent person. You'll be courteous, and you'll tell Meghan how happy you are that she's here to teach in Burton."

Before I could get out an answer, she added one final shot. "And you'll apologize, right now."

"He doesn't have to do that." Meghan fiddled with the strap of her handbag. "He was right. I shouldn't have gotten so carried away that night. I was upset, and I used that as an excuse. I put Laura in a bad position."

If she 'd acted like a spoiled brat or let Ali force me into an apology, I could've hung onto my resentment. But agreeing with everything I'd said that day made me feel like scum. It didn't help when Ali put an arm around her shoulders and rubbed her back.

"Oh, aren't you sweet to let him off the hook ... but you shouldn't. Trust me, my dear brother has had his share of getting carried away, as you put it." Ali shot me a dark look. "Why're you just standing there, with no shirt on? Go get showered. I'm going to show Meghan to her room and then get started on dinner."

60

"Where's Bridget?" I stopped at the bottom of the steps.

"One of the girls from the stand is dropping her off after they close up. I wanted Meghan to be able to get settled before we let Bridge at her." Ali picked up the small suitcase that sat by the front door. "Your room's this way, Meghan."

I watched her follow my sister around the staircase and down the short hall that led back to the only downstairs bedroom. She didn't look my way, but I couldn't tear my eyes away from the swing in her hips.

And if I groaned as I stomped up the steps, who could blame me?

"... SO WHEN I HEARD about ArtCorps, I was really excited. The kids in Burton can't wait to meet you. We've got a room set up for you at the elementary school, and don't worry, it's air conditioned." My sister hadn't stopped talking for a solid ten minutes, and when she paused to take a breath, Bridget took over. Meghan hadn't said much beyond "Yes" and "Thanks." I hadn't said anything at all.

"I'm looking forward to meeting everyone." Meghan smiled at my niece. "What's your favorite medium?"

Bridget's eyebrows drew together, and Meghan hurried to clarify. "I mean, what kind of art do you like best? Drawing, oil color, watercolor, sculpture ... ?"

"I like to paint." Bridget took a bite of lasagna.

"That's my favorite, too. I like watercolors." Meghan wiped her lips. "Maybe we can do some painting around the farm while I'm here. What's your favorite subject? Uh, what do you like to paint? The sky, or plants, or animals?"

"She likes horses." I hadn't meant to speak until I heard the words spurting out of my mouth. All three females at the table turned to look at me.

"Yup, I like to paint Mr. Fred's horses. Uncle Sam won't let them come live here, even though this is a farm and the only animals we have are Loopy and Butler, and even though they're in Old MacDonald—" She shot her mother a reproving look. "They aren't real farm animals."

Meghan laughed. "What are they, then?"

"Loopy's a dog, and Butler's my cat. They live in the barn."

"Ah." She nodded. "But at least you have them. I never had any pets growing up. Oh, except my brother had a hermit crab one summer."

Ali stood up to clear the table. "So where are you from originally, Meghan?"

"Florida." She glanced away, her mouth tightening, and I remembered her friend Laura's words.

Her dad died almost two years ago, and last fall, her mom got re-married, to one of their best friends. Meghan likes him, but you know ... it's still difficult.

"And do you have just the one brother?" Ali was in full discovery mode. I watched Meghan to see if it was bothering her, but her face was pleasantly blank.

"Yes, just one. Joseph. He's younger than me." She laid down her fork, lining it up with her knife.

"I wish I had a brother." Bridget picked up a piece of tomato from her salad plate and popped it into her mouth. "Or a horse."

We all laughed, and Ali shook her head. "Sweetie pie, I think you have a better shot at the horse at this point. If you're finished eating, bring your plate over and then run upstairs for your bath."

"But I want to talk to Meghan." I heard the hint of whine and stepped in to save her from the wrath of her mother.

"Hey, squirt, she's not going anywhere. You heard your mom. Get moving." I gave her a light swat on the backside.

"Okayyyyy." Bridget dragged out the last syllable and favored us with a sigh that was laden with drama. "Promise you won't go to bed before I come back down?"

"I promise." Meghan nodded with all due solemnity and picked up her plate as Bridget scampered away. Holding it in one hand, she leaned to pick up a bowl, and I tried not to notice how the neckline of her green shirt sagged, giving me a tantalizing glimpse of cleavage.

"Sit down, Meghan, you don't have to help. Sam, you do. Get off your ass."

Meghan kept clearing the table. "I like to be useful. Oh, and I have years of experience waiting tables, so I want to keep my hand in."

"When did you work as a waitress?" Ali took the dishes from her and rinsed them under the water.

"Pretty much from infancy on. My family owns a restaurant on the beach in Florida."

"Oh my gosh, really? How fun. What's it called?"

"The Rip Tide. My great-grandparents started it, and now my mom runs it. Well, my mom and my brother and sister-in-law, I guess."

Ali turned to grin at me. "Sam, isn't that cool?" She slid more plates into the dishwasher. "Sam loves the beach. When he was a teenager, he wanted to move to California and become a surfer."

I rolled my eyes. "I think I was ten." I pushed my chair back. "I'm going to walk over to the stand and make sure they locked everything up."

"Oh no, you're not. Everything's fine over there." She closed the dishwasher and then leaned against it, hands on her hips. "I need to go up and make sure Bridge is actually getting clean in the bathtub and not just drawing with the bubbles." She pointed at me. "You're going sit right back down and do your best to be a decent person. Show Meghan that you're not the total dick you might seem to be."

"He doesn't have to stay. I don't need a babysitter." Meghan softened the words with a smile. "I'll just go unpack or something."

I ignored her and addressed my sister. "Ali, you know I won't sleep tonight if I don't check on the stand. Cassie Demeyer might be a very dependable high school junior, but she's not you. I'll be ten minutes, tops."

"Fine." Ali smiled, and for the space of one inhale, I actually thought I'd won. And then she added, "Take Meghan with you. It'd be nice for her to see a little of the farm."

"Ali." I ground out her name. "Stop this. You're not my mother, and you don't have any right to try to teach me a lesson. Or make me pay for what I said."

"Maybe that's something you need to remember, brother dear. But I'm not trying to punish you. I just think Meghan might enjoy the walk."

"I would." Meghan surprised me by taking Ali's side. I had expected her to want to be as far from me as possible. "And I'd like to scout out some possible places to paint while I'm here. Maybe see some spots I could take Bridget."

"Fine. Whatever. God knows I can't fight two stubborn women." I strode out the kitchen door, letting the screen bang close behind me.

"Samuel Pierce Reynolds, our mother is rolling over in her grave right now." Ali's furious face looked at me through the open window over the sink. "You mind your manners."

The door opened again, and Meghan stepped out. A light breeze stirred her hair, and the last rays of sunshine glinted on the red curls. She paused, regarding me steadily.

"If you don't want me to go with you, it's fine. I'll just look around on my own. Your sister doesn't have to know anything."

"She'd know," I muttered darkly. "She always knows."

Meghan lifted one shoulder. "Well, I'll go with you then, but you don't have to talk to me. You can walk in front, and I'll be quiet. I do know how to do that."

If that was a dig at me, I chose not to respond. Instead, I began walking across the yard, cutting through Ali's herb garden and one of the empty fields. Over the last eighty years, my family had worn a path between the house and the main road, where our stand was located. I followed it without thinking, my mind preoccupied with the girl meandering behind me.

We skirted around a field of trees, and I paused to point it out to Meghan. "This is the peach orchard. It's part of our land, technically, but I leased it out to another farmer. For now, at least. One of these days we'll be ready to deal with fruit again."

She stood next to me in silence, close enough I could breathe in her scent. It was musky and warm, making me think of the fields in high summer, when everything smelled alive and vibrant.

"When are the peaches ripe?" She squinted, checking out the trees.

"Ah, about another month or so. Clingstones are already being picked, but these are Semi-Freestones." I reached for a branch and examined the fruit. "Yeah, maybe three weeks. When they're ready, go ahead and help yourself to these trees. It's part of our agreement with the renter."

"Good to know." She smiled, and I thought of that night, holding her in my arms, when she'd reached up to touch my face. "I do love peaches."

Because I got a sudden image of her biting into a peach with juices dripping down her chin, running between her breasts, I only grunted and started walking again.

The Colonel's Last Stand wasn't fancy. We still operated out of the original lean-to shed that my grandfather had put up during the Depression. Over the years, each generation had added a little more, though: it was enclosed on three sides now, and we had a fourth wall that we slid across when day was done. The register was against the back, and we had several permanent shelves that held jellies, pickles and local honey.

I pulled keys from the pocket of my jeans and opened the padlock fastened on the front sliding wall. It rolled back easily, revealing the tables of produce and baskets of fruit.

"Wow." Meghan stood in the doorway, watching as I made

sure the register had been shut down and locked. "It smells like heaven in here."

I breathed deep and nodded. Strangely it mattered to me that this girl who I'd only met three times—and only twice sober—understood at least a little of why this place was special. She wandered among the tables, running her fingers over the tomatoes and picking up a bunch of onions to examine them.

"Do you get a lot of fresh produce where you live?" When I thought of the beach and the food there, I only pictured fish and seafood. But it was Florida, too, so I guessed there was more to it than that.

"Oh, yeah. Depends on the time of year, but we get strawberries in February, corn by early May, and oranges on and off as they get ripe. My mom has contracts with local farmers for other food, too. You know, like lettuces, tomatoes, cucumbers, whatever."

"Yeah." I gave the shadowed building a quick scan and assured myself that everything was all right. When I headed back out, Meghan followed me, stepping into the waning sunlight. I rolled the door back over and locked it. "Okay, we're good to go here." I turned back to the path.

"The stand looks like it's been here for a while." Meghan was walking next to me now instead of a few steps behind. I tried not to care about that.

"My great-grandparents opened it with a few baskets of peaches, tomatoes and onions back in 1936. It's come a long way."

"Who's the colonel?" Curiosity tinged her voice.

"That would be my many-times over great grandfather, Colonel Pierce Reynolds. He fought in the War Between the States."

"You mean the Civil War?" She grinned, and I was hard-pressed not to return the smile.

"I mean, the War Between the States. Or as some people around here still call it, the War of Northern Aggression."

Meghan laughed, and the sound made me want to grab her

and pull her to me. That reaction in turn made me angry at myself. She was just a girl. Just a college girl, way too young for me. That is, she'd be too young for me if I were looking for that kind of entanglement, which I wasn't.

"After going to school in Savannah for three years, I've come to the conclusion that the war, whatever you want to call it, isn't really over for some people. And that even though I live geographically farther south, Florida isn't as much South as Georgia is."

"You're probably right. I haven't spent much time in Florida, but it seems like there're more Yankees there than Southerners." I leaned forward to grab the branch of a bush that was about to snap back to hit Meghan. "Did you like it? Growing up there?"

"Oh, yes. Living on the beach was wonderful. Summers were the best—we'd wake up, put on our bathing suits and just swim all day. Hang out at the beach. Even when I got older and worked summers at the Tide, I'd pull my shift and then go right down to the ocean. All my friends were there, too, and it just felt ..." She cast her eyes up, thinking. "Safe. And like home."

I nodded. "I get that. It's how I feel about the farm. There was something about growing up here, knowing it was where my dad and my granddad had lived before me, doing the same things, more or less. I belong here."

"That's exactly it." We were approaching the house, and she stopped, leaning against a tree. "Belonging. I love Savannah, and going to school there's been amazing. I've met so many people, and I've gotten to do things I never would have done if I'd stayed in Florida. But I still don't feel like I belong there."

"So do you think you'll go back to Florida after you graduate?" I stuck my hands in the pockets of my jeans and widened my stance, watching her.

Meghan made a face. "I don't know. Probably not. The things that used to fit me there, that made it home, aren't around anymore. Or they've changed. When I go back now to visit, it doesn't feel the same."

I remembered that Laura had mentioned Meghan had just returned from a trip home the night she'd gotten so drunk. I felt another twinge of regret for what I'd said to her at Boomer's.

I knew I should just leave it alone, say goodnight and go back into the house, but I didn't. "What's changed?"

Her chest rose and fell as she inhaled deep, and her teeth worried at the corner of her mouth. "My dad died, about two years ago. He'd had cancer, and he was sick for a long time. And then last fall, my family kind of imploded. My mom got married again, and my brother found out he was a father. He ended up marrying the girl, and she's really nice, but still   ... lots of change."

"Yeah, I can imagine." The sun was setting, and the last rays caught her curls until they were ablaze. Her green eyes were fastened on the ground, lost in some private thought or memory.

"I really didn't want to come here." Her voice was low, and I had to lean forward to make out what she said.

"Because of me?" It sounded incredibly conceited, but I was pretty sure it was true.

"Yes. Well, partly. I thought if I went farther from home, I'd have a better chance of ... I don't know, re-inventing myself, I guess." She shook her head and met my eyes. "I mean, how weird is it that I'd be sent here? I've never even heard of Burton. Then Laura's hairdresser tells her about that bar, and our car breaks down, and we meet you ... and the next thing I know, I'm spending the summer here."

"Coincidence is a strange thing." It was all I could think of to say.

"It really is." She was quiet again, staring over my shoulder. "I'm sorry if me being here is a problem for you. I know we started off on the wrong foot, but maybe ..." She trailed off. "At least I can try to stay out of your way."

It was what I wanted, but perversely, hearing her say it stung. I tightened my jaw and turned toward the house. "I work pretty hard during the summer. I don't think it'll be hard to stay out of each other's way."

I almost felt her quick intake of breath, the stab of hurt. But I didn't turn around again before I went inside the house and straight upstairs to my room.

Chapter SEVEN

Meghan

"**N**OPE, I'M NOT KIDDING. It was the same Sam Reynolds." I held my cell phone away from my ear as Laura expressed her surprise. Loudly.

"How the hell did that happen? And how did you not know you were staying at his house?"

I shifted on the soft mattress and worked to keep my voice down. It'd been all I could do to not text Laura as soon as I'd realized I was going to be spending the summer with Sam Reynolds. I'd managed to hold off on calling her until everyone was in bed.

"All the paperwork had his sister's name on it, and she's divorced. So her last name is different than his. I knew it was a small town and I'd probably run into him this summer, but I never in a million years thought I'd be living with him."

"And he didn't know either?"

"Apparently not, judging by the look on his face when he walked in and saw me sitting in his living room. And think about it, why would his sister mention me by name? So he comes strolling in—oh, and did I mention he wasn't wearing a shirt at the time?"

Laura laughed. "No, you didn't mention it. But why is that pertinent?" There was a teasing note in her voice.

"Honey, when any guy built like him has his shirt off, it's worth mentioning. I noticed his abs even that day at Boomer's, but I'm willing to admit it was hard to keep my eyes on his face today. And he had that sweaty look—he'd just come in from the fields." I fanned myself with my hand.

"Don't tease, Brian's not going to be here for another week." Laura sighed. "Did he freak out when he saw you?"

"A little, but then his sister jumped in and made us explain everything. She's awesome, by the way. She's not much older than you and me, but she's definitely the one in charge here. And her little girl is adorable."

"So what are you going to do?" Laura cut right to the chase.

I hesitated, thinking about our walk out to the stand earlier in the evening. For a few minutes, I'd thought he was going to be human. We'd had what passed for a real conversation, and then before I knew it, he was telling me that he'd stay out of my way. That I'd probably not see him very much, which was clearly stupid since we were going to be living in the same freaking house. Eating our meals together. Sleeping under the same roof.

"I guess I'm just going to take one day at a time. I like Ali and Bridget, and I'm here for the summer. I'm not going to run away just because I got assigned to a house where the guy hates me. That's his deal. I'll be as pleasant as I can be, and the rest is up to him."

I tried to keep that in mind over the next few days. It wasn't hard, because it seemed that Sam had been right: he was up in the morning before I came out to the kitchen looking for coffee, and only sat at the dinner table long enough to eat. Ali didn't seem upset, and she explained it to me after I'd been there three days.

"We're in the thick of onion harvest right now. It has to be done by hand, and we can only afford to hire help for a week. So they work as long as there's daylight. As a matter of fact, I'll probably go over tonight and tomorrow night. I know Sam's a little nervous about getting them in, and he needs every hand."

"Can I help, too?" I surprised myself by asking the question. Ali raised her eyebrows. "Have you ever picked onions?"

"No." I shook my head. "But you can teach me, right?"

She smiled at me over the rim of her water glass. "Sure. But you know, you don't have to do this. You're our guest."

"I'm not doing anything yet but planning the classes. Believe me, I have plenty of energy. Unless you'd rather I stay back here with Bridget?"

"Nah, Bridge is going to come pick, too. She's a pro." Ali pushed back her chair and picked up her plate. "Okay, let me get these dishes rinsed off, and you go change. I suggest an old pair of jeans you don't mind getting really dirty. And sneakers."

I frowned. "Not shorts?"

"Not unless you want to get eaten alive. I'll spray you down with bug repellant, but the mosquitoes are fierce. Cover up as much as you can. It shouldn't be too hot by the time we get there."

I was happy I'd followed Ali's advice by the time we got to the field. I batted at the annoying whine in my ear and itched at my arm. "And I thought the bugs were bad in Florida."

"Once you get some onion juice on you, they won't bother you so bad. It's just the walk over and getting started. Come with me, and I'll get you set up."

She grabbed us each a lightweight basket to carry over our arms and led me to a row that was empty of people. A few of the other workers looked at me curiously, but no one said anything. I spotted Sam at the far corner, moving in rapid and fluid movements. If he'd seen us, he didn't give any indication. I turned my attention back to Ali and the ground, which looked like it had been turned over already.

"Why are they all dug up?" I toed a big clump of soil.

"Part of the process. The onions have to be undercut and the soil loosened a few days before we actually pick them. They air dry for about three days, and now our job is to get them into the baskets and then into the barn. We have people in there who'll cut the tops and roots, then bunch and bag them." She leaned to the ground, grasped an onion plant at the juncture of the greens and white top. Gently, she shook off the dirt and laid it on its side in the basket. "See, it's easy, but you have to make sure you pick it up in the right place. Why don't you take over from here, and I'll do the row next to you in case you need anything."

It did seem easy, but still, I was much slower at it than Ali or even Bridget. I saw the little girl out of the corner of my eye, cruising down a row a few over from me. I scowled and tried to pick up the pace.

"Don't let her intimidate you. She's been doing this since she could walk, pretty much." Sam's voice behind me made me jump.

I straightened and looked at him over my shoulder. He was working on the row to my left, and he didn't pause as he spoke.

"She's fast." I shook the dirt off the next onion and laid it in the basket. "I'm afraid I'm not much help."

He flickered his eyes to my face briefly. "You came out to help. That counts. We're doing well, actually. Should finish up tomorrow."

"Does that mean you'll be around the house more?" I blurted out the words and felt my face heat. "I mean, you won't have to work so hard, right?"

Sam laughed, and I smiled in spite of myself. I hadn't heard that sound before, and it turned out that he actually had a pretty great laugh.

"Summer on a farm means all hard work. No let up, really. But yeah, I'll be around a little more. I won't have to run off after dinner every night." He slanted me another glance. "Why, did you miss me?"

"Don't flatter yourself." I smirked. "I don't even really know you. But I was afraid maybe you were avoiding me. I don't want to make things difficult for you."

Sam straightened and stretched his back. "Like you said, we don't really know each other. We got off on the wrong foot, and I jumped to some conclusions. I'd have to be pretty stupid to let you push me out of my own house just because of that."

I smacked my forehead where a particularly aggressive mosquito was attacking. "Okay. Just checking. Because if I do make you uncomfortable, I can always see about living somewhere else this summer. There's got to be another family who'd host me."

"Don't you like living out here? What's the matter, not exciting enough for you, city girl?"

I dropped another onion in my basket. "See, that right there, that's what's wrong with you. You come over here, you're nice to me, sort of, in your own special way, and then you say something like that. You don't know anything about me, as I think we established that day at Boomer's, but you make assumptions. For your information, I love it out here. I couldn't think of a better place to spend the summer. The farm is beautiful, and I want to explore it. I want to paint the orchard at sunset and that empty side pasture at sunrise. Ali's been sweet to me, and I love Bridget already. And I'm not a city girl. I go to school in Savannah, and yeah, it's bigger than Burton, but it's hardly New York City, is it? I grew up on the beach. Oh, and I might be slow at onion harvesting, but I'm a damned hard worker."

"Whoa, there." We'd come to the end of the rows, and Sam held out one hand toward me. "Nobody said you don't work hard. You're the one who brought up moving."

"Only because I'm trying to be nice, dumbass!" I stamped my foot, which in the soft dirt had far less effect than I might have wanted. "I'm giving you an out. To say—yes, Meghan, you make me uncomfortable and I don't like you, so take your stupid self off to another place."

He frowned and glanced over the field. "I didn't say you were stupid."

I set my jaw and rolled my eyes. "Oh my *God,* you are the most irritating man. Fine. I'm not stupid, and I work hard." It struck me what he hadn't denied. "But I do make you uncomfortable? Why? Because of the drinking still? I promise you, I don't make a habit of it. You don't have to hide the vodka while I'm here."

"No, not because of the drinking. I told you, I realized I was wrong to say what I did that day. Your friend—Laura—she told me you didn't get drunk very often."

"Then what is it?" My basket was getting heavy, and I set it on the ground, rolling my shoulders. Sam's eyes dropped to my chest as the motion drew the cotton T-shirt tight over my boobs. I watched in fascination as his Adam's apple bobbed and he licked his lips. Interesting.

"I don't know." He closed his eyes and ran a grimy hand through his hair, leaving it standing on end.

"If you don't know why I make you uncomfortable, then I don't know how to stop doing it." I took one deliberate step closer to him, standing on the lumpy ground where the onion plants had been. His eyes widened slightly, and he stiffened.

"Are you more uncomfortable now, Sam?" I realized this was the first time I'd called him by name. It gave me an odd thrill. "Does it make you nervous when I stand this close to you?"

He looked down into my eyes as though he had no other choice. "Only because you smell like bug spray and onion juice."

I let a smile curve my lips, and I stood on my tip-toes so that my lips were even with his ear.

"Liar."

I stepped back, still smiling, as Ali came over. "What's going on?"

"Nothing." I picked up my basket again. "Sam was just giving me some pointers."

"Really?" Ali didn't look convinced, but she only held out a hand to me. "Here, let me have your basket. I'm taking mine over to the truck. Just get a new one and you can start on the next row, if you want."

"No problem." And because he was still standing there motionless, I made it a point to step close enough to Sam that my arm brushed him as I passed.

Just because I could.

I HELPED WITH THE onions again the next night and was there when Ali carefully loaded the last basket into the truck. A little cheer went up from the eight of us who'd been working.

"Onion harvest is officially finished for another year." Sam stood by the truck. "Thanks, everyone. I'm going to get these over to the barn."

"Sam, Bridge and I are going home so she can go to bed. Art class starts tomorrow, and I want her to get a good night's sleep." She slid her eyes in my direction. "Meghan, why don't you ride over to the barn? You can see what happens to the onions in the next step and give Sam a hand with unloading."

If looks could kill, Ali would have been flat on her back in the soft dirt. Sam glared at her and opened the door to the truck cab. "I'm good. I have help over there already." He glanced at me for a scant moment. "Besides, if class begins tomorrow, maybe the teacher needs her rest, too."

"Oh, I'm good. I don't need much sleep." I went to the other side of the truck. "And I really wanted to see what happens to all those onions I picked." I climbed onto the wheel well so that I could see him over the truck bed. "Unless you're not *comfortable* with me riding over with you, Sam?"

Ali laughed. "I'll leave you two to work this out. Bridget, get a move on, darlin'."

I looked down at Sam, one eyebrow raised. "Well? What's it going to be? Are you man enough to handle a little ride to the barn with me?"

He growled and swung up into the cab. "Get in the damn truck. I don't have time for this."

I jumped to the ground, opened the passenger door and hoisted myself in to sit next to him. "See, that wasn't so hard."

Sam turned the key in the ignition and shifted into gear. "I don't know why you're making this such a big deal. It's onions. There'll be people cutting tops and roots. It's not that exciting."

"I just want to see the whole process." I leaned back against the door and drew my knees up onto the seat. This was the old farm pick-up that they only used to transport things back and forth on the property. The paint was chipping on the exterior; in fact, in some places it was completely worn away. The inside smelled of cigarette smoke and sweat, and the seatbelts had been cut out years before. There was something about seeing Sam in the driver's seat, with one elbow bent over the rolled down window and the other hand resting on the wheel, that really turned me on. I had a sudden vision of the two of us parked in some hidden corner of the farm, making out in this cab. The idea of Sam's hands on me definitely made me hot and bothered. I shifted in the seat.

Sam glanced at me, the dark expression still on his face. "If you wanted to see the whole process, you should've been here last winter when we planted. Or in the spring when we weeded. Or even last week when we started undercutting. You're getting the tail end of it. I don't get why it matters to you."

That was an easy one. "I like to learn. I want to know how everything works, and why. It makes me happy to think that the next time I pick up an onion in the grocery store, I'll have a better idea of how it came to be there."

Sam grunted. "Wonderful. Glad we could help with your education." He sounded anything but glad, and I smothered a sigh as we stopped at the barn.

The sun had already set, leaving us in the dim twilight, but the interior of the big building was flooded with lights, and the wide doors were propped open. Three women stood at a long table, their hands moving so fast as they trimmed the onions that I nearly couldn't see them work. They called greetings to us as Sam and I got out of the truck.

We unloaded the bed in silence. I liked to tease Sam, and I was enjoying seeing how far he'd let me push before he either gave in and admitted he felt some attraction to me or began to push back. But I didn't mess with his work. I wanted to be helpful, so I did exactly as he told me and carried baskets to the end of the work table.

When we'd delivered the last load, one of the women looked up at us, grinning. "Sam, you got yourself a new helper, eh? Pretty new girlfriend?"

"Not my girlfriend." Sam's jaw was clenched. "She's just a college student, staying with us for the summer to teach art."

The woman only shook her head and winked at me. I smiled back, even as I felt Sam's obvious rebuff. *Just a college student.*

"Maddy, you'll finish up here and lock up? Turn everything off?" Sam addressed the woman who'd been teasing him.

"Sure thing, Sam. Just like every night. I got it covered. You look like you're dead asleep on your feet. Better go home and get some rest."

Sam nodded. "Yeah, last day of onion season's a killer. Thanks, Maddy." He waved to the other two women and headed back to the truck.

I walked behind him and got back into the cab in silence. Sam started it up again without looking at me. I snuck glances at his profile and realized Maddy was right: he did look exhausted.

"So was onion harvest everything you'd hoped it would be?" He was trying to be sarcastic, I knew, but I decided to pretend otherwise.

"Yup. I now feel qualified to call myself an onion expert."

"Huh." The side of Sam's lip curled. "If that's what it takes to make you think you're an expert, I'm a little worried about these art classes you're supposed to be teaching."

"Hey." I sat up straighter in my seat. "You can make fun of me trying to help with onion harvest, you can say I'm immature or whatever because I got crazy drunk one night, but don't mess with my art. I take my craft seriously. And I'm very, very good at it."

He had the good grace to look contrite. "Sorry, low blow. I'm tired. I don't do well with tired."

"Yeah, I get that." The house came into view, and I took a deep breath before I asked my next question. "Is that really all you think of me? Just a college student who's staying at your house while I'm teaching art?"

Sam parked the truck by the shed, but he didn't open his door. I didn't move either.

"What else do you want me to say? That's who you are."

"But ..." I wasn't sure how to put into words what I wanted to express. "But from the other times. We met twice before I even got here."

"Yeah." He nodded. "But the first time, you were too hammered to open your eyes, let alone talk. And the second time ..." He stared out the windshield into the dark. "I was yelling too much to get to know you. So even though I saw you before, I don't know any more about you than I would if I'd met you for the first time the other day in my living room."

I played with a loose piece of plastic that had peeled up from the seat. "I guess that makes sense. I think—" I paused, trying to choose the right words. "I think I feel like you made an impression on me. Even though I really didn't remember anything about the car breaking down that night, I still had a memory of you the next morning. Just a flash, but it was there. That's why I got so hurt when you yelled at me at Boomer's. I thought you were a nice guy, and then you weren't. At least, not that day, to me."

Sam's cheek twitched. "I can see that. But, well ..." He

shrugged. "What does it matter?"

I ran my tongue across my bottom lip. "Maybe because I think I'm kind of attracted to you. And I think maybe you are to me, too. That's why you got all over me that day, and that's why it upset me when you did."

He didn't rush to deny it, as I thought he might. For a full minute, he didn't respond at all. When he did, his voice was flat.

"Listen, you don't know me at all. I don't know you. So any, um, attraction we might feel is probably just circumstantial, and we need to ignore it and move on. I'm much too old for you, and I can tell you for sure, I'm not interested in someone like you. So if you stick to your art lessons, which is why you're here, and I concentrate on my work, the summer'll be over fast enough."

I slid a little closer to him on the seat. "You said you're not interested, but you didn't say you weren't attracted."

He finally looked at me, and the angry passion nearly made me shrink back. "Who the hell wouldn't be attracted to you? You're beautiful, you must know that. And you give off this vibe ... I don't know what you'd call it, but it's there. Doesn't matter, though. Just because you feel something doesn't mean you have to act on it. And trust me, I'm not."

He opened the door, got out of the truck and slammed it behind him. I watched him stalk into the house. He didn't look back to see if I were following him inside.

I sat for a long time in the dark cab, alone.

Chapter EIGHT

Sam

I WAS USED TO living with women. My grandmother had lived with us until her death, so between her, my mom and Ali, Dad and I had been outnumbered. And even after she wasn't around, it always felt like the females were predominant in our home. I was okay with that; they treated me well, fed me and kept me from making stupid mistakes most of the time.

After Grandma and then my parents were gone, it was just Ali and me. She was young, but she'd picked up where Mom had left off, taking on the cooking and most of the housework. Her marriage to Craig was a little bit of a surprise, and it left me with a house that felt empty. I learned to get by on my own. When Ali and Bridget moved home, my sister'd picked up her role in my life as if she'd never left, and there was no doubt her little girl had me wrapped around her finger. I was used to being in the minority. I could deal with it.

Or so I'd thought.

In the two weeks she'd been living in our house, somehow Meghan had shifted the balance so that sometimes I felt like I was an interloper in my own home. I thought I knew what it must be like in a college sorority, thanks to the giggling, the private jokes and the chick flicks on TV in the evenings. My sister had morphed from the mature, responsible woman I'd known for the past seven years to a teasing, winking teeny-bopper.

And Bridget wasn't any better. She was thriving with the extra attention and was quick to tell me each night how much everyone at school loved the new art teacher. She brought home different projects each day, and even I had to admit that it was cool to see the improvements in her work when she pointed them out to me. But the breaking point came one late afternoon when I came in from the fields to find the three of them in the living room, with the carpet rolled up, dancing to some crazy music from Meghan's iPod blaster.

Seeing them jumping and gyrating around was the final straw. I needed to escape all the estrogen that was flowing through my house before it consumed me and I found myself doing the cha-cha slide or whatever the hell they called it. So as we finished dinner, I announced that I was going into town to run some errands.

"Tonight?" Ali frowned at me. "Can't it wait until tomorrow? I can pick up what you need. I'm helping Meghan at the school for a few hours in the afternoon."

"No, it really can't." I spoke more adamantly than I'd intended, and they all three looked at me in surprise. "I mean, I need this part for the tractor first thing in the morning. I've got to go round to Boomer's and then to the hardware store and talk to Mitch. And I want to see if Mr. Harper's around, so I can ask him about the bees."

"Okay." Ali shrugged. "I was just trying to save you a trip."

"Yeah, thanks. I'm going to head out now. See y'all later." I practically ran through the door, and I was pretty sure I heard giggling behind me as I got into the truck. The sound went right up my spine and bounced around in my head. God, did I need this break.

I stopped at the hardware store first and picked up a few things I knew I was going to need in the coming weeks. None of it was pressing, but Ali would grill me if I came home empty-handed. I spent a solid half-hour shooting the breeze with Larry, the store's owner. I worked for him part-time in the winters to make ends meet when the stand was closed, and he was a decent guy. It was a relief to talk baseball, whatever bugs were trying to eat my cucumber plants and even a little town politics. He didn't once mention art, pop culture or nail polish, and for that I was grateful.

I swung by Boomer's after that, catching him just before he closed up.

"Hey, boy. Whatcha need?" He leaned back against his paper-strewn desk, keys in his hand.

"Hey, Boomer. Do me a favor and take some part you have laying around that you don't need and toss it in a paper bag for me."

The older man folded his arms across his broad chest and cocked his head. "Say what? Little early for drinking, isn't it, Sam?"

I shook my head. "Haven't had a drop. But I told Ali I was coming out tonight to pick up a part I needed first thing tomorrow morning, and if I come home without a bag from you, she'll know."

He shifted his weight from one foot to the other. "So you're lying to your sister, huh? You got a girl out here in town, boy? Who're you seeing?"

"God almighty, no. Last thing I need is another girl. That's why I had to get out." I shuddered, and Boomer chuckled.

"Ah, I see. You got that pretty little art teacher living out with you now, and the females are ganging up on you, huh?"

"Not so much ganging up as ... giggling. Boomer, you don't know. They talk about the stupidest things, and then they laugh like it's hysterical ... they're making me nuts. I just had to get away tonight."

"Hmm." Boomer eyed me up and down. "Funny thing, wasn't it, that girl getting the job here in Burton. You think that's why she was here that night, scouting us out?"

"Nah." I shook my head. "It was just one of those things. Coincidence."

"Well, I wouldn't have figured her to stay around once she knew it was your house she was living in. The day she came to pick up her car, I was afraid to leave the two of you alone. Wasn't sure if I'd come back to see you in a knock-down brawl ... or on the floor doing some *other* kind of wrestling." He smirked.

"What the hell are you talking about, Boomer?" He was too close to touching on the truth, and it pissed me off. "I was just telling her how she'd left her friend in a bad way, and she took it wrong. We were yelling, sure, but it wasn't any more than that. I didn't even know her. Still really don't."

Boomer guffawed. "The hell. You don't need to know someone to feel the pull. I'm not saying anything about now, but that day, right here in this room, you were looking at that girl the same way I look at the cherry pie down at Kenny's."

"You're crazier than they are." I stuck my hands deep down in my pockets. "Are you going to give me a bag or not? Because if you're just going to stand here and tease me, I may as well go home."

He waved a hand. "Calm down, calm down. I'm going to get you covered." He opened up a desk drawer and dug around for a minute and then came up with an old crankshaft. "Will this do?"

I nodded, grateful. "Yeah, that's perfect. Thanks, Boomer."

"Any time, boy. And if things get bad with all them women, just give me a call and I'll come rescue you." He came around the counter and slapped a hand on my shoulder. "Four daughters and a wife, remember? I feel your pain."

I grinned. I'd forgotten that Boomer would definitely be the one who'd understand. "Thanks, man."

"I got your back. Now get on out of here so I can close up, or the wife'll be calling to see if I'm dead."

I waved and headed back to my truck. Tossing the bag onto the passenger seat, I started up and headed out of town. The testosterone infusion had done its job, and I was feeling more relaxed than I had in weeks. I thought of Boomer's words about Meghan. He was crazy. Ridiculous. I didn't look at her any particular way. And if I did, what did it matter? It didn't mean a damn thing.

I wasn't one of those guys who needed drama as a side dish to women. The relationships I'd had in the last few years were low-key, quiet and kept far away from my family. The last had ended amiably back in the spring when Jaycee Mathers had decided to move to Nashville for a new job. Since then, with the planting and upkeep on the farm, I hadn't had time to get involved with anyone else. Truth to tell, I didn't miss it.

It was full on dark by the time I got back to the farm. Ali had left a light on in the kitchen for me, but I didn't go in the back door. I rounded the house, climbed the front porch and dropped into the old wicker chair, setting the two paper bags on the floor and stretching my legs out in front of me.

"Hi."

The voice came from the dark corner, making me jump a mile. At the same time, I heard the squeak of the swing that hung there. As my eyes adjusted, I could just make out Meghan's shape, curled in the corner of the swaying bench.

"God, you about gave me a heart attack. What the hell are you doing out here?"

She sighed, just a breath that carried to me across the night air. "Ali wanted to get Bridget to bed early. She's lying down with her upstairs, but I think she might have fallen asleep, too. It's such a pretty night. I just wanted to come out for a little air." She unfurled her body, letting her feet hit the floor. "I'll go back in now and let you have your privacy."

"No, don't go in." I spoke without thinking about it. "You were here first." I paused for a minute, and then added, "Do you want me to leave?"

She shook her head, and the chains on the swing groaned again as she resettled herself. "No, it's okay. I don't mind company."

"Guess it's strange for you here, not having a ton of people around all the time. Do you miss it?"

She laughed and stretched her arms over her head, dropping one arm along the back of the bench. "You seem to have a skewed sense of what my life in Savannah is like. I live in an apartment with Laura, not in a crazy dorm. We're pretty quiet. She's practically engaged, and we both work hard at school. We're not exactly party girls."

"Do you date?" I wasn't sure why I asked the question or if I even wanted the answer.

She hesitated. "I do. Probably more than I should." She leaned her head back and stared up at the velvet sky. "Laura says I leave a trail of broken hearts in my wake."

"I bet you do." I kept all condemnation out of my voice.

"I don't know why. I just ..." Her finger came up and traced a link of the chain that suspended the swing. "I don't mean to do it. I meet someone, and we go out, have some fun, and then, I don't know. I guess it stops being fun, and I don't want it anymore. So I end it." She shrugged. "Sometimes it's okay, and we stay friends. Other times, not so much."

"Maybe you just haven't found the right one." What the hell was I saying? I must've been picking up more from their Lifetime movies than I'd realized.

Meghan laughed. "You sound like Laura. She swears I'm going to meet some guy, and he'll turn out to be the one I've been waiting for. But then, she can afford to be a romantic. She's been with the same guy forever, and they're perfect together." She glanced over at me. "What about you? Do you date?"

I shifted, uncomfortable. "Not really. Not like you're thinking. I have ... friends who are women, though."

"Ah." There was a hint of amusement in her tone. "Do those friendships have benefits?"

There was something about the dark that made it easier to talk. "Some of them. I don't have time for the kind of relationship where there are, uh, expectations. Right now, my priorities are my family and this farm. Ali and Bridget are the most important things in my life. And I've been working to keep this farm together for twelve years. I can't afford to let up now."

"Ali told me about your mom and dad. I'm sorry." The soft vulnerability in her voice made me want to fold her into my arms and offer the same comfort she was expressing. I laced my fingers over my stomach to keep from moving.

"Yeah. I guess you know something about that."

She shrugged. "A little, but not both parents at once. I still have my mom. I can't imagine being eighteen and not only being completely on your own, but having to take care of your little sister, too."

"It was what I had to do." I smiled a little, thinking about my parents. "You know, the only saving grace is that I'm positive they were absolutely happy to the end. They'd gone away for their twentieth wedding anniversary, taken a trip to Gatlinburg, and they were on their way back when the accident happened. They were still so much in love, you know? They still did the stuff that makes kids pretend to be grossed out, even when they're happy their parents do it."

"My mom and dad were the same. They'd been together since they were kids." She paused, and then added, "And I guess my mom and Uncle Logan are like that, too. When Mom walks into the room, Uncle Logan gets this look on his face ... like he can't believe how lucky he is."

"That's your stepfather?"

She made a face. "I guess so. I never think of him like that. He's still Uncle Logan, only now he lives with Mom."

"Still. I never had to deal with that. I wouldn't want to see my mother with someone else, even with someone I like."

For a few minutes, nothing broke the silence but the creak of the swing as Meghan swayed back and forth on it. When the breeze blew across the porch, I could smell her unique scent, that musky undertone with just a hint of orange. Sitting on that bench swing, curled up with her head tilted to the side, she made such a tempting picture that I had to grip the arms of my chair to keep from getting up and joining her.

And then what would I do, I wondered. I'd pull her toward me, use my finger to lift her chin and I'd kiss her. I remembered the feel of her softness against my chest, and I wanted it again. I wanted to kiss her until her eyes went hazy and her lips were swollen.

I was just about to lose the battle with myself when she spoke, shattering my preoccupation.

"The farm—that's why you don't really date, right? Because you feel responsible for what your parents left you?"

"Yeah, I guess so." My voice was rough with desire, and I cleared my throat. "It's a full time job, and then some. But I owe it to my parents, and to Ali and Bridget, too, to make sure it stays with us. I can't lose it."

"And you think this is what your parents would want? They'd want you to sacrifice your life to hold onto the land?"

"They gave up the right to have an opinion on the subject when they died and left me." I knew my words were harsh, but I trusted that Meghan would understand what I meant. "At one point ... maybe I thought things might be different. After Ali got married and moved out, I considered leasing more of the farm and renting the house. Trying something different. I was in college then—"

"You went to college?" She sounded amazed.

"Yeah, why the shock? Because you figured me for a dumb country farmer?"

"No." Meghan shook her head emphatically. "Not at all. I just figured you never got the chance. Ali said your parents died right before your high school graduation."

"I went to night school, and I took some courses online. Took me a little longer, but I got a degree in business."

"Not agriculture?"

I laughed and crossed one leg over the other. "No, why would I study something I already knew? I live and breathe agriculture. The Guild suggested business, and they were right."

"The Guild? What's that?" She stretched one leg onto the bench, flexing her bare foot. Her shorts had ridden up, and I could see the top of her thigh, the fascinating ridge of tendon that disappeared into the denim of her pants.

Suddenly my chair was just a little less comfortable. I hoped she couldn't see how the zipper of my jeans was bulging more than normal.

"Uh, the Guild? It's a group of business owners in town. They've been supporting each other, helping newcomers and contributing to the community for years. When my parents died, they jumped in to help me keep the farm. I couldn't have done it without them."

"Oh, I see. That's like my uncle Matt. He and the rest of the posse kind of take care of Crystal Cove. Whenever someone's having a hard time or just needs a little help, they make it happen."

"Yeah, that sounds like the Guild. What's the posse?"

She smiled, her eyes lighting up. "That's what my dad's friends call themselves. It was my father, my uncle Eric and a group of guys they've known from the time they were all little boys. They've been part of my life since I was born."

"Feels good when people have your back." I sat forward and leaned an elbow on my knee. "Really is a pretty night."

"It is. Reminds me of the nights growing up when I used to sit out on the deck at the Tide, with my family and a bunch of friends. The grown-ups would talk, and we kids would play games. Sometimes my dad would bring out a grill, and we'd toast marshmallows. Those were happy times." Her eyes were faraway, staring into a distance I couldn't see.

"I never thanked you." It was an abrupt change of subject, and she jerked her gaze to my face, confused. "For helping with the onions, I mean. You didn't have to do it, but you stepped up. I appreciate it."

"Really?" She smiled, and her whole face lit up with it. "You do?"

I smiled back at her. "Yeah, really."

"Does this mean we're friends?" She sat up, too and used her feet to stop the swing from swaying. The moonlight shone on her hair, and her eyes were luminous.

I considered for a minute and then nodded. "Yeah, I guess so."

"Okay. That makes me happy." She brushed her hair back behind her ear. "I don't expect everyone to like me, but you matter. I'm going to be here for the rest of the summer, and I'd hate to live here with someone who couldn't stand me."

"It's never been that I couldn't stand you, Meghan. It's just ..." I couldn't explain how I felt without saying something I knew I'd regret, opening a door I couldn't afford to walk through. "Maybe it's that you remind me of myself when I was your age."

"Oh, because you're so much older than me now." She was teasing, and one side of my mouth lifted in response.

"I am. Too old for you."

"That's a matter of opinion, and I don't agree with yours. Besides, why would I remind you of yourself? You were always so responsible."

"On the outside, I was. But inside ... and sometimes the outside, too, on Saturday nights ... I was kind of wild. I raised my share of Cane, like Ali would say."

"You know, that makes me like you even better." Meghan stood and stretched her arms high over her head. Without missing a beat, she bent at the waist and leaned to touch the tops of her feet. I watched, my mouth hanging open, as the neck of her shirt sagged. I could see right down the front, to the swell of her breasts over the cups of a black bra and the flat of her stomach. The denim shorts tightened over her pert little ass, and again I was having a hard time sitting still.

She straightened and caught me staring. Taking a step forward, she stood about an inch away from my knees, close enough for me to touch if I just reached one hand forward.

"I'm glad we're friends now, Sam." She spoke softly, and the whisper caressed my face. "You know, we could be the kind of friends who ... well, your kind of friends. No complications. No drama. Just fun and ..." She exhaled and ran a hand over her curls, bunching them at the back of her neck. "Maybe letting off a little steam."

All I had to do was reach up and put my hand to her waist, tug her forward, and I knew she'd melt into me. It was what we both wanted, I knew, but it was what might happen after that that kept me from moving.

"Meghan, what I said before stands. I'm too old for you. And you're a guest in my home, so I'm not going to take advantage of you. That wouldn't be right."

"It's not taking advantage if I offer. If I want it, too. I'm not asking you for a commitment here, Sam. I'm just saying, we could give each other what we both need."

I had to get away, now, or I was going to give in. Her scent filled me, and she was so close that I could feel heat coming off her body in waves. I clenched my teeth together and stood up, moving her back gently with my hands on her upper arms.

"I'm going inside now, before I do something that you and I would both end up regretting. I'll be your friend, Meghan. But that's all I can do."

I released her arms and turned to go back inside. As the screen door closed quietly behind me, I cursed myself as a fool and stomped upstairs toward a cold shower that had nothing to do with the air temperature.

Chapter NINE

Meghan

I LAY IN BED awake for a very long time that night, reliving every minute from the conversation on the porch. I'd been startled when Sam had appeared around the corner of the house and climbed the steps to the porch. I knew he hadn't seen me; if he had, he wouldn't have sat down. For a few minutes, I was tempted to keep quiet and just watch him. There was a definite allure to his face when he was relaxed, not on alert as he usually was around me.

But I was curled up on the hanging bench swing, and I knew it was only a matter of time before a twitch of my body or the movement of my breath made the chain squeak. And then he'd be angry at my silence. I wouldn't be able to blame him for that, since it'd be more than a little creepy-stalkerish to sit in the dark watching him.

I fully expected him to let me go inside without saying anything when I offered, but he didn't. And whether it was the dark, the cool of the evening breeze or something I didn't know about, he was more open and talkative than he'd ever been around me.

When he'd said my name ... *Meghan, what I said before stands* ... I couldn't breathe for a moment. He'd never said my name before. He talked to me, he talked about me, he talked around me, but he'd never addressed me directly that way. I was so taken by that fact that I nearly missed what he said afterward. *I'm too old for you.*

I didn't understand his preoccupation with our age difference. If he didn't like me, fine. If he could say, honestly, that he wasn't attracted me, that he felt nothing, I'd leave him alone and accept his offer of friendship. But he never said that. I could feel his want when we were close; it was a nearly tangible thing, more than just a reflection of my own desire. Tonight, he'd been on the verge of giving in.

And yet, I had to admit that I wanted it to be more than him giving in to me. I didn't want to be the seducer. I'd been there before, more times than I chose to remember. I always regretted it, particularly when I was forced to end the relationship, as inevitably I did.

I must have dozed off at some point, because when I opened my eyes again, the sky outside my window was painted in breathtaking shades of pink and purple. I rubbed the grit out of my eyes and stood to pull back the curtains. The wide blue expanse beckoned me, and without pausing, I picked up my messenger bag and slung it over my head, then hunted for flip-flops. Once I had them on my feet, I slipped out of my room as quietly as I could manage.

The house was silent. I didn't know whether or not Sam was already up and out in the fields, but I didn't smell coffee, which probably indicated he was not. I went out through the front door and across the porch, heading for a large rock in the center of the side yard.

I didn't have time to unpack my paints and set up the easel before the sky changed, so instead I pulled out my watercolor pencils and a large pad. I sat on the rock and allowed the beauty to wash over me. Without looking away from the sky, I let my fingers fly over the page. There was no sound but the scratch of the pencils on paper and the chirp of early morning birds.

I was in another world, completely absorbed in the sky, the air on my skin and the teasing scent of flowers wafting on the breeze. Like magic, the colors translated into my drawing, capturing a piece of the glory I'd spied through my bedroom window moments before.

"That's incredible."

Sam spoke softly, but I jumped nonetheless, dropping the rose-colored pencil I held.

"God, you scared me."

"Seems like we're forever sneaking up on each other." He held a steaming mug in one hand and sipped the coffee as he gazed down at my pad.

"Maybe it's a metaphor for our relationship." I dared to use the 'R' word, and Sam didn't contradict me. Well, friendship was a sort of relationship, too.

"You're up early." He was standing so close behind me that I could smell the coffee on his breath.

"I didn't sleep very well." I'd let him draw his own conclusions about why. "I happened to open my eyes at one point and saw the sky. I couldn't do anything but come out here and try to put it onto paper."

He nodded. "I've never seen anything like it. I mean, yeah, I've seen art. But I've never seen it in progress. It's beautiful." He sat down behind me on the rock, close but not touching me at all.

"Thanks." The light was changing as the sun rose fully, and I laid down my pencil. The sketch had turned out well, though not quite the same as I imagined it would look in paint.

I dropped my head back and let it roll, working out the kinks from thirty minutes of looking up. Without breaking the movement, I reached for Sam's mug. "That smells heavenly. Can I have a taste?"

His brown eyes darkened as they wandered down my face to my lips and back up again. He held the mug to my mouth and tilted it until I tasted the hot sweet liquid on my tongue.

"Mmmmm." I closed my eyes in appreciation and ran the tip of my tongue over my top lip.

Next to me, Sam made a noise deep in his throat. When I opened my eyes and turned my head to look at him, he was closer than I'd expected. He stared down at me before his gaze dropped lower to my body. I'd run outside in the same clothes I'd worn to bed, my favorite soft white tank, with no bra underneath, and an old pair of green cotton shorts that barely covered my ass. It wasn't appropriate outside attire, clearly, but that wasn't bothering Sam.

Or maybe it was. His throat worked as his eyes made their way back up to my face. I held my breath, and for the space of a few rapid heartbeats, he didn't move. And then slowly, so slowly, he snaked the hand not holding the coffee cup around my shoulders and caught my chin between his thumb and forefinger. With just the slightest pressure, he coaxed it up, leaned forward an inch and touched his lips to mine.

I wanted to move my arms around his neck, open my mouth and deepen the kiss. But I held back, afraid of spooking him. Instead, I closed my eyes, waiting for the touch of his tongue to my bottom lip, and let him tug my chin to open my mouth.

His lips were firm but languorous, moving as though we had all morning to do nothing but sit here, connected only at our mouths. His tongue teased, first stroking the inside of my lips, then circling around my tongue, seeking and taking. His fingers splayed over my jaw, moving my face up a little to give him even more access.

He didn't touch me anywhere else, but I felt the kiss in a line of fire down my body. I wanted to grip his shoulders and pull him down on top of me in the grass. I wanted the weight of him on me, to feel him against my breasts and between my legs.

But I didn't move. At the same time that I wanted more, this kiss was enough, because it was Sam, and because he had initiated it. With his arm still around me, I felt cherished and protected in a way I'd never known I wanted. His chest pressed against my back and along my side, cocooning me.

I knew the minute he began to pull back. He moved away from me, and I felt the brush of his breath over my still-parted lips. When I opened my eyes, he was staring into them under brows that were drawn together. I didn't look away, and for a few seconds, he didn't either.

"I need to get to the fields." Without warning, he dropped his hand from my face and stood up. I'd been leaning on him more than I'd realized, and I had to catch myself from tumbling off the boulder in his absence.

"Okay." I looked up at him, waiting. I wanted to push him. God, how I wanted to rise up on my knees, even knowing how the rock would bite into my bare skin, wrap my arms around his waist and make him kiss me again. I craved the touch of his hands down my back and on my ass.

"I need to go." He repeated the words, but still he didn't move. I stayed silent this time. His hand reached out toward me, and for a dizzy second I thought he might draw me close again, but he only touched his fingertip to one of my red curls. I held my breath.

His face was shuttered again, but his chest rose and fell rapidly, making me think his heartbeat probably matched my own. I lifted my hand to cover his where it hovered near my shoulder, but he stepped back, fisting both hands at his sides.

"I'll see you later." He spun and stalked off around to the back of the house. The screen door squeaked open and slammed, and I remembered his coffee cup. He must've opened the door to set it in the kitchen. A moment later, I heard the distinctive engine of the farm truck and the peel of tires on gravel.

My body sagged as though Sam had been holding it up. I brought my fingers to touch my lips, still buzzing from the kiss. It had been so unexpected and so simple ... maybe the most uncomplicated kiss I'd had since I was fifteen years old. He hadn't touched me except on my face. Yet it shook me more than if he'd had his hands down my shirt.

I retrieved my pad and returned the pencils to their case with hands that weren't quite steady yet. Once I had everything packed up, I went back inside. The house had come to life in the near-hour I'd been drawing; Bridget lay on the floor in front of the television, watching morning cartoons. Ali was pouring a cup of coffee as I walked into the kitchen.

"Hey, early bird." She unhooked another mug from the cabinet and poured me some coffee. "Getting a little, uh, art time in this morning?" Her voice was teasing, and I glanced over to see one eyebrow raised.

"Yeah. The sky was beautiful." I took my coffee and added milk. "Thanks, this smells wonderful."

"Oh, yeah, you were definitely checking out the sky. Mmmhmmm." She nodded, a smile playing on her lips.

"What's that look for?" I leaned back against the counter, crossing my arms over my chest and blowing on my coffee mug.

"Nooothing." She stretched out the word. "Only you know, I happened to look out my window this morning right after I got out of bed. Just checking on the day. And I saw you holding your sketch pad, and I saw my brother ... holding you."

"Oh, God, Ali." I covered my face with both hands. "Don't tell him you saw that. He'll freak out. Well, more than he already probably is." I peeked at her through my fingers. "Are you mad at me?"

"Lord, no. Why would I be?" She mirrored my position across the kitchen, sipping on her coffee.

"Because he's your brother. And ... and. . I don't know. I was mad when my friend Suzanne kissed my brother when we were in high school. There could be an ick factor."

"Maybe that's because you were young, and he's your little brother. I don't have any illusions about Sam's virtue." She leaned forward to glance into the living room, making sure her daughter was still paying attention to the television. "He's always been very discreet. He never brings girls around here, ever, but I know when he's seeing someone in town."

I frowned. "Is he seeing someone now?"

Ali shook her head, smirking. "Not since Jaycee Mathers hightailed it to Nashville back in March. And believe me, she wasn't anything special." She took another drink of coffee. "So you want to tell me what's going on with you two, and how long it's been going on?"

"I have no idea, and just since this morning." I traced the seam at the edge of the counter. "We talked last night on the front porch after you fell asleep and abandoned me down here."

"You talked? Without yelling at each other? Wow."

I grinned. "I know, right? He seemed ... mellow."

"Yeah, because he'd been in town hanging out with Boomer and other males. He got his testosterone fix. So what'd he say?"

I hugged my arms around my middle. "We talked about losing parents. And living in small towns. He thanked me for helping with the onions. Oh, and we decided we were going to be friends."

Ali's eyes widened. "That's a big step for my brother. So did the talk on the porch lead to anything else I should know about?"

My mind flashed to standing in front of him, bending over to stretch out my stiff back. The expression on his face when I'd caught him staring down my shirt—and then checking out my ass—had nearly dissolved me into a puddle right then and there.

"No. We said good night and went to bed. Alone. In our own beds, I mean."

"And made plans to meet this morning?"

I rolled my eyes. "No. That was accidental. I woke up, and the sky was just so gorgeous. I grabbed my stuff and went outside to sketch it before I lost the color and the light, and Sam came out with his coffee just as I finished. Maybe he saw me from the window, too."

"Could be. And then what?"

I shifted my weight from one foot to the other. I liked Ali. We'd become fast friends in the few weeks I'd lived here, and it was wonderful to have another girl around, particularly since Laura was preoccupied with Brian up in North Carolina. I'd never hesitated to rehash my romantic interludes with my friends; we all talked about dates and boys and our sex lives. But what had happened between Sam and me this morning was not something I wanted to share, especially with his sister. My reluctance must have shown on my face because Ali smiled and shook her head.

"Okay, I'm sorry. Nosy sister. I'll mind my own, unless and until you want to share. But I'm here, if you need someone to talk to. And I promise, I'm completely impartial."

I pushed off the counter. "Thanks, Ali. I'll keep that in mind. It's just that—maybe this is nothing. Sam kissed me this morning. But I don't think he wanted to."

"Sweetie pie, I've known my big brother for a very long time. He never does anything he doesn't want to do. Not like that, at least. He may not have thought he wanted to kiss you, but if he did, on some level, he wanted to do it. Trust me."

"I do. But don't say anything to him, okay? If he thinks I'm making a big deal about it, I'll be back to square one with him." I finished my coffee, rinsed off the cup and set it in the sink. "Right now, I need to get ready to introduce the young minds of Burton to the wonders of charcoal sketching."

TEACHING ART WAS NOT something I'd thought seriously about doing until this past year. When I'd started college, it had been with the same grand illusions of other art students: I would live in an attic in Paris, surviving on crusty bread and cheap bottles of wine, until I was discovered and became a Famous Artist. Happily, SCAD did a good job of introducing us to the realities of life. Most of us would end up using our talents and degrees in art-related fields, like design, advertising or illustrating. A few might nab jobs at museums.

But none of those fields interested me in the least. Neither had teaching, but when I looked at all my options, it seemed like the lesser of several evils. At least I'd still be creating, and I'd get summers off. A good part of my motivation for signing up with ArtCorps had been to see if I could handle working in a school setting.

As it turned out, though, I loved it. The kids were so excited every day when I announced our project, and they worked hard. I had a few volunteer parent helpers in the classroom, and I'd found them enthusiastic as well.

"Art wasn't like this when I was in school," one of them confided to me as she helped me clean up. "It was just crayons and construction paper. Scissors and glue. This is cool."

I laughed. "I figured this summer should be an overview for the kids, introducing them to as many different mediums as possible." So far we'd done watercolor, pencils sketches and collage, in addition to today's charcoal drawing. I was excited to see what they would do with pottery and 3-D sculpture next.

"Such a shame that we can't do this all year around. Some of the kids are really talented." The mother sighed as she dropped chunks of charcoal into a bucket. "I'm happy to see so many of the older children get involved, too. You do a good job teaching so many different grade levels."

"It's fun." I slid a stack of paper into a drawer. "Kind of like what it must have been like on the frontier, you know? In the one room schoolhouses."

"Exactly." A loud crash sounded out in the hallway, and she rolled her eyes. "That's got to be my two hellions. Two hours of sitting still translates into an afternoon of frenetic activity to make up for it. Thanks, Meghan. See you next week."

"Thanks for your help." I began packing up my bag to leave, making sure everything was neat and tidy. Having a classroom of my own was fun, I decided. Although if I were teaching here for real, during the school year, I'd set up my bulletin boards differently. And I'd have tables instead of desks ...

A knock on the open door broke my reverie. I looked up to see Sam standing just outside in the hallway, his worn blue baseball cap twisted in his hands. He shifted from foot to foot and glanced around as though he expected the principal to appear and ask him for a pass.

"Hey." I came around to the front of my desk and leaned against it, although what I wanted to do was sprint over to him, take his face in my hands and kiss him senseless. He looked taller than ever in this setting, with the miniature chairs all around us. His brown T-shirt had smudges on it, but the way it clung to his chest more than made up for that. And his jeans ... soft old blue jeans ... fitted him perfectly in places that I didn't want to think about.

"Hey." He gazed around the room. "Class is over? Everyone's gone?"

"Yup." I smiled. "Were you planning on doing some charcoal drawing today? Sorry, too late."

His eyebrows knit together. "Charcoal?"

I pointed to the bulletin board on the far side of the room, where today's projects were displayed. "The masterpieces."

"Oh. Cool." He spared them a glance before he came inside the room, being careful to stay at least five feet from me, with desks between us. "I wanted to talk to you here, away from the house. About this morning."

I frowned and tilted my head, as though every second of that kiss weren't burned into my memory. "This morning?"

"Yeah. Outside." He swallowed. "When I kissed you."

"Kiss? Hmmm. Not sure I know what you mean. Maybe you need to refresh my memory."

He exhaled, smacking the hat against his thigh. "Meghan ... what I mean is, it was a mistake. I'm sorry. I shouldn't have done it."

I'd figured this was coming. "Okay."

"What?" His eyes widened, and he took a half-step back, nearly losing his balance and falling into a desk.

I spread out my hands in front of me. "Okay. You shouldn't have done it, you're sorry. No big deal." I hoped he couldn't hear the pounding of my heart that contradicted my words.

Sam's eyes narrowed. "It isn't a big deal?"

I laughed. "No, it isn't. You were pretty clear last night about what you want—or rather, what you don't want from me. I'm a big girl, Sam. I'm not going to cry and carry on like a lovesick teenager, just because you got a little carried away this morning." I pushed off the desk and stepped forward until I was standing nearly on top of him. I could smell sweat and soap and maybe even a hint of rich soil. I touched him in the center of his chest with just my finger.

"After all, it was only a kiss."

I bit back a smile at his quick hiss of breath. His hands clenched on the hat, and his lips parted. For a second, I thought he might grab me, but when he didn't, I moved around him to the windows, where I pulled down the window shades.

"What are you doing in town, anyway?" I snapped the last one shut and returned to the desk to get my bag. "You didn't come all the way in here just to tell me you didn't mean to kiss me, right?"

Sam shook his head a little, as though clearing it. "No. No, I had to, uh, drop off a soil sample at the Farm Bureau."

"Oh, good. Well, I'm done here." I held up the ring of keys and let them jingle. "I need to lock up the classroom. After you?"

He stared at me a minute more before he nodded and walked back out to the hall. I followed, clicking off the lights and shutting the door behind us. I turned the key in the lock and dropped the ring into my handbag.

"I guess I'll see you back at the house." I started walking toward the front door as he trailed behind me.

"Yeah. I'll see you there."

It took every bit of my self-control not to turn around to see if he watched me walk to my car. I drove out of town under the speed limit, but once I reached the open back roads, I rolled down the windows, blasted the radio and floored it.

This man was driving me crazy.

I'D CALMED DOWN BY the time I pulled up in front of the old white farmhouse. Bridget was in her mother's herb garden, watering the plants, and she gave me a happy wave as I rounded the house and went into the kitchen.

"Hey, there. I heard charcoal was a big hit." Ali turned from the stove, where she was frying battered green tomatoes. She spotted my face and her smile faded. "What's wrong?"

I waved my hand. "Nothing. Not really. Well ..." I hesitated. "No. It's nothing."

Ali put one hand on her hip. "What did that dumbass brother of mine do now?"

I opened the fridge and pulled out the water pitcher, got a glass out of the cabinet and poured. "Why do you think it's something to do with him?"

"You have the look of a woman pissed off at a man. And since to the best of my knowledge, the only men you've met in Burton are Sam and Boomer, and since Boomer is a pretty amiable guy and sticks to only pissing off his own wife, Sam seems like the most likely candidate."

I took a long drink and set the glass back on the counter. "He's maddening, Ali. I know he's your brother, but it's the truth. And the most frustrating part is that I knew exactly what he was going to do. Well, I didn't know he was going to come to the school to do it, but I knew he was going to back-peddle and tell me it was a mistake. The kiss, I mean."

"He went to the school?" Ali's mouth dropped. "He left the

fields in the middle of a sunny day to drive to town?"

"He said he was coming in anyway to drop off a soil sample." I wasn't really sure what that meant, but it sounded like something a farmer would do.

"Bullshit. The Bureau's closed on Fridays. He went to see you, and that's all." She laughed and turned back to flip the tomatoes. "Hoo boy, does he have it bad. This is the best thing ever."

"I'm pretty sure he wouldn't agree."

"Probably not. So what did you say? When he told you he didn't mean to kiss you? What, did he trip and fall onto your lips?"

"He didn't say that exactly. Just that he was sorry, it shouldn't have happened, blah, blah, blah. I just said ... okay."

"You did?" Ali turned down the flame under her pan and stirred another pot.

"Yeah. And you should have seen the look on his face. He expected me to pitch a fit, and when I didn't, I think he was a little disappointed."

She laughed again, almost a cackle. "Perfect. I can't wait to see—oh, shhh. Here he comes."

The old farm truck rumbled into the backyard, and Sam climbed out. He was considerably dustier than he'd been earlier in the afternoon, and the look on his face was anything but happy. I watched him stride over to the outside shed sink, strip off his shirt and wash up. And all I wanted at that moment was to be able to walk outside, slip my arms around his damp waist and rest my head on his muscled back. To do that, knowing he would turn in my arms and look down at me with a desire that matched my own ... I sighed.

"I have an idea." Ali leaned toward me, keeping her eyes on the window. "Just follow my lead, okay? Trust me. And Jesus, girl, rein it in. You're looking at him like you want to slurp him up with a spoon."

I didn't have time to answer her before the screen door

squealed open and then slammed shut. Sam stomped into the kitchen. Droplets of water glistened on his chest, and his light brown hair was darker at the ends where it was wet. I clutched at the counter edge behind me.

"Hey, good timing. Supper's about ready."

Sam scowled at her. "I'm getting a shower. Start without me." He started through the doorway to the living room until Ali's sharp voice stopped him.

"No, sir, we will not. Grab a clean shirt and come sit down. These tomatoes will get soggy if we don't eat them now, and we're not being rude and eating without you." She rapped on the window to get Bridget's attention and motioned her inside.

Sam muttered something low under his breath, but he stepped into the small laundry room off the kitchen, chucked his dirty tee into a basket and took a clean one from the pile Ali kept there for him. I couldn't help licking my lips as I watched him pull it on.

"Meghan, will you please put the potatoes on the table?" Ali thrust a steaming bowl in front of me, and I had no choice but to take it. I set it down in the middle of the long plank table just as Bridget came dancing in.

"Wash up, Bridge, we're going to eat. Here, Sam, take the meat."

In a few minutes, under Ali's expert prodding and direction, we were all sitting down around the table. Sam asked the blessing on the food, in the words I was sure were an exact duplicate of the prayer his father and grandfather had used. As soon as we began passing platters and bowls, Ali glanced at me.

"Meghan, you know, I was thinking. This is your third Friday night in Burton, and all you've been doing is sitting at home."

Across the table, I saw Sam's arm freeze in mid-action as he spooned out boiled potatoes. I slid my eyes to Ali.

"Yeah, I guess you're right." I had an inkling of where she was going, but I also knew it was likely doomed to failure.

"Why don't you go out tonight? You told me you love to dance, right? And you've been to the Road Block. You should go back there, go dancing."

I wasn't sure how to reply. "Uh, that sounds like so much fun, Ali. But I'm not sure I want to go over there by myself, and I don't know anyone else in town. Or at least, no one to take me dancing. I've only met students and parents, and none of them seem like they'd make good dates."

Ali swung bright eyes toward her brother. "Sam, you should take Meghan dancing tonight."

He was shaking his head before the words left her mouth. "Nope. No way. I don't do dancing, and I'm too tired to go out tonight. You might remember I've been out in the hot sun all day, in the fields?"

"*All* day?" Ali's tone was arch, and Sam flushed.

"I'm not going."

"Really, Ali, it's okay. I'm fine to just—"

"What's the matter with you, Sam? Are you afraid to take her out? Afraid of a little dancing? I remember when you used to be fun."

At this point, Bridget and I were watching the back and forth like a tennis match. The little girl's eyes, wide and wondering, met mine. I gave a little shrug.

"Ali, give it up. I'm not going out tonight."

Temper flared in Ali's brown eyes, so like her brother's. "Fine. Then I will."

"What?" All three of our voices joined in combined surprise.

"I haven't done anything fun with a friend for so long I can't remember the last time. If you're not going to take Meghan dancing, then I'll go with her. I wanted to check out the new bar, anyway."

"What in the hell are you talking about, Ali?" Sam brought his hands down on the table. "Since when do you go to bars?"

"You might remember, brother dear, that I'm young. Maybe I've wanted to go out and kick up my heels for a long time, and maybe this is my chance. You're not going anywhere. You can stay home with Bridget. Put her to bed at eight. And don't wait up. We're going to be late." She dropped her fork onto her plate with a clatter. "Oh, and you can do the dishes, too. C'mon, Meghan. Go get dressed. We're leaving in fifteen minutes."

She pushed back her chair and stamped out of the kitchen. I watched her go, my mouth open. When I turned back to look at Sam, he had resumed eating.

"Sam, I didn't—I mean, I never thought—"

He shook his head. "You better go get ready. When she says fifteen minutes, she means it. And you need to make sure she doesn't get into trouble. She's not lying when she says she hasn't been out in a long time." He added something about the blind leading the blind, but I headed to my room before he could elaborate.

Fourteen minutes later, I was back in the kitchen, wearing a denim mini-skirt and green tank top. Ali was there already, in a pretty flowered sundress that hit her leg high above the knee and hugged her curves. Her cowboy boots were feminine, with lots of silver topstitching over the black leather. She'd pulled her long brown hair into a curly ponytail.

"Wow, hot mama!" I whistled as I checked her out and then guiltily looked for Bridget. To my relief, she'd already gone upstairs.

"You look good, too." Ali eyed me critically. "Except you need different shoes. Your feet'll get stomped in those sandals." I held out one foot. "Sorry, I don't have any. I didn't pack anything but these and my flip flops."

"That's okay, I have the perfect pair. Be right back." She skipped past me toward the stairs.

Sam was standing at the sink, up to his elbows in suds. I cleared my throat. "Thanks for doing the dishes. We won't stay out long. And I promise, I won't have anything to drink."

He glanced at me over his shoulder. "Just don't drive drunk.

I don't want to have to wake up Bridget to go bail you and my sister out of jail." His eyes traveled down my shirt, where it clung to my boobs, to the skirt that barely covered what it had to. His lips pressed together. "Meghan—"

"Here we go!" Ali reappeared with a pair of bright red shoes. "We're about the same size. Try them and see."

I kicked off my sandals and stepped into the sky-high heels. I'd expected them to be tight and uncomfortable, but they actually fit me like a glove and felt perfect.

"Awesome. Okay, let's go." She paused at the back door. "I have my phone, Sam. Bridget's in the tub, and she'll be ready for bed in a little bit. You know what to do." She held the screen for me.

I glanced at Sam. "See you later."

"Yeah." He spoke low, but I heard him anyway as we stepped into the fading light.

We drove my car, and once we were clear of the farm, Ali let out a long sigh. "Oh my God, I didn't mean that to happen like it did. I thought I could talk him into going with you, but then when he was so stubborn ... I figured he'd jump in to stop me." She laid her hand on my arm. "I'm sorry, Meghan. If you really don't want to go, we can turn around."

I looked at her out of the corner of my eye. "Hell, no. Are you kidding? I've been dying to go dancing. And going with you is even better."

She smiled. "To be honest, once Sam made it clear he wasn't going, I was pretty excited. I haven't been out in years, except to meetings and baby showers. This is going to be fun."

The parking lot at the Road Block was even more crowded this time than it had been when Laura and I were there. The difference was that once we'd parked and begun walking in, Ali knew just about all the people we passed. She called out and waved as we made our way to the door. I just tried to keep up with her.

Inside, the music was loud, and the dance floor was crowded. Ali grinned as we pushed our way through to the bar and ordered beers.

"You have no idea how much I needed this!" She stretched out her arms and let her head drop back, yelling the words over the noise.

"I'll only have one drink," I shouted into her ear. "So you can relax and have as much as you want."

The bartender slid the bottles across to us, and Ali tilted back the bottle, taking a long pull and closing her eyes. "God, the last time I got drunk was the night Bridget was conceived. It's been a long eight years."

I grinned. "You've been busy being mommy. And you're good at it."

"Yeah. I love her to bits. But sometimes I forget that I'm only twenty-six, not forty." Pain shadowed her eyes, but she blinked it away. "Hey, look, there's a table by the wall. Let's grab it before someone else does."

We darted around people standing near the bar and others trying to get to the dance floor. Ali dropped her handbag on the table, and we both pulled out chairs.

I watched her take another hit of beer. "How long have you been divorced? If you don't mind me asking."

Ali cast her eyes up. "Let's see ... I got married when I was eighteen. Had Bridge when I was nineteen. Craig left when she was five months old. So almost seven years."

I shook my head. "And you haven't dated that whole time?"

"Nope. No time, with us trying to make the farm work."

"Did he break your heart?" I peeled a little bit of the label from the sweating bottle.

"Hardly." Ali huffed out a short laugh. "No. Honestly, I was just as happy to see him go. I'd never have walked out on him, but ... it was a bad idea, the two of us getting married." Something flickered in her eyes, and she upended the beer, chugging it down. "I'm ready for another."

I stood up. "Stay here. I'll grab you one and get myself a

soda." I threaded my way through the crowd.

"Hey, sexy." A hand on my ass made me halt, and I spun to see who was touching me. My heart sank when I recognized Mr. Sexy Cowboy, the guy from my first visit to the Road Block. From the surprise on his face, I realized he remembered me, too.

"Uh, hi. Nice to see you again." I tried to move forward, but he had me by the hem of my skirt.

"Wait a minute. You were supposed to be, like, one of those religious ladies. Your friend told me."

"Ah ..." Damn Laura and her creative lies. Couldn't she just have told him I had a jealous boyfriend? "Yeah, that didn't work out."

"Well, I'm glad." He tugged me closer to the chair where he sat. "We can pick up where we left off."

"Thanks, but I'm here with a friend." I pointed back to the table where Ali was waiting. "Maybe another time."

"She won't mind." He gripped me harder and pulled so that I stumbled backward, landing on the edge of his lap.

"I think I said no." I pushed against his shoulder, struggling to stand up.

"Hey, Trent, the lady wants to go. Give it up, bud." The guy who spoke was about my height, with blond hair styled in that deliberately tousled way. He stood next to me and gripped Mr. Sexy Cowboy's arm. "She's not playing hard to get." He glanced at me. "Are you?"

"No." I stepped back. "Definitely not."

Trent raised both hands in surrender. "Okay, okay. We had a good time before. I was just trying to, uh, let it continue." He looked a little abashed as he slanted his eyes to me. "No hard feelings?"

"Sure." I turned to go, and my blond rescuer stayed next to me as I walked away from their table.

"Sorry about Trent. He's harmless, but he can be persistent, particularly after he's had a few."

We reached the bar, and I caught the bartender's eye and

ordered a beer and a soda. Trent's friend reached for his wallet. "Make that two beers and a soda, please. My treat, to make up for Trent."

"You don't have to do that," I protested.

"My pleasure." He handed a twenty across the bar and then turned back to me. "I'm Alex, by the way."

I offered my hand. "Meghan. Thanks again." I looked over my shoulder. "I really am here with my friend Ali, but you're welcome to join us."

Alex followed my gesture and smiled. "Hey, I know her! She's my next-door neighbor. And a good friend. I was planning to get over to see her this weekend."

"Then you have to come over and say hello." I led the way, and Ali's eyes brightened when she saw us.

"Alex! When did you get back into town?" She jumped up to give him a hug and take her beer from me.

"Just last night. I figured to come by the stand tomorrow to say hey. How's everything with you? Sam doing okay? And the baby?" We all sat down, Alex angling the chair to stretch out his long legs.

Ali laughed. "Same old here. Doing the mommy thing, working the farm, running the stand. Sam's still driving me crazy and working too hard. And Bridget's seven now—no more baby."

"Geez, that's crazy." He grinned and shook his head. "And what about your love life? Any bouncing going on in that lonely bed?"

My eyebrows rose in shock, but Ali only giggling. "Nah. Would you believe this is the first time I've been out just for fun since before Craig? I'm nearly a lost cause." She took a swig of beer and then lifted it toward me. "I'm sorry, Alex, have you met Meghan? She's living with us for the summer."

Alex turned his bright blue eyes my way. "Yeah, I had the pleasure of helping her escape the clutches of Trent Wagner." He looked me up and down, but it didn't make me uncomfortable. I got the feeling he was only curious, not creepy. "So what brings you to the metropolis of Burton, Georgia this summer?"

"I'm teaching art at the school, just for a few months." I glanced between the two of them. "I take it you've been out of town for a while?"

"Alex lives in Atlanta." Ali reached across to squeeze his arm. "He left for college and never came home. Well, for good, I mean. He comes back every summer since Fred and Missy won't go visit him in the big city."

"Ohhh." I nodded. "You're Mr. Fred's son. Mr. Fred who owns the card-playing horses." I'd heard Bridget rhapsodize over the horses next door since I'd been here.

Alex laughed. "Well, they're not card-playing, that I know of. But yeah, Dad named them after card games. It was a joke, because his mother was raised Methodist, and they weren't allowed to play cards. He did it to get her dander up, he says."

"Bridget totally covets them all. The running argument in our house is between Sam and her, about how we really can't have a farm without horses." Ali finished her beer and stood up. "I need another drink."

"Want me to go?" I watched to see if she was swaying, but she seemed steady.

"Nah, I'm good. Plus I'd have to send Alex to protect you from grabby cowboys. Maybe I want to see if one of them wants to get grabby with me." She winked and slipped past me.

"Good to see her having fun." Alex sipped his beer. "She and Sam had a rough time there for a while."

"They're great people. I'm glad I'm staying with them."

He nodded. "So what's up with old Sam these days? Anyone bouncing on *his* bed?"

I almost choked on my soda. "Um, not to my knowledge, no." I felt the red creep onto my cheeks and hoped Alex wouldn't notice it.

"Hmmm." He narrowed his eyes. "Got your eye on that, do you?"

I opened my mouth, but nothing came out. Was I that transparent? "I don't know what you mean."

"Aw, honey, I recognized the look. C'mon, you're living in that house ... I take you're unattached yourself. Have you seen him with his shirt off?"

I thought of Sam walking in wet before dinner, and I might have hummed a little. Alex chuckled.

"I'll take that as a yes. Ah, that boy. I had a crush on him from the time I was thirteen. Never looked my way, of course. He's a hundred percent hetero."

Ali came back in enough time to hear his last statement. "You're so right, my friend. You never had a chance there. But you heard it here first: I think my go-it-alone big brother just may have fallen hard for our Miss Meghan."

Alex wiggled his eyebrows. "That *is* news. Are we talking serious?"

Ali sat down again and scooted her chair closer to Alex. "He told her he only wanted to be friends, but he kissed her early this morning while they watched the sunrise, and then he informed her that it was a mistake. But get this: he drove all the way in from the farm to town in the middle of the day to tell her that it was a mistake."

Alex whistled. "Sounds serious to me." They looked at me expectantly.

"I think you're both crazy. I'm not looking for serious, and I can tell you for sure Sam isn't. And I'm not talking about him anymore. I'm here to have fun tonight." The music changed from the twangy old-school country to a song with a good dance beat, and I took advantage of the opportunity to stand up. "I'm going to dance. Who's with me?"

We stayed on the dance floor for a long time. Ali had a few more beers, and I noticed her dancing became much less inhibited as the night went on. But Alex stuck close by us, and when Ali began to bump and grind, it was with him. When any other guy got near us, he edged him out, making sure we were protected.

At the first slow song, Ali backed away from us. "I'm hitting the ladies' room and then getting some water. You two dance."

I grabbed her arm. "You want me to come with?"

"No, I'm good." She smiled at me and slipped through the crowd.

Alex drew me close, and I closed my eyes, laying my head on his shoulder. He moved with grace and finesse, his feet seeming to know just where to go next, and it was relaxing to dance with someone who had no expectations of me. His hands stayed at my waist, and he never tried to press his hips to mine.

"Are you serious about Sam? I know what you said ... but are you?"

I leaned back so that I could see Alex's face. "You're making me gooey with all this romantic talk."

He smirked. "I've heard that before. But don't change the subject."

I lifted one shoulder. "I don't know. I like him. I mean   ..." I tightened my hands on the back of his neck. "This is going to sound crazy. The first time I met Sam, I had actually just left this bar, with my friend Laura. I was so wasted. The car broke down, but I was passed out in the front seat. I don't remember any of it, except the next morning, when Laura told me the story, I had a flash ... of Sam's eyes. Of him holding me. And then I ran into him when I went to pick up my car, and he yelled at me for being so irresponsible."

Alex laughed. "That sounds like Sam. He and I had a similar chat when I was in high school, and he caught me getting high out near our property line. Told me that I was letting down my parents, and he wouldn't allow me to hang around Ali if that was the kind of guy I wanted to be. I acted like it didn't matter, but damned if I ever did it again."

"Glad to know I'm not the only one. It bothered me, though. More than it should have, coming from a virtual stranger. And then I ended up here, which was just bizarre. I don't know.

There's something about him, and even though most of the time he acts like he can't stand me, I know he feels it, too. This pull."

"Maybe it's just animal lust, pure and simple. Once you get it out of your system, the pull may go away."

"I guess it's possible." The song ended, and I followed Alex back to our table to sit down. "But I think it's more than that. I like Sam. When we were sitting on the porch talking last night, it felt like we were friends."

Alex leaned back in his chair. "I think you should go for it. Rock his world a little. I haven't seen him in years, but the Sam I knew could use a little shake, rattle and roll."

Ali fell into her chair. "Who's shaking and rolling?"

Alex patted her arm. "Your brother and Meghan."

"Awesome! Someone should be. Okay, let's dance more."

I pulled out my phone. "Ali, do you think we should go home? It's getting late."

"After we dance. I've got eight years to make up for."

She wasn't kidding. It was another hour before we left the dance floor, thirty minutes more before I got her out the door and to the car, with Alex's help.

"Are you sure you can get her home all right?" He closed the passenger door.

"Oh, yeah. I'm perfectly sober. And I've got my phone if we have any problem."

"Okay." He looked back toward the bar. "I'm going to go back inside for a little while. I saw some interesting prospects, and I'm going to pursue them, see what happens." He nudged me with his elbow. "Might I suggest you go home and do the same?"

I grinned. "I just may do that. It was good to meet you, Alex."

"You, too. I'm going to be in town for two weeks, so if you need anyone to talk to or to take you dancing ... you know where I am. One farm over."

"Got it. Good night."

The car was silent as I drove through town. I thought Ali had fallen asleep, so I jumped a little when she spoke.

"Isn't Alex great? I've missed him."

"Yeah." I fumbled with a way to bring up a sensitive topic. "Ah, couldn't have been easy to grow up gay in a small town in Georgia."

Ali's laugh was laced with sleepiness. "Yeah, but nobody bothered him. Not really. He was always just Alex. He's so cool. He was there for me ... during a bad time."

I frowned. "He was in your high school class, right? So didn't you say he went away to college? Was he around when you were getting divorced?"

"No. No, that wasn't a bad time, that was only a course correction. It was the best thing for Bridge and me, when Craig left."

"Does Craig ever see Bridget? Where did he go, anyway?"

"He moved to Arkansas. No, he doesn't see her. Hasn't since she was a baby." She was quiet for a few minutes, and then I heard the unmistakable sound of a single sob.

"I'm sorry." I kept one hand on the wheel and my eyes on the road as I reached over to pat her arm. "I didn't mean to bring up a sensitive subject."

"No. You didn't. I always get—" She hiccupped. "I get weepy when I drink." She sighed, her breath shaky. "Craig doesn't see Bridget because she's not his daughter."

"Ah. Oh." I worked to keep my voice even.

"No one knows, except Craig and Alex."

"And Sam?"

She shook her head. "No, Sam doesn't know. I was afraid if I told him the truth, he wouldn't let me marry Craig, and he'd go after—her real father. And that was the last thing I wanted."

"Who is her real father? Is he still around?"

Ali bit her lip. "He was my boyfriend for a long time. But he left Burton the day after high school graduation, and he never came back. We had a fight, and that was the end. I didn't know about Bridget. By the time I did, it was too late. I was dating Craig already, mostly because I was still so hurt, and when I told him ..." She shrugged. "He asked me to marry him. He thought it would be fun, I guess, to try to make a family. It didn't work. But Alex was there for me in those days when I was trying to figure out what to do."

We were both quiet until I turned off the road and onto the driveway that led to the farm. "I'm so sorry, Ali. That must have been incredibly hard."

She turned to grip my wrist. "You can't tell Sam, okay? Some day I will. But now, it would crush him to find out I didn't tell him the truth back then."

"I promise, I won't say anything." The headlights of the car swept over the house as we pulled to the back, and I thought I saw someone sitting on the front porch. Sam, watching to make sure we got home, I assumed. I parked the car, and Ali and I snuck into the back like kids after curfew.

"I'm going right upstairs to bed." She stopped suddenly and pulled me into a tight hug. "Thank you, Meghan. I had so much fun tonight. You have no idea." She released me and turned to climb the steps.

I waited until I heard the click of her bedroom door, and then I shut off the lights Sam had left on for us. Taking a deep breath, I headed for the front porch.

Time to shake, rattle and roll.

Chapter TEN

Sam

THE MUCHKIN WASN'T HARD to put to bed. One boring storybook later, she was sound asleep, snoring softly, with her mouth open. Whether it was the fact that she was worn out from art class and her chores today, or just that she knew I wasn't going to take any nonsense, I didn't have the same problems her mother did with bedtime. I went back downstairs and wandered. I should have been exhausted, too, but I couldn't settle. I tried to sit down with a book I'd been reading for the last month, but every time I heard the slightest noise, my ears perked up, wondering if the girls were home.

Finally, just before midnight, I stalked outside to sit on the porch. The night was still, but every now and then, a breeze blew up to rustle the trees. Stretching out my legs, I dropped my head onto the back of the rocking chair and closed my eyes.

I wanted to think about baseball and the tomato plants bursting with robust red fruit and the next Guild meeting. But even though I kept forcing my mind in those directions, it seemed determined to wander back to this morning, and the undeniable softness of Meghan's lips. The silk of her hair. The scent of her, fresh from sleep, sweet and warm. The heaviness in her eyes when she lifted them to look at me after I'd stepped back, as though I could lay her out on that rock and do whatever I wanted with her full approval.

I should've laughed it off and gone in to have breakfast with her. But instead I'd run away and been the first one at the farm stand, putting up with the girls who worked for us when they commented on my snappishness as I took out my frustration on them. All morning, whether I was on the tractor or on the ground, I thought of her. That told me one thing: this was a mistake. Touching her had been crazy.

I don't know when I decided to go into town, but there I was, in the truck, heading to the school. I knew what time her classes ended, roughly, but there were still kids and moms trickling out of the building when I pulled into the parking lot. I watched, parked in the shade of a tree, until I figured the last of them was gone.

The school office was open, but although I heard voices from within, I couldn't see the secretary or the principal. I strode down the hall, wondering which classroom was Meghan's, when the sound of singing reached my ears. It wasn't necessarily the best I'd ever heard, but I knew it was her; the song was one I'd heard her playing on her iPod around the house. I followed the sound around the corner and spotted the open door.

She was straightening up her desk, packing her bag, and I didn't think she even realized she was singing. Her lips moved, but it was absent-minded, almost without thought. I took a minute to watch her unawares. She walked around the room with grace and purpose, smoothing back her hair from her eyes. She'd put it up in a ponytail today, and it looked cute, swinging in time with her steps. Her jeans hugged that tempting little ass, but her green shirt looked professional and grown-up. I guessed it was a compromise, with the jeans as her casual, artistic side, and the top her concession to being a teacher.

I knew it was a matter of time before she glanced over and I scared her out of her mind, so I raised my fist and knocked.

She jerked her head up, startled, and then her eyes went soft again and those lips curved into a smile. She circled the desk and came around front to lean against it, crossing her arms, which only served to put her boobs on display. *Shit.* I couldn't think like that.

It was true that I'd expected her to argue with me when I told her the kiss had been a mistake. But instead, she only smiled and agreed. She wasn't mad or upset, at least not so I could tell. She didn't try to change my mind. And then the next thing I knew, she was practically pushing me out the door and into my truck.

It was annoying when she didn't act like I thought she should. Or at least like I thought she would. I'd driven back to the farm in a worse state than I'd left it, dropped my pickup behind the barn and switched it for the farm truck, moving fast to avoid running into Ali and having to explain to her why I'd left in the middle of the day to drive all the way into town.

I knew Meghan would be home by the time I ran out of things that could be done away from the house, and I weighed the mixed anticipation and dread of seeing her against Ali's temper if I missed dinner without a good excuse. Ali won. Besides, why the hell should I let this little redhead keep me from my own house and my own supper? I hadn't done anything wrong. Or if I had, I'd fixed it by our conversation this afternoon. Now I needed to just get on with it, forget how she'd felt beneath my hands and my lips, bull through the next two months. I could do it.

When Ali brought up dancing, it was easy to say no. I never went to bars, not anymore. Not in years. The men I hung out with were a generation older than me, and we drank coffee instead of beer. Besides, there was no way I was taking Meghan dancing. I knew where that would end. I'd made up my mind that nothing would happen between us, but if I had to hold her close on the dance floor ... or worse, watch while someone else did ... there was no way I'd be able to keep from kissing her again. Better to just stay away from any situations that were fraught with temptation.

I was shocked when Ali announced that she was going out with Meghan instead. And by the time I'd thought of all the reasons she shouldn't, they were gone, Meghan dressed in some tiny skirt that barely covered her ass, a shirt that made her tits shout, "*Grab me!*" and fuck-me heels my sister had loaned her. I was left with a sleepy kid, a sink full of dishes and a growing frustration. Sitting out here on the porch might have been cooling off my body, but it wasn't cooling off the frustration I'd been fighting all day.

I heard the sound of a car on the gravel driveway, and Meghan's headlights swept over the house. I was sitting in the corner of the porch, so I doubted they'd spotted me. Still, I stayed put, hoping they would both go to bed fast. Once I knew they were in their rooms, I could sneak into mine with no one the wiser. I didn't need the two of them teasing me for waiting up like I was their father.

The kitchen door squeaked, and I heard the click of heels across the floor. After a minute, one set changed, moving farther away. Ali climbing the stairs, I decided. Good. The other pair of feet began moving, too, and the lights I'd left on went out. I waited for the sound of Meghan's bedroom door opening and closing.

Instead, the screen door opened, and Meghan stepped out onto the porch. Her eyes sought me in the dark corner, and I realized she must have seen me from the car.

She didn't say anything. Standing a few feet away from me, lit only by the pale moonlight, she was ethereal. Her hair spilled over her shoulders, not quite disguising the swell of her breasts under the clingy shirt. I let my eyes wander down her legs, from the edge of the denim to my sister's red high heels. The frustration that had been coiled in my gut all day found an outlet in a sudden stiffness between my legs.

Meghan took one step forward. She toed off her shoes, setting them by the door. Her eyes never left me as she took one step and then another toward me.

I swallowed and tried to remember the many reasons why this was a bad idea. Since all of my blood was currently residing somewhere south of my belt buckle, my brain couldn't seem to come up with even one thing.

She stood in front of me, inches from my knees, just where she'd been last night when she'd offered me more than just friendship. Then I'd pushed her away. Tonight, I wasn't sure I could do it again.

"Hi." Her voice was low, and one side of her mouth lifted in a smile.

"I see you girls got home. Finally." I didn't mean to say them, but the words came blasting out before I thought about it.

Because she was Meghan, and she never did what I expected, she only lifted one eyebrow.

"I brought your sister home as promised, safe and sound. I had one beer, hours ago, and my car didn't break down." She slid her foot between both of mine, her eyes still steady. "This is where you say, 'Thank you, Meghan.'"

I let out a breath. "Yeah. Thanks. How drunk is she? Did she get groped?"

"Not by me." Her smile grew, and she pivoted sideways and dropped onto my lap. Out of instinct, I caught her by the hips.

"What are you doing?"

"You brought up groping. It seemed like a good idea." She leaned onto my chest and twined her arms around my neck. "You kissed me this morning. I know you said it was a mistake, and maybe you meant that. But right now, I don't care. I want to kiss you." She brought her lips to my jaw, nipping along the line until she reached my ear. "What do you think, Sam?" Her whisper sent a shot of want straight to my cock.

I gripped her hips and pulled her closer, twisting her body so that she was forced to straddle me. Her denim skirt was tight, and it rutched up to the top of her thighs. I ran my hands down the expanse of bared white skin, teasing the inner muscles until she shivered. She tightened her hold on me and pressed her breasts against my chest.

"I guess I'll take that as agreement." The words drifted to my ear as Meghan kissed down my neck, sucking gently on the pounding vein there. The tip of her tongue darted out to touch and tantalize.

I took hold of her face and brought it to mine, holding her chin as I kissed her with abandon and reckless need. I pulled down to open her mouth and plunged my tongue inside and then held the back of her head, tilting it enough to let me get even closer. My lips moved to devour her, as I moaned. All I wanted was her, laid out before me, legs open and eyes begging. My body wanted to slam into her, mark and brand her as mine.

Sucking her lower lip into my mouth, I circled it with my tongue and caught it between my teeth, swallowing her answering moan as the vibration of it swam down my throat. She wriggled even closer, rubbing the warmth between her legs against the stiffness between mine. Blood pounded in my ears as I realized that only a thin wisp of material covered her.

There was still a part of my brain that tried to remind me I'd decided not to do this. That whatever pull I felt toward Meghan was wrong and leading straight to a dead end of possibilities. But I was having trouble hearing that caution over the overwhelming urge to touch her. I tried to compromise. *I'll just touch her boobs. Just one touch ... then I'll stop.*

I let my hands fall away from her face, dropping them to her shoulders and then lower, to the straining green cotton over her bra. I palmed both breasts, my breath catching at their fullness and weight. She made a small sound in her throat and sat up a little, dropping her head back, eyes closed. I took advantage of her position to sweep my thumbs over her nipples, rubbing back and forth as they hardened under my touch. I curled my fingers beneath the neckline of her shirt and tugged it down, along with the lace bra under it, so that she was bared to me. My breath was coming in pants, and I lifted her slightly, bringing her even to my mouth and capturing the stiff peak.

Meghan's hands grasped my head, as though she were afraid I'd move my mouth away from her. I tongued her nipple, pressing it into the roof of my mouth and then sucking it hard. She began moving against me, rubbing her center against my hard cock in a way that was going to make stopping almost impossible.

I kept my mouth on one breast, my hand on the other for the space of a few more breaths, before I slid both hands to her ribs and then around to her back. "Meghan. We need to take a break here or I won't be able to stop."

She lifted her head and opened her eyes, smiling at me. "Why would you want you to?"

I shook my head. She wasn't going to make this easy. "Because while I have no objections to a heavy make-out session at midnight on the front porch, I'm not up for having sex on the floor here, where my sister or my niece could wake up and come down to see what all the racket is."

She sighed, dropping her forehead to my shoulder. "Okay, I get that. But damn, you feel good." She trailed one hand down my chest, over my stomach, to where the zipper of my jeans was straining. I sucked in a sharp breath as her fingers rubbed me. "I was given a strict mandate tonight to rock your world. I could still do that."

"I think you already have." I caught her hand and held it between both of my own. "I'm not that guy. I don't want you getting me off if I can't do the same for you. And dammit, Meghan, all the things I said before still stand. I'd be lying if I said I didn't want you, but it's not right. Not for either of us."

She stared down into my face, her eyes unreadable. "Maybe it's right for now. Maybe we just need to get each other out of our systems. You know? Like scratching an itch." She traced my mouth with the tip of her finger. "We could try it."

"And what if that itch needs more than one scratch?" I opened my lips, snaked out my tongue to touch her finger. She slid it inside my mouth, and I sucked at it, feeling the corresponding pull between my legs.

"Then ... we have the summer. Sam, trust me, I'm not looking for anything serious. If you knew me better, you'd realize that. I never date anyone for more than a few weeks. It's kind of a rule with me. I get bored easily, and when I'm done, I'm done. But we're both adults, and we're both unattached. Why shouldn't we have some fun this summer?"

I knew all the reasons I should tell her no, and they were good, strong reasons. But I also knew there was no way I was going to make it the rest of the summer without touching her. Maybe it was better to lay down some ground rules.

I grazed my hands up to frame her face. "I don't want to hurt you. But I also have to look out for Ali and Bridget. If we do this ... we need to be discreet. They can't know that anything's happening."

An expression of amusement flittered over her face. "Have you met your sister? Do you think anything happens around here that she doesn't know about? I think you're kidding yourself."

I lifted one eyebrow. "I've been able to have other relationships without her knowing. I'm just smart about it."

Meghan laughed, and the movement brought her body closer to me again, making it hard to pay attention to what she was saying. "Really? Does that include ... hmmm, what was her name? Casey? Jaycee?"

I stiffened. "How do you know about her?"

She cuffed my shoulder. "How do you think, doofus? Ali told me. She said she didn't think you'd been dating anyone since Jaycee or whoever she was left town."

"Shit." I closed my eyes. "She's better than I thought. How could she know about that?"

"Sister intuition?" Meghan smirked. "I get that. I know I was shocked when I found out about Joseph—that's my brother—getting his girlfriend pregnant. I hadn't even suspected, and usually I knew all his secrets." She smoothed her fingers over my hair, almost absently. "But what you mean is, you don't want to make this a big deal. You don't want to take me on dates or hold my hand when we're walking around the farm, right? Nothing that'd make anyone think we might be a real couple."

Meghan's voice held no condemnation or hurt, but I still winced. She made it sound so harsh. "It's just too hard to explain things like this to Ali, and Bridge would start designing you a wedding gown. She's young, and she's impressionable. For her, there's a strict order to life. You kiss a boy, you wear a white dress, and you live happily ever after. I don't want to disillusion her yet."

"I understand." Meghan slid her hands behind my neck. "So we're talking clandestine make-out sessions in the orchard? Sneaking around after bedtime, meeting in the barn for a quick roll in the hay?"

I trailed my fingers down her side, over her ribs and then back up to her still-exposed breasts. They were too tempting, and I leaned forward to touch my lips to one stiff nipple. "We don't have hay in the barn. Just farm equipment. Nothing that would be comfortable enough for what you're suggesting." I bit gently on the rosy peak.

She smiled and massaged the back of my neck, holding me in place as her eyes drifted closed. "What kind of farm doesn't have hay in the barn?"

"The kind that doesn't have animals. And if you object to our hay-free farm, you can join Bridget's campaign for horses. Won't do any good, though. We can't afford to feed them yet. Maybe someday." I eased her bra and shirt back into place. "God, I could sit here all night with you on my lap, doing this. Except I'd be so tired in the morning, I wouldn't get anything done tomorrow."

"I think tomorrow is today." Meghan shifted to adjust her bra, cupping her hand around my jaw with gentle fingers as she leaned back. "And I know you need your sleep."

"Yeah, I do." I wasn't sure exactly where we stood. Were we going to be summer fuck buddies, for as long as I could hide that from my snooping sister? Or were we back to being just friends again?

"This is your show, Sam." Speaking as though she'd read my mind, Meghan eased off my lap and stood up. "When you want me, you know where I am. I won't push. If you wake up tomorrow—well, in the morning, at any rate—and decide it's a bad idea again, you don't have to explain anything to me. I'll figure it out." She laid her hands on my shoulder and bent so that her lips were against my ear. "But if you need something to help you make up your mind, to help you sleep, know that in my bed tonight, I'll be thinking of you." She straightened, keeping her eyes pinned to mine as she ran her tongue over her lips and then skimmed fingers over her own breasts.

My mouth went dry. At that moment, I didn't care about waking up Ali, Bridget or everyone in ten-mile radius. I wanted her on the porch floor, under me, writhing. I needed to be inside her, making her scream my name, more than I needed my next heartbeat.

But Meghan only smiled and touched one finger to my cheek. "Night, Sam. Sweet dreams."

I watched her hips sway back across the porch and through the front door. She held it carefully so that it didn't slam, and then her footsteps disappeared in the direction of her bedroom.

God, what kind of self-flagellating fool was I?

I DIDN'T SLEEP WELL. Every time I closed my eyes, I saw Meghan touching herself, and I woke more than once with a painful hardness between my legs. I mumbled a curse against her and all women as I rolled over and tried to get comfortable. It was a losing battle.

I gave up at sunrise. After a quick shower, I dressed and snuck down to the kitchen to make a pot of coffee. I was going to need at least that much today. The rest of the house was silent. I expected my sister would sleep in after her big night out, and Bridget was never an early riser. Slipping into Meghan's room and taking care of what seemed to be a permanent erection was tempting but too risky. In the light of day, I knew I'd been right about keeping whatever happened between the two of us a secret from Ali. And maybe if I kept my distance from Meghan, I'd be able to avoid doing anything that would have to be kept a secret.

I left the house with my coffee and drove to the field farthest from the house. Yeah, distance was the best thing. I liked to think I was strong, but the last few weeks had let me know that any time I was close to Meghan, my self-control seemed to vanish. Staying out of her path today, when I wasn't sure exactly where we stood, felt like a good plan.

By the time I ran out of excuses to keep me away from the house, it was past dinner-time. I parked the truck by the shed as usual and washed up, taking my sweet time doing it. Ali was going to blast me for being late for a meal, I knew, so why rush toward trouble?

To my surprise, though, it was laughter that I heard when I swung open the screen door to the kitchen. My sister and Meghan were standing at the counter, peeling and chopping carrots and cucumbers. A huge salad bowl sat between the two cutting boards.

" ... and then Trent says, 'But I'm hotter than he is. What does he have that I don't?' And of course I'm laughing so hard, and Flynn's giving me the look of death—" Ali broke off mid-sentence when she saw me. Meghan glanced up, the knife in her hand coming to a halt in mid-air. Her eyes met mine, and the air in the room was suddenly steamier than it had been outside.

"There you are." Ali looked nearly as flustered as Meghan and me, and I realized what she'd been saying when I'd interrupted. I hadn't heard that name on her lips in a very long time. What had happened between my sister and her high school boyfriend all those years ago had never been clear to me. All I knew was that for four years, they'd been inseparable, and then on graduation day, something had gone wrong and Flynn Evans had left. His parents still lived in town, but to the best of my knowledge, their son hadn't ever returned.

"Yeah, here I am." I reached over my sister's shoulder and snagged a cucumber slice. "I thought I was going to be late for supper, but it's not even ready. What's up with that?"

Ali smacked my hand away. "Stop it. Yes, we're running a little late. Bridge and I went over to Fred's with Meghan, to paint his horses."

"I didn't know they needed a touch-up." I traded my dirty shirt for a clean one in the laundry room, aware of Meghan's eyes following me. The tip of her tongue shot out to wet her upper lip, and my stomach turned over. I had to focus hard to avoid walking across the room and pulling her against my body. I wanted every inch of her touching me.

"Smartass." Ali shook her head. "You know what I mean. Meghan gave Bridget a lesson on scale and proportion. And they painted on canvas, too. The pictures are in the living room. You should go check them out."

Getting out of the kitchen seemed like a very good idea. I turned my back on the women and went to examine two canvases propped against the sofa. It was apparent which one my niece had painted, though I noticed an improvement over her other horse drawings. But Meghan's made my jaw drop. It was like I was standing in my neighbor's pasture, and I half-expected Rummy, the horse in the foreground, to lift his head and whinny at me. This girl's talent blew me away.

"Okay, we're ready to eat." Meghan leaned through the doorway to call me. She smiled, brushing an escaped strand of hair behind her ear, and pointed at the paintings. "So what do you think?"

"Freaking amazing. How do you get it to look so real?"

She shrugged. "Years of training and hard work. And trade secrets. If I told you, I'd have to kill you." She winked at me. "Bridget did a good job, too, didn't she? I think she's got talent. I know she has a good eye."

"Yeah." We stood for a minute, staring at each other, neither of us moving. I let my gaze sweep down her, taking in the clinging white T-shirt and cut off denim shorts that made her legs look endless. I pictured them wrapped around my waist, and breathing became an issue.

"Hey, are we eating or what?" Ali stood behind Meghan, the salad bowl in her hands. "I know it's a cold dinner, but I'm starving. Come on, you two."

Bridget chattered through most of the meal, telling me about everything she had learned from Meghan that afternoon. I saw the gleam of hero worship in my niece's eyes and thought I'd been right on with what I'd told Meghan the night before. If Bridge thought I was dating her beloved art teacher, she'd start imagining weddings and new cousins. This was a kid who craved a big family, and I couldn't deal with the inevitable disappointment I knew she'd suffer.

Dinner finished, Bridget cleared the table and ran outside to do some sketching before the sun went down. After the screen door slammed behind her, Ali leaned back in her chair and studied me.

"So, big brother, I have to say I was kind of shocked you weren't waiting up for us last night. I expected a full interrogation when we got home."

I folded my napkin into a small square, not meeting her eyes. "You're both adults. I'm not your father or your husband." I was both surprised and relieved that Meghan hadn't told her that I had in fact been waiting on the porch to make sure they made it home alive.

"Hmmm." Ali tilted her head. "And you're not at all interested in what happened at the bar?"

I lifted one shoulder. "I figure if it's something I need to know, you'll tell me. You came home, so obviously you didn't get picked up by some drunk cowboy."

"Well, *I* didn't." Ali smiled at Meghan, one eyebrow raised. "I mean, don't get me wrong. I had fun. But Meghan ... she's the one who made the conquests. The guys were all over her."

I glanced across the table in time to see a flush cover Meghan's face as her eyes dropped. Suspicion, heavily laced with jealousy, snaked into my chest. I pictured her coming home last night, straddling my lap, primed and ready for whatever I did to her. I'd thought it was her attraction to me making her so eager, but was it maybe someone else who'd gotten her hot, and I was just convenient.

My mouth tightened. "Yeah? Guess it was good to have some real fun finally, huh? Get away from this boring old farm." Temper simmered in my gut. "Did you leave a trail of broken hearts? Or did you just get them riled up and then leave them thinking they were going to get lucky?"

"Sam!" Ali's expression was incredulous, her mouth gaping and brow furrowed. "What the hell?"

"You're the one who said she had guys all over her. I'm just drawing logical conclusions."

"You mean stupid conclusions. If you want to know the truth, there was really just one man Meghan paid any attention to. They danced together all night, and I think he would have gone home with us, if she'd given him the green light. I wouldn't be surprised to see him coming around here. He's from Atlanta, and he couldn't keep his eyes off her."

My heart pounded. Why was I surprised? I'd predicted this. She was a city girl, no matter what she claimed, and she liked to have fun. I was just a stupid farmer in a backwater town, and she'd been messing with me.

"Good." I swung around to glare at Meghan. "If it'll keep

you out of my way, I don't care how many guys come sniffing around here after you. Do 'em all. Screw your way through the rest of the summer. It's what you do, right?"

I knew I'd gone too far, hit too many tender places that she'd shared with me, but I couldn't help it. Rage and frustration spilled into my growled words.

Meghan met my eyes, and hers were filled with hurt. With a sound deep in the back of her throat, she pushed back her chair and ran from the house, the door slamming again. In the shocked silence of the kitchen, I heard the sound of her car starting up and gravel flying.

"What in the goddamn hell were you thinking?" Ali hissed at me. "Why would you say those things to her?"

I ran a hand through my hair, regret and guilt beating back at the jealousy now. "I don't know. There's just something about her that sets me off." I glared at my sister. "But you don't know the whole story. She came home last night, all soft and wanting to kiss me, and then you tell me she'd been making out all night with some guy at the bar—"

"It was Alex." Misery clouded Ali's face. "Alex is home, and he hung out with us last night. I was just messing around. I thought if you were a little jealous, you might make a move for Meghan. But she wasn't with anyone else last night but Alex and me. And you know you don't need to be threatened by either of us."

"Fuck." I dropped my head into my hands. "Ali, why the hell would you do that? You can't play with people like this."

"I didn't know about last night. I mean, whatever happened when we got home. She didn't say anything to me. The only thing I knew was that you were kissing her yesterday morning. I saw you from my bedroom window, but then it seemed like you pulled back, and I thought maybe you needed a little nudge." She closed her eyes. "I didn't mean to go so far."

"Yeah." I stood up, shoving away my chair, and grabbed my keys from the hook. "I'm going after her. Any idea where she might go?"

Ali shook her head. "No. She wouldn't go back to Savannah, would she?"

"I doubt it. I'll drive around and see if I can find her." I shot a finger at my sister. "If she comes back or you hear from her, call me right away, you hear? And get ready to grovel when Meghan comes back. You owe it to her."

"What about you?" Ali rose, her hands on her hips. "I may have gone a little too far, but I'm not the one who basically called her a slut."

I clenched my jaw. "I already know what I have to do."

Chapter ELEVEN

Meghan

I PRESSED THE GAS pedal to the floor of the Honda, ignoring the trees flying by me as I swiped at tears that ran down my cheeks. My hands shook as I gripped the steering wheel.

I had no idea where I was going. Burton was surrounded by two-lane roads that led north to South Carolina, west toward Macon, east to Savannah and south to Florida. I wasn't sure which one I was driving on at the moment, but I knew eventually I'd have to stop and figure it out. The only important information right now was that I was driving away from Sam Reynolds.

Even thinking his name wrenched another sob from my throat. I thought I'd been mad and hurt that day at Boomer's, but I hadn't really known Sam then. He'd been a virtual stranger making judgments on me, which was annoying and infuriating. But over the last weeks, Sam and I had opened up and gotten to know each other. Our porch talks had been surprisingly intimate, and especially after last night, when it seemed we'd come to some kind of understanding about this irresistible pull between the two of us.

I didn't have any idea that Ali was going to tease him about what had happened last night at the Road Block. When she'd begun talking about me dancing with one particular guy, I figured she was talking about Alex, using him to make Sam jealous. I kept waiting for her to explain, but before she could, Sam was saying the most horrible things I could imagine. Each word stabbed into my heart, cutting me until I couldn't breathe. I could only think of getting away.

The road curved sharply, and my car skidded on the shoulder, kicking up dirt until I got it under control. I eased up a little on the gas as I came to a crossroads. A familiar pick-up sat at the stop sign on the right of the intersection, and my heart skipped a beat. I floored it again, blowing past Sam's truck. There wasn't a chance he hadn't seen me, given that there weren't any other cars on the road. The sun was setting, but it was still light enough to make out my Honda. I could only hope that he'd choose to leave me alone.

I should have known that was too much to wish for. Moments later, his headlights were in my rearview mirror, flashing on and off. I ignored him, pressed my lips together and gave the car a little more gas. Sam kept up with me, laying on his horn. I hit the button on my window and stuck my arm out of the car, flipping him off. But taking my hand off the wheel made it harder to control at this speed, and I swerved onto the shoulder again. For a dizzying minute, I thought I was going straight into the trees, but I managed to tap the brake enough that the car only did a ninety-degree spin and ended up facing the opposite direction as I was slammed against the door.

Sam's truck screeched to stop about twenty feet ahead of me—well, actually behind me now, since I was situated the wrong way. I heard a door slam, and I fumbled to unlatch my seatbelt. I had just opened my own door and put my feet on the ground when he reached me.

"What the *fuck* do you think you're doing?" He seized my

arm, almost shaking me before he stopped himself. His hand gentled, and he scanned me up and down. "Are you okay? Did you hit your head? Does your neck hurt?"

I leaned back against the car. "No, I'm fine." I shrugged his hand away, and his mouth clamped down.

"You're goddamned lucky you're not dead. Are you fucking crazy?" Sam scraped his hand through his hair. "I swear to God, Meghan, you make me insane. You could've killed yourself."

"Why would you have cared? I'm just in your way, remember? I was heading off to find some guy to screw since that's all I'm good for—"

"Would you shut the hell up?" He grabbed me again, this time by both arms, and before I could maneuver away, he pulled me against him and covered my mouth in a bruising kiss.

I fought him for the span of two heartbeats, and then a tidal wave of want overwhelmed me. I clawed at his back, trying to get closer. Sam slid his hands from my arms down my back until he gripped my ass and held me tight against him. I felt his hardness at my hip and ground into it so that he moaned.

His mouth was aggressive and demanding, lips moving against mine and tongue demanding that I open to him. When I did, he explored the inside of my mouth, stroking and coaxing. I circled my tongue around his, matching his desperate need with my own.

When I brought my hands up to his face, cupping his jaw, he spread his hands on my butt and lifted me. Instinctively, my legs circled his waist, putting my pulsing center even with the ridge beneath the fly of his jeans. I rocked, needing that friction more than I needed my next breath. Sam tore his mouth from me and stared down into my eyes.

"I want you. I'm not waiting any more." He ground out the words as though I'd been the one holding us back.

"Like I've been—" I began, and Sam hitched me higher against him, making me gasp as the throbbing between my legs scraped across his middle.

"Shut up, Meghan." He took my mouth again and holding onto me, strode down the shoulder of the road to where his truck stood idling. Without lifting his head, he balanced me with one hand and used the other to open the passenger side door. His fingers circled to cup my ass, just barely skimming between my legs. My breath hissed as he set me down on the car seat.

I wasn't sure what he intended to do, but at this point, I was beyond caring. Him, hard and ready inside me, was my only goal. So when he grasped the hem of my shirt and tugged it upward, I raised my arms in silent obedience. Sam tossed the shirt behind us, and it snagged on the steering wheel.

"My God, you're beautiful." He didn't stop to admire me, just mumbled the words as he filled both hands with my breasts. His thumbs circled the sensitive peaks over the lacy blue material of my bra until my head fell back and I squirmed on the seat.

"Sam." His name seemed to be the only word I was capable of saying. He didn't answer, only pushed my breasts together and leaned to take one nipple into his mouth. His fingers pulled down the cup on the other side and rolled the stiff nub, just hard enough to make me cry out but not enough to really hurt.

I clutched at his sides, bunching the material of his shirt in my fists. My breath was coming in short puffs, hitching now and then when Sam bit down on my nipple or sucked me into his mouth.

He put a hand to my shoulder and lowered me to lie down on the seat. He stood between my legs and skimmed the backs of his fingers down my stomach to the button of my denim shorts. My eyes closed against the onslaught of sensation, I felt the release when he unfastened the button and slid down the zipper. He took off my shorts and underwear in one motion, and I opened my eyes to see them fly over my head, landing behind me on the driver's seat. He parted my legs further, making teasing circles up the inside of my thighs.

I knew if he touched me at all, I was gone. I'd been so turned on for so many weeks, all he'd have to do is breathe on me to make me come. I suspected that he felt the same way, since instead of exploring the folds at the juncture of my legs, he undid his own pants, pausing to pull a condom out of his wallet. Somewhere in the back recesses of my mind, I wondered if he was always so prepared, but at this second, I could only be glad he was.

"Next time, I promise, more. More everything. For now, I have to be inside you."

I wasn't going to complain. He lowered his jeans enough that his cock emerged, hard and jutting forward. I watched through lowered lids as he rolled on the condom and then took me by the hips.

He paused and met my eyes. For the first time since I'd skidded off the road, I saw something in his face beyond intense passion or anger. He swallowed and licked his lips.

"This ... this is okay?"

I reached my hand to stroke his forearm and smiled as I repeated back his words. "Shut up, Sam."

Without another word or hesitation, he lifted my hips and plunged into me. I arched my back, trying to draw him even deeper, but he held my hips and controlled our rhythm. His eyes never left mine as he thrust and rocked.

I gripped the back of the seat with one hand and my own hair with the other as pure pleasure built within me, spiraling me upwards. I was so close, so ready to fall over the edge. Sam was moving faster, and then he used one hand to touch me at the spot where we were joined. The brush of his fingers over my clit sent me rocketing, soaring as I cried out his name, my mouth open as I fought for air. I shattered into a million shining pieces as Sam's body tensed. He groaned just a single word—my name—and I felt him spasm within me.

For a moment, all was silent except for the chirping of the birds and the far-off sound of frogs, singing to each other at a lake somewhere. The blood rushing through my ears subsided, and I closed my eyes, not sure what would come next.

Sam withdrew from me, stepping back from the truck. I heard him zipping up and buttoning his jeans and the crunch of his boots on gravel, stepping away briefly. And then there was the lightest touch on my thigh.

"You okay?"

I opened my eyes and nodded, suddenly self-conscious that I lay mostly naked on the seat of his truck while he looked down at me. Given our history, I expected him to turn cold, tell me to get dressed and go home. But instead, he lifted my legs and climbed into the truck, shifting me so that I lay partly over him. He reached around me to take my shirt from the steering wheel and helped me pull it over my head, giving me at least partial coverage.

"If it were my choice, I'd sit here all night, just looking at you lying naked in my truck. Damned if it isn't the sexiest thing I've ever seen." His voice was low.

I tried for a smile. "I guess we're lucky nobody really drives these roads this time of night. That would have been an awkward explanation."

A pained expression crossed Sam's face. "Meghan, I'm sorry. That wasn't—I mean, I'm not sorry about what just happened. But I should've been man enough to make sure it happened somewhere more private. If someone *had* come along and seen us, it would've been my fault."

I ventured to touch his arm, fingering the hard muscle where tanned skin disappeared into the tight sleeve of the shirt. "At the time, I didn't care. And since no one did come along, I still don't care. So stop beating yourself up."

A flush crept up his neck. "Yeah, I guess I'd have to agree. I was pretty far gone. I'm not sure anything or anyone could've stopped me." He reached his other hand to cover mine where it still rested on his arm. "But Meghan, I *am* sorry about before. About tonight. I was way, way out of line, and I was wrong. I don't have any excuse. When I heard what Ali said, I just couldn't think straight."

I struggled to sit up a little, keeping my hand within his and pushing up on the other elbow. "Sam, nothing happened last night. Ali and I hung out with her friend Alex, and yes, we danced, but he definitely isn't interested in me."

Sam's lips curved into a smile. "Yeah, my sister told me. She felt awful." He snorted. "Serves her right, trying to play around with people's lives. Maybe she learned a lesson."

"I doubt it." I grinned, and Sam laughed.

"You're probably right." He looked out the windshield, down the road to where the last lingering rays of the sun danced between the trees. "Anyway, I didn't mean what I said. None of it. I was hurt, I guess, thinking you'd been with some other guy and then coming home to me."

"I don't play like that." I kept my voice even and serious. "I do date a lot. I've been upfront about that with you. But I never see more than one guy at a time, and cheating is never okay. Not for me, not anyone I'm with."

"I know that." He cupped my face in one large hand, and I leaned into his palm, letting the gentleness of his touch undo me. "So what happens now?"

I turned my head to kiss the center of his hand. "What do you want to happen next, Sam?"

His eyes were steady on mine. "I want to take you home and let my sister know you're okay. She's probably going crazy, worrying." He paused, and I could almost see the wheels turning in his head. "And then ... I want to be with you, for this summer. I don't want to hide anything, or make it something shameful, something to keep secret."

"We're both grownups," I agreed. "No reason to hide, as long as everyone knows ... it's just a summer thing. Just for now."

His eyes flickered. "Yeah." He rubbed his face and sighed. "It's not that I don't feel something for you, Meghan, but the farm, and Ali—"

"And Bridget. They all have to come first. I get it. And you know I'm not looking for anything serious. I just want to enjoy whatever this is between us. I don't want to fight it, or fight you."

Sam pulled me up against his side. "I don't know, if a fight leads to something like what happened tonight, maybe it's not a totally bad thing."

I laughed. "Okay, point taken. But maybe it doesn't have to get so serious before we let off that steam."

"Yeah." He shook his head. "Jesus, you scared me, Meghan. When you went past me, you had to be doing over ninety. And when I saw you go into that skid—" He shuddered. "I don't think I've ever been so scared in my life."

"I'm sorry." It was my turn to apologize. "It's kind of my thing. When I get mad, or sad, or upset, I go driving. I blare the radio and just wander. Usually not so fast, but you really got to me tonight. I was ... hurt."

He winced. "I'm an idiot." His hand caressed my face again. "How can I make it up to you?"

"I'm sure I'll think of something. For now, maybe you should try to find me my shorts."

WHEN WE GOT BACK to the house—me driving slow and sane, with Sam sticking close behind me—Ali was sitting on the steps to the kitchen. As soon as I opened my car door, she flew across the yard.

"Meghan, I am so, so sorry. I never meant to push it that far. I was stupid. And—" She glanced over my shoulder, to where Sam was approaching us. "And I shouldn't have tried to interfere in your life. Or my brother's."

Sam stepped close enough to me that I could feel the warmth of his body against my back. We'd decided not to keep any secrets from Ali, but I wasn't sure if he wanted to actually come out and tell her anything. And when I thought about it, what was there to tell? "Hey, Ali, so I'm going to screw your big brother senseless all summer, with no strings attached. You cool with that?"

Clearly Sam had no such qualms. He slid his arms around me from behind and leaned to murmur into my ear, loud enough for Ali to hear him. "I don't know, Meghan. Do we trust her? Do we think she learned her lesson?"

I watched her eyes widen, and a grin spread across her face. "Oh my God, did you two finally give it up? No more sexual tension at every meal? Staring at each other when you think the rest of us don't see?"

Sam shook his head. "Don't make a big deal of this, Ali. It's just—" He caught my eye and paused. "Just what it is. Don't break out the wedding magazines or go telling everyone around town that I've got a girlfriend. Understand?"

"As if I would." Ali rolled her eyes. "Please. I'm just relieved not to be caught in the middle anymore."

"If you were in the middle, baby sister, you put yourself there." Sam tweaked her nose. "Now if you ladies don't mind, I'm going to bed. It's been a long and eventful day." He smirked at me, and then dropped a light kiss on my lips as he released his arms from around me.

I watched him head into the house, jeans tight on that ass I'd had in my hands less than an hour ago, T-shirt clinging to the muscles on his back. If I'd thought that having him once was going to make this intense want lessen, I was sadly mistaken. If anything, it had only whetted my appetite. I needed more.

Ali followed my gaze. "Oh, girlfriend, you've got it bad."

I jerked my eyes back to her. "What? No. I mean ... you heard Sam. This is casual. It's a limited-time-only-deal, and when summer's over, so are we. He's got a farm to run, and I've got another year of college. This is just ... fun."

"Mmmhmmm." Ali nodded, pretending to take me seriously, but I spied the spark of humor.

"Really, Ali. That's all. Oh, and don't worry, we'll be dis-

142

creet around Bridget. She won't catch me sneaking into her uncle's bedroom, I promise."

Ali laughed. "You better hope she doesn't, 'cause if she did, she'd think it was a slumber party and invite herself along. Relax, Meghan. I'm not worried."

We made our way inside, and as Ali held the door, she laid a hand on my arm. "I really am sorry about before. I had no idea my brother would go all jealous-caveman-mean. Can you forgive me?"

I thought about lying on my back in the cab of Sam's truck, my legs around him, and I smiled. "Yeah, I definitely forgive you."

Chapter TWELVE

Sam

OVER THE PAST TWELVE years, I'd become an expert at keeping my so-called love life separate from my family life. I guess that's what they call compartmentalizing. Whatever it was, I liked it fine. I'd go into town one night every week or so and spend the evening with a woman, and then I'd come back home a happier and more relaxed man, able to take on the stresses of the farm and family. I didn't have to worry about what Ali thought of the girl I was sleeping with or whether that girl would get her nose out of joint when I sat for hours drinking beer and watching a baseball game on television. I didn't have to take anyone's feelings into consideration. It was easy. Simple.

The morning after Meghan and I had screwed our brains out on the side of the road, I awoke with a distinctly uneasy feeling. Whatever this was between us, there was no keeping it apart from the rest of my life. I'd not only brought my love life to my doorstep, I'd given her my grandma's bedroom.

I lay in my bed as the gray light turned pink with the sunrise, wondering if Meghan had expected me to sneak into her room last night. Was she going to be disappointed with me, or pissed that I'd just come up and gone to sleep? I'd never stayed the night with any woman I'd slept with, but Meghan was right here, one floor down. What if she gave me the cold shoulder this morning? And was I expected to do anything special, like take her breakfast or offer to come see her during the day? No way I could do that. I had work to do, a farm to run. I couldn't hang around here all day.

I got up and showered, still brooding. Standing in the stall, I remembered Meghan spread out on the seat of my truck last night. I'd known from the minute I'd laid eyes on her, passed out in the car alongside the road, that she'd had a good body, but I'd never guessed how completely fucking beautiful she was. My cock hardened, remembering her gorgeous breasts and the long legs that had clutched around me as I drove into her ...

"Shit." I closed my eyes and leaned one hand against the wall of the shower, wondering what Meghan would do if I just showed up in her room right now, crawled into bed with her and took care of this massive hard-on. For one crazy minute, it sounded like a decent idea. And then I remembered that my sister and my niece were in the house, too, and the thought of getting caught by either one of them skulking out of Grandma's old room made my erection a little less erect.

I finished in the shower, got dressed and went down to the kitchen. It was silent as it usually was at this time of day. I liked the quiet, because it was when my house belonged to me. Any other time, it was Ali's and Bridget's, too, and I didn't mind that, but it was nice to have a few minutes of peace. I made the coffee and poured it into my mug while flipping through yesterday's newspaper, catching up on scores and highlights, letting the day settle into my bones.

After I'd finished my coffee, I lingered a few extra minutes, just in case Meghan decided to wake up. If she were mad that

I hadn't come to her room last night, I'd rather know now than have it on my mind all day long. But she didn't come out. I even crept to the front of the house and put my ear to her door, just in case she might be awake, reading or drawing. But I didn't hear anything from within.

Finally, I gave up, went out the back door and climbed into the old farm truck. I had plenty to do today, and giving myself over to the normal routines of my work was how I coped. Why should today be any different, just because I'd slept with a girl last night? Or rather, hadn't slept with her. I'd banged her and then left her with my sister.

"Put it away," I growled to myself, and starting up the truck, I headed over rough dirt roads out to the stand.

No one was there yet, of course. I was always first on the scene, there to unlock the sliding wall and make sure everything was set up for the day. We had two high school kids who worked for us during the busy summer months, and Ali spent most of her time at the stand, too. But I liked to keep my eye on things, check on stock and inventory as well as basic upkeep.

This morning, after I knelt down to oil the wheels of the slider, I went to the back and examined the supports around one of the shelving units. Last winter, we'd been hit with a massive ice storm, and when everything had melted, water had leaked into this part of the small building, warping some of the wood and making it necessary to replace some shelves. Because this was the area that held our locally produced jams and honey, along with other fairly heavy products, I needed to make sure that the repairs were holding.

Cassie Demeyer showed up just as I'd finished my rounds. She was a pretty blonde girl, with a friendly smile and bright blue eyes that made her a customer favorite.

"Morning, Sam." She slammed the door of her old Buick. "Are we all set?"

"Yeah, I think so. Jim Newman says he'll be bringing the first of the semi-freestone peaches over today. I looked at them yesterday, and I think it's a good crop this year. Make sure you push them with customers who're looking for local fruit."

We talked about pricing for the peaches and what produce was reaching the end of its season, so she could try to sell out what we had on hand. As soon as Lynne Bower, another of our high school employees, pulled up to join Cassie, I left them to their work and headed out into the fields to do my own.

By four-thirty that afternoon, I congratulated myself. I'd made it through the day without obsessing over Meghan; even if she'd crossed my mind once or twice—every hour—I was still willing to call it a victory. I could do this. Whatever this was.

I drove back to the house, parked the truck and went through my normal wash-up routine at the outdoor sink. I was just drying my face when I heard steps behind me. I turned to see Meghan coming up the path that led to the house from the stand. She was carrying a basket of peaches, and her eyes were fastened on me. Or more accurately, on my chest, still damp from the splashed water.

My heart thudded as I watched her approach. She wore a paint-spattered blue tank top, and it clung to her in a way that made me hope she hadn't seen any men today. None at all. And those shorts ... they were almost riding up her ass. I felt myself harden, and it only got worse when she stopped a few feet away from me and ran her tongue over her lips.

"Hey." I shut off the water and leaned against the sink. "Where've you been?" I heard the words come out of my mouth and hoped they didn't sound as accusatory as I feared.

Meghan's lips curled into a smile. "I went over to help out at the stand for a while this afternoon. Bridget stayed with me in the morning so we could do some drawing, and then I walked her out there after lunch." She lifted the basket of fruit. "They were still busy, so Ali sent me home to put on the chicken for dinner. Oh, and she had me bring us some peaches, too, because they're selling fast."

"Good." I slung my sweaty shirt over my shoulder. "So are

you, uh, okay today?"

"Okay? Why?" Her forehead furrowed, and then smoothed as understanding dawned in her eyes. "Oh, you mean after last night."

"Yeah. Last night." I nodded like a freaking bobble-head doll.

"I'm good." Her smile widened to a grin. "I don't want to disillusion you, Sam, but that wasn't my first time."

"I know. But it was your first time with me. *Our* first time." My voice was rough with remembered passion. "And I was gone all day. I didn't know ... if you expected anything."

Meghan set down the peaches and put her hands on her hips. "Anything like what? An engagement ring? A declaration of undying love? I thought we'd worked out our expectations yesterday."

"No, not like that. I mean, like for me to be hanging around. Or ..." I glanced toward the house. "Or coming to your bedroom last night. Sleeping with you. Staying the night."

She laughed. "Oh, Sam. You're making this so much more complicated than it needs to be. Were you worried all day that I'd be mooning around the house, waiting for you to show up and be my boyfriend?"

"No. Yes. Hell, I don't know. I've never done this, been with a girl who lived in my house. It's—" I glanced around, searching for the right word. "It's weird, is what it is. I have no clue how to treat you. How you expect to be treated. Do we hold hands at the dinner table? Do I kiss you goodbye in the morning before I leave for the fields? Do you want me to check in at lunch time?"

"What do you want to do? Because that's what I want, too. I don't want you kissing me or holding my hand or anything because you think it's what you're supposed to do. Only do it if you want." Meghan took another step closer to me, her eyes roaming down my body again. "For instance, how would you feel if I saw you washing up out here, and I just waved and walked right into the kitchen?"

I considered. "I guess I'd feel okay with it. Why wouldn't I?"

"Right. Because that would be natural for me to do that. But what you don't know is that every single time I see you here at the end of the day, stripping off your shirt and getting all wet, the only thing I want to do is ... this."

She reached out one finger to trace the path of one small water droplet as it ran down from my neck and across my chest. I shivered at her touch. Her fingertip took a detour around my pecs and up to circle one nipple, teasing ever closer to the center of the disc but never actually touching it. I closed my eyes as she ventured farther down, over my abs to stop at the waistband of my jeans.

"The first time I saw you out here washing up, all I could think was that I wanted to come up behind you, wrap my arms around your middle and lay my head on your back. Just to breathe in your scent after a day in the fields, and touch your chest ... your abs ... any part of you ... as long as I wanted."

My mouth was dry, and my cock strained against the zipper of my jeans. I couldn't think of anything intelligent to say. Shit, I couldn't think of anything stupid to say.

"So if I'm in the kitchen looking out the window when you come in from working, I just might come out to do that. Okay? Not because I think it's what I should do, or what you expect me to do. But because it feels good. It's what I want to do."

I nodded. "God, I hope you want to do that every single day."

Meghan nodded. "I can tell you it's a strong likelihood. But don't worry, if Bridget is out here or in the kitchen, I'll keep my hands to myself." She ran her fingers up my arms, and I thought I heard a little hum under her breath. "So what about you? What have you been fantasizing about doing if we ever got together?"

I caught her hand and dragged her closer. "Exactly what we did last night in my truck."

Her eyes went soft for a moment. "Yeah, that works for me,

too. What else?"

I reached behind her head, where her red curls were gathered into a messy ponytail. Pulling out the hair band, I combed my fingers through the strands, gentling when I hit snarls that needed to be unraveled.

"Hmmm ... let me think." I squinted. "I want to sit out on the front porch with you after dinner. While Ali's putting Bridge to bed, and the day's work is done. I want to hold you in my lap on the swing and make out until neither of us can think straight."

"Didn't we do that Friday night?" She was teasing, but I nodded.

"Yeah, but when we're so turned on we can't breathe, this time I want to be able to pick you up and carry you to your ... hmm. No, that won't work."

She tilted her head. "What? What won't work?"

I ran one hand over my damp hair. "Your room. It used to be my grandmother's, before she died. And call me crazy, but the idea of having sex in her bedroom just isn't something I can do. It would be like she was still in the room, you know what I mean?" I shuddered.

Meghan shook her head, an expression of distaste on her face. "Oh, yeah, I get that. Eww. Just even with her stuff still there ... yuck."

"Which is a problem." I sighed. "You're living with Grandma, and I'm upstairs right next to Bridget's room. I know I said the porch floor wasn't an option the other night, but desperate times and all that. Maybe I could bring down a blanket."

"Sam, relax." She stood on her tip-toes and kissed me, just the barest of touches on my lips. "We'll work it out. Ali and Bridge aren't here all the time. Right now, for instance, we have an abundance of privacy."

"Damn, that's right." I was mentally kicking myself. "All this time we were standing here talking about stupid stuff, and we could have been taking advantage of this opportunity. I could have you upstairs, naked on your back. Or ..." I smiled, thinking of the possibilities. "Maybe on your stomach, with your ass in the air."

Meghan's lips parted, and her eyes dilated. "I like the way you think."

I was just about to grab her arm, drag her inside to my room and put my plan into action when I heard the sound of voices. I recognized my niece's excited chatter and her mother's answer.

"Shit!" I moaned the word and tugged Meghan close to me again. "We waited too long. Listen, the next time I'm about to miss a chance to make love to you because I'm talking too much, stop me. Tell me to shut up and get busy."

She giggled. "Okay. Same goes, all right?" She made as though to slide away from me, and I caught her arm, lowering my head to nuzzle her neck.

"Porch tonight, after dinner. Yes?"

"I wouldn't miss it." She rubbed her body against mine as I let go of her arm, and my whole body lit up when I felt her little grind over the bulge beneath my fly.

"You're making me crazy." I smacked her on that tempting little backside as she bent to retrieve the peaches, making her yelp in surprise.

"Good. It's all part of the plan." She winked and skirted around me, making sure to keep well out of my reach.

God, I couldn't wait until after dinner.

"SHHH! YOU'RE MAKING THE chains squeak. Don't wake up Ali and Bridge."

I shifted in the swing, trying to keep quiet while I did so. But it wasn't simple, since I was holding Meghan in my lap at the same time.

"This isn't as easy as it looks." I kept my voice to a whisper and lifted her hips to resettle on top of me. "Keeping the swing quiet when you're one person is hard enough, but when you have a whole other person to balance—"

"Hey!" She leaned back away from me, her mouth turned down and her eyes dangerous. "What are you saying? I'm too heavy to sit on your lap? To be on the swing with you? Are you calling me fat?"

"God, no." I'd lived with women long enough not to fall into that particular trap. "Why would you think that? I was just saying it's a matter of finding my center of gravity."

"Are you sure?" She still looked worried.

"Meghan, are you kidding me? You're perfect. You can't really think you're heavy."

She stuck out her lip. "My boobs are too big."

"No such thing." I hoped she picked up the fervent tone in my voice. "Babe, I fucking love your boobs." I slid my hands up to demonstrate, lifting them together and then rubbing my palm over the stiff nipples. "If I tell you that the first time I saw you, passed out in your car, I noticed your—um, assets right away, will you get mad and call me a pig?"

Meghan shook her head. "Nope. I'd only ask why it took you so long to actually touch them."

"Because I'm an idiot, remember?" I lowered my mouth and laved one nipple through her shirt and bra. She moaned a little, just under her breath.

In the ten days since we'd begun ... doing whatever this was, our after-dinner porch time had become the highlight of my day. Unfortunately, it also represented the only private time we'd had, since everyone's schedules had conspired to keep one extra person at home any time Meghan and I were here together.

I was getting desperate. We'd managed to find some creative ways to get each other off during our porch make out sessions, but it wasn't the same. By a long shot. I felt like a kid again, stuck with dates that ended in chaste goodnight kisses and blue balls.

Meghan slipped a hand between us, her fingers teasing my

stiffened cock over my jeans. "If we were alone ..."

I groaned. It had become a game for us, to drive each other crazy by describing what we'd do if we were alone. She could get me hard just by whispering, "IWWA" when we were sitting at dinner or if she walked past me at the stand.

"Yeah?" I rubbed her nipple between my finger and thumb. "What would you do?"

Her lips curved on one side. "I would sink down to my knees, and I'd unzip your pants. Drag your jeans down your legs ... slowly. Rub my boobs across your boxers, and then I'd take your dick out ..." She increased the pressure of her fingers a little, and I think I went cross-eyed. " ... and I'd hold you by the base. Cup your balls. Curl my fingers around the shaft and move up ... and down. And then I'd take you in my mouth, swirl my tongue around the head, go down, down, down." Her voice, already low, dropped to a whisper. "And then I'd suck you on the way back up."

"You're going to kill me." I gripped her ribs and moved so that her damp core sat over my erection. Meghan began moving in slow, agonizing circles, her eyes drifting shut.

Inside the house, a door slammed, and we both startled. Meghan nearly fell off the swing in her hurry to climb off my lap, but I caught her by the waist. "It's okay. Probably just Ali getting up for the bathroom. She usually has a window opened, and the breeze could have closed the door."

Meghan dropped her forehead onto my shoulder. "I don't want to complain, Sam, but I had more privacy when I was in high school."

I brushed her hair back, letting it cascade behind her shoulder. "Really? Where did you go to make out in those days? The beach?"

She snorted. "Never. Not unless you wanted to end up with sand in some very uncomfortable places. No, we had a few spots. There's a little apartment above the Tide—it was actually where my parents lived when I was born. When I got old enough that

Mom let me close by myself, sometimes I'd take my boyfriend upstairs afterwards. Of course, we had to leave the lights out, because if anyone in town noticed activity, they'd have called my parents." She smiled, almost dreamily. "But we never got caught."

"You were lucky." I wound a curl around my finger.

"What about you?" Meghan drew her knees up to her chest and curled into my chest, laying her head over my heart. Seeing her like that, safe and ensconced in my arms, gave me an odd feeling I wasn't ready to name yet.

"Ah, you know. The typical. Parking out in the woods, or sneaking off to a barn."

She frowned up at me. "I thought you said you didn't have hay in the barn."

"We don't. But other farms do."

"Oh."

We were quiet for a few moments, enjoying the breeze as it played across the jasmine next to the porch. I ran my fingers up and down Meghan's spine and smiled at her shiver.

"I have an idea." It had come to me when she asked about our make out spots. "Want to go out on a date with me?"

She looked up again, eyebrows raised. "A date? Like ... what kind of date?"

"Come on, Meghan, I know you've been on dates before."

"Well, yeah, but at home. Or in Savannah. What do y'all do out here in Podunk?"

I shook my head at her teasing. "You'll have to trust me. But I promise you, it'll be like no date you've ever been on."

"Hmmm." She swiveled so that her chin rested on my breastbone. "Okay. You've got yourself a deal. What should I wear?"

"Dress comfortable." I wriggled down so that I could reach her lips and kissed her. "Meet me at my truck tomorrow night at eight. And don't be late."

I KNEW MEGHAN WOULD be in town at school until at least four the next day, and Ali was working the stand as usual. So after I finished my work in the morning, I drove back to the house and began getting ready for our date.

I opened up the old cedar chest in the upstairs hall and pulled out four old quilts. Dropping them at the top of the steps, I went into the bathroom and dug around the cupboard until I found the bottles I needed. Just before I went back downstairs, I remembered to grab two pillows off my bed and add them to my pile.

It took some doing to get the truck ready, but once it was, I unwrapped a brand-new tarp and spread it over the back. I needed one more trip into the house for matches, candles and the bottle of wine Ali had bought last month. I'd replace it on my next trip to the liquor store. The last item I needed was in Meghan's room, and I walked in cautiously, as though at any minute she might jump out and ask me what the hell I was doing in there. I hadn't been inside Grandma's room since Meghan had arrived, and it was weird to see her things over the familiar furniture.

Blank canvasses were propped up against the hope chest at the end of the bed, and a bunch of brushes dried on a towel by the windowsill. Piles of books dominated the dresser. For the most part, Meghan was neat; there were no dirty clothes on the floor, and her bed was made. But she must have had trouble deciding what to wear that morning, I thought, because I saw a couple of discarded shirts tossed over the coverlet. A pink lace bra sat there, too, and I picked it up, running my fingers over delicate fabric. I'd seen some of her underwear by now, on nights when we got particularly daring on the porch, but not this one. Just imagining her within the cups made me hard.

I tossed it back onto the bed, remembering my mission. Meghan's music blaster was on the nightstand, and unplugging it, I carried it out to the truck.

155

Mission accomplished, I thought. Now I just had to wait until eight o'clock. This was going to be the longest day ever.

Chapter THIRTEEN

Meghan

"**N**O, GRAHAM, DON'T TOUCH anything!" I made a desperate grab for the seven-year old terrorizing the kids around him. "Or anybody."

"I'm a monster!" He roared, darting around the desks and evading me once again.

Truer words, I thought, but I didn't have time to laugh. This child was determined to spread his finger paint over everything and everyone in the room.

"Whoa there, tiger." A tall woman in jeans and boots caught Graham and swung him up, holding him by his middle. "Time to wash up."

"Thanks." I hurried over with wet paper towels and wiped off as much of the paint as I could manage with the boy batting and kicking. I glanced up at his captor. "I appreciate the help. Are you a mom? I don't think we've met yet."

"Nah, not a mom. Just an aunt." She let Graham down, holding his hand in a death grip. "To this little cherub, actually."

"Oh." I grinned; it was clear that this chick had her nephew's number. He wasn't going to get away with anything. "Everything okay with his mother?"

"Yeah. She's my sister, and her husband surprised her with a trip to Hilton Head for a long weekend. Anniversary deal. They left this little prize with my mom, and for some reason I'll never understand, she gave him a donut for breakfast. Sugared him up before she sent him to you. So ... sorry about that."

"No problem." I dried my hands. "I did notice he was a little more, ah, active today."

The woman grimaced. "You're being too nice. He's a brat sometimes. He's the only grandchild, and so he's more than a little spoiled." She sighed. "I can't say anything, I do it, too."

"What are aunts for, if not to spoil? My nephew is just a little over a year old, and I could just eat him up whenever I see him." I stuck out my hand. "I'm Meghan Hawthorne, by the way. The art teacher."

"Maureen Flynn. Veterinarian and auntie to horrible monster children." She shook my hand as I laughed.

"Graham's really not that bad, not normally. He's actually got some talent, when I can get him to sit down and concentrate."

"Doesn't surprise me a bit. My dad's an artist, of sorts. He's a mason, and he designs these beautiful fireplaces or walls for people. He's got the eye, Ma says." Maureen examined me a little more closely. "You're not from Burton, are you?"

I laughed. "No, why? Am I missing a special symbol marking me as part of the town?"

"Nah, I just realized I didn't know anyone related to you. So what brought you to our bustling city?"

"It's a long story." I moved to my desk and began to sort through the day's projects. "But basically, I'm part of a program that places art students in communities that need them. I'm only here for the summer."

"Ah." She nodded. "Do you live nearby?"

"I go to school in Savannah, but right now, I'm staying out

at Sam and Ali Reynolds' farm."

"Ohhh." A shadow passed her face so quickly, I wasn't sure I hadn't imagined it.

"Do you know them?" I had a hunch maybe she knew one of them a little better than the other.

"I ... did. Not so much anymore." This time the discomfort lingered.

I sighed. "Sam? Did you date him?"

Her brow knitted together. "What? Sam? Oh—no. No, I 've never had the pleasure." She winked at me. "But by the way your face is turning that lovely shade of red, I'm guessing you have."

"I'm not—I mean—"

Maureen laughed. "No comment is a perfectly acceptable answer. No, I knew—know, that is—Alison. But it was years ago." She paused, as though remembering. "We sort of drifted apart. But at one time, I thought she was going to end up part of my family."

I was confused for the space of a moment, and then everything clicked. *Evans.* Of course. This woman must be the sister of Ali's lost love, Bridget's real father. Examining her more closely, I thought I saw a tiny bit of resemblance.

And if this were Bridget's aunt, and Graham was the child of her sister ... that meant Bridget had a first cousin, right here in town. In her class. I blinked, wondering if Ali knew about this. Of course she had to. This was Burton. Nothing was hidden.

Maureen was speaking again. "Nice to meet you, but I need to get the paint monster back to my mom before he does real damage. Graham! Get a move on, we're going to Granny's house."

The other parents were straggling in to retrieve their children, and by four o'clock, my classroom was empty. I finished cleaning up and lit out for the farm. I had a date, and I needed time to prepare.

No one was home yet when I got back to the farm. Ali had

put pork chops in the slow cooker for dinner, and they smelled delicious. I high-tailed it to my room, where I stripped off my teacher clothes and jumped into the bathtub.

Tonight wouldn't be our first time having sex, but in my mind, that night in the truck on the side of the road only partly counted. We'd almost been animals that night, mad for each other, and while the intensity was still there in spades, tonight we'd have time to enjoy each other. So I wanted to be perfect. I used my favorite citrus body wash and shaved every part of my body that qualified for that attention.

I had just climbed out of the tub and wrapped myself in a towel when I heard Ali and Bridget get home. Ali stuck her head through the doorway. "Hey. Whatcha doing?"

"I ..." Licking my lips, I tried for a smile. "I have a date. So ... I was getting ready."

Ali's eyes wandered down my body, and she grinned. "My brother's taking you on a date?"

"Yeah. I don't know where or what. He just told me to meet him at the truck at eight."

Her eyebrows went up. "Oooooh. Well, then I guess I'll just say I won't be waiting up."

My face burned, and Ali laughed. "In case you're wondering, no, I'm not going to make this any easier on you. It's too much fun, seeing the two of you tortured with having to behave yourselves."

"Thanks." I tucked the edge of the towel in to the top, securing it against my chest. "I have no idea what to wear, since I don't know what we're doing."

Ali came in and flopped onto the bed. "Around here, you can't go wrong with jeans. If you're leaving at eight, he's not taking you into the city for a fancy dinner. There's a movie house in Summerville, but jeans would work for that, too."

"Good thinking." I pulled out my favorite pair of soft and faded denim and flipped hangers in the closet, looking for a shirt. "Hey, can I ask you something?" I glanced over my shoulder.

"I'm not helping you pick out sexy underwear for tonight. Sorry, I know it's a girlfriend thing, but when it's for my brother to see—there's way too much eww."

"No, silly." I shook my head. "I don't need help with that." I thought of the expression on his face whenever he lifted my shirt and saw a new bra, and I smiled. "I know what he likes."

"Way TMI." Ali shuddered.

"Speaking of which ... I met Maureen Evans today. She came by to pick up Graham."

Hurt and sadness flickered over Ali's face. "Oh."

"I didn't make the connection at first, but then when I told her where I was living this summer, she got the same look on her face that you have now. She said you used to be friends."

Ali grabbed one of my pillows and turned onto her stomach. "Yeah, we were. Until her brother left town, and me, and their whole family. I think they blamed me, which was ironic, considering I was the one trying to talk him into staying."

"I'm sorry. I didn't mean to bring up a painful subject." I drew a black lace bra and a matching scrap of material that passed for panties out of my drawer and stepped into the bathroom to change, talking to her through the door.

"It's not your fault. I was really close to all of the Evans until graduation, and then ... I wasn't. They were like my surrogate family. Maureen was okay with me until I married Craig."

"And none of them suspected ... ?" I pointed out toward the living room, where I could hear the TV show Bridget was watching.

"I don't think so. No one ever said anything to me."

"So Graham is her cousin." I kept my voice quiet.

Ali laughed, but the sound didn't have much humor. "Yep. Her one and only." She shot me a meaningful look. "For now."

I raised my hands. "Oh, no, my friend. No strings attached, remember? Summer-only deal. No babies. You're on your own."

"I'm not that sorry Bridge doesn't know he's related to her. That kid's a piece of work."

"Yeah, even Maureen said that. She said he's spoiled because he's the only grandchild."

"I know. And don't think that doesn't make it tougher ... the thought that my kid's only grandparents live ten minutes away, and they don't know it."

"Do Craig's parents keep in touch with her?" I thought of my huge extended family back in Florida. The idea of not having any grandparents was inconceivable.

"Not really. Cards at her birthday and Christmas, but I think Craig probably told them the truth after he left. They were great while we were married, but after he moved away, they did, too."

We both turned our heads at the sound of the kitchen door. "Hey, where are my women?"

Ali and I both laughed, and she climbed up from the bed. "I think that means us. I better go finish up dinner so you two can enjoy your ... date." She winked at me.

I stood for a minute without moving. Hearing Sam's words and knowing he was including me in them—his women—gave me a strange feeling that was a mix of longing and panic. I liked the idea, more than I should. The panic came because I dreaded what might happen if Sam began to want more—and I couldn't give it to him.

I pushed the thought away. Tonight was about romance and fun and just being present in the moment—no worries about the future or the past. And I was determined to make it perfect.

I finished dressing, put on a little makeup and brushed my hair, leaving it down and curly around my face. When I stepped out of the room to go help Ali in the kitchen, I ran full-force into Sam, who was still shirtless and slightly damp.

"Hey." He caught me by the arms. "Where's the fire?"

"I think it's in the kitchen, cooking your dinner." I grinned up into brown eyes that were devouring me. Taking a step back, I held out my arms. "So? Do I look okay for tonight? Or do I need to be fancier?"

Hunger that had nothing to do with pork chops burned

from his face. "You don't need to be anything else. God, you look good." He glanced around me at the huge oak grandfather clock that dominated the living room. "How many minutes until eight?"

I laughed. "What's going to happen at the magical hour of eight? I'm still in the dark about what we're doing tonight."

A slow smile spread over his lips, and heat flooded my face. "Okay, so I'm not *completely* in the dark. I have some ideas."

He stepped closer to me, until I was backed against the wall that was shadowed between my bedroom door and the turn to the kitchen. "In the dark is the key phrase. But I don't want you to worry. Maybe I should give you a little preview."

My heart stuttered a little at his nearness. His chest, bared at my eye-level, sent a scorching rush of desire between my legs, and I couldn't help running my hands over his skin.

Sam tucked me into his body so that I could feel every inch of him. With one finger, he tilted my chin upwards and kissed my mouth. He started slow and sweet, but when I wrapped my arms around his lower back, he growled low and pushed his tongue between my lips.

When we came up for air, I dropped my forehead to his chest. "I need to go help Ali with dinner."

"Yeah. I need to get a shower." Neither of us moved.

I lowered my hands to his ass and pressed him closer to me. "IWWA ..."

"We're changing that, right now. Today it's not IWWA, it's WWAA."

I frowned, and he leaned to whisper in my ear. "When we are alone."

I sighed. "I can't wait."

He slapped me lightly on the butt and stepped back. "Then let's get through dinner so we don't have to."

I was pretty sure Ali's pork chops were excellent that night, tender and tasty, but they could have been sawdust for all I knew. I ate mechanically, trying to keep up with the conversation and act normal. I didn't think Ali was fooled, but Bridge didn't seem to notice anything amiss.

I helped with the dinner dishes, and by then it was nearly seven. Sam was sitting at the kitchen table, playing cards with Bridget.

"That's enough Go Fish," he announced after four hands of the game. "Choose something else."

"Oh, I know! How about Old Maids?" She scrambled down and ran to the cupboard where all her games and books were.

"I don't know how to play that." Sam frowned at the deck of unfamiliar cards.

"It's basically Go Fish, but with different cards." Ali dried her hands. "They're all word plays. See, there's Ben Dover. And Tully Vision. There's only one Old Maid card, and whoever ends up with it loses."

"Mama, what's an old maid?" Bridget began dealing the deck.

"It's what they used to call women who never got married, sweetie."

Bridge glanced up at me. "Meghan, are you an old maid?"

I held back a giggle at the horrified look on her mother's face. "Bridget! No, Meghan is *not* an old maid. And it's not a very nice thing to say."

I decided this was an opportunity to educate her. "Bridge, when this game was made up, women felt like they had to be married to amount to anything. But now women can do whatever they want. They can get married or not, they can have any career ... so that's why we don't say old maid anymore."

She nodded, but I wasn't sure she understood. "I want to get married when I grow up. I'm going to marry Parker Smith, and we're going to live on his farm because it has horses and pigs, and we're going to have lots of babies."

Ali rolled her eyes, but I hurried to answer Bridget. "That's great, honey, if that's what you want to do. But there's a ton of other things out in the world, and you might decide you want to do them, too."

"Don't you want to get married, Meghan?" The little girl picked up her cards and scanned them.

The room was silent, and I felt as though everyone was waiting for my answer. "Um, probably. Some day. When the right person comes along, and when I'm ready. But right now I'm too young."

She cast me a skeptical look. "You're not too young. Mama was younger than you when she got married." She laid down a pair of cards and gazed pointedly at Sam. "*You're* not too young, Uncle Sam. Are you going to get married ever?"

Silence fell again, and I saw Sam's throat work as he swallowed. "Maybe someday, peanut, but for now, you and your mom are plenty of women for me."

"And Meghan," Bridge added.

Sam glanced up at me, his eyes unreadable. "Yep. And Meghan, for sure."

That same mixed feeling settled in my stomach, and I took a deep breath, wiping my suddenly-damp palms on my jeans. *Just for now*, I reminded myself.

Sam made it through two hands of Old Maid before he stood up, announcing that he had to get some things ready outside. Before Bridget could ask what he was doing, Ali interrupted and reminded her that it was time for a bath and reading.

"Have fun tonight," she whispered as her daughter dragged her toward the steps. "But don't tell me about it. I'd like to stay blissfully ignorant if you don't mind."

I wiped off the table and stood uncertain in the middle of the kitchen. It was nearly eight, but I wasn't sure whether or not Sam wanted me outside. I heard him around the truck, and my curiosity was running high.

Before I could peek out the window, the screen door opened, and he stuck his head inside. "Okay, I'm ready. C'mon."

"Do I need to bring anything?" I rubbed my arms, wondering if I needed a sweatshirt.

"Nope, just yourself." He held out a hand, and I took it.

The pick-up truck was just outside the door, and two fishing poles leaned against the bed. Sam squeezed my hand and looked down at me with questioning eyes.

"Okay, so if I'm way off base here and you don't want to do this, I've got a plan B. But tell me the truth: are you all right with some night fishing?"

"Are you kidding me?" I reached for the pole nearest me and ran my hand over it. "I'm a beach girl. I love to fish."

The relief on his face was adorable. "Good. I thought it would be fun. I've got a special place picked out, and I think you'll like it." He pulled me around to the other side of the truck, tossing the fishing stuff into the back over a tarp as we rounded the tailgate.

Sam started up the engine and within a few minutes, we were bumping along a rough dirt road, heading into the woods. He'd taken my hand again when he started driving, and now he pressed it to his thigh.

"In case I forget to say it later, you look gorgeous tonight. I couldn't stop looking at you when we were eating dinner."

I tightened my fingers around his. "I've been rushing through this whole day, just to get to tonight. I don't even remember eating dinner."

He turned sharply, and we were deeper into the trees. The canopy of branches hid the stars and moon, and the night was full-on black. I closed my eyes and leaned my head back against the seat.

"Are you tired?" Sam's thumb rubbed the top of my hand.

"No." I turned my head and smiled at him. "Just enjoying the present. The quiet and the dark."

"Well, look ahead now, just for a minute." He took a left, and suddenly we were in a clearing. The sky stretched over us with a million stars, and before us, moonlight gleamed on a beautiful expanse of blue water. I caught my breath.

"Oh, Sam, it's so pretty." I leaned forward, checking out

the sloping bank that led down to the river. "Is this where we're fishing?"

He nodded. "Yeah, this is my favorite spot." He pulled the truck alongside the water, as close as he could get without getting stuck. "Wait here a second."

Sam jumped out on his side and circled around to open my door for me. He laced our fingers together again as he helped me out and led me to the river.

"If you sit down here, I'll bring the fishing gear over." He pointed to a flat rock that sat on the edge of the water.

"I can help you," I offered, but he shook his head.

"Nope, just stay put."

He didn't have to tell me twice. There was something about moving water that spoke to my soul, and I realized how much I'd been missing the ocean this summer. I leaned down to let my fingers trail in the rushing bubbles. It was icy cold, and I shivered.

Sam joined me with our fishing poles. He insisted on putting the bait on my hook for me, even after my assurances that I always did my own hook at home.

"I'm not that much of a girl, Sam." I took the offered reel.

"I didn't think you were, but this is a date, and maybe you don't want to get your fingers all slimy."

I couldn't think of an argument, so I smiled. "Thank you for that."

We cast out and watched the bobbers bounce as they landed. I settled myself between Sam's legs, relaxing my back against his chest. "This is the best date ever. Thank you."

The fingers of his free hand wrapped around my stomach. "This is just the beginning. Don't thank me too soon."

"But it's perfect. Most guys would take me out to a restaurant or some place like that, and I'd have to pretend to like it. But this is exactly what I wanted. What I needed."

"I'm glad to hear that, because I'd have hated to put on a stupid tie and go to a fancy place to eat." He leaned in to trail his lips down my neck. "I would have done it, if it were what you wanted. But I'm glad it isn't."

My line tugged sharply. "Hey! I think I got something." I sat forward and pulled up, cranking in slow and steady. I liked that Sam didn't try to take the pole from me; he just watched me, smiling, as I slowly reeled in a good-sized trout.

"That's a nice one." He watched the fish flop on the river bank. "I've got an ice chest in the truck if you want to keep it."

I shook my head. "Nah. Let's let him go. He's been a good sport."

Sam removed the hook and tossed the trout back in the river. I watched him swim away. "Do you think he's going back to tell his friends how he was abducted by aliens?"

"Maybe." He laughed. "I've never thought about what the fish think when they're thrown back in. Do you ever eat what you catch?"

I shrugged. "Sometimes, but usually not." I ran the tip of my tongue along my top lip. "It's the catching that I enjoy, you know? I guess I always think the best part of anything is having fun while it's there, and then being smart enough to walk away when it's over. Or toss it back."

Sam watched me for a minute and then nodded. He picked up my rod. "Want to cast again?"

I looked at him, kneeling next to me, those brown eyes hungry as he glanced up at me. His T-shirt stretched over his shoulders, and I knew I didn't want to wait another minute.

"No, I don't think I do." I slid from the rock and knelt in front of him. "I think I want to enjoy what I hooked. And guess what, Sam?" I kissed up his neck until I got to his ear lobe. I bit it gently, sucking it into my mouth. "WAN."

He pushed back to see my face, and he was grinning again. "WAN. We're alone now."

"Yes, we are." I slipped my hands into the waistband of his jeans and tugged him as close to me as I could. "So what are you going to do about it?"

Sam lifted me up, his hands cupping my backside. "Come and see."

Chapter FOURTEEN

Sam

ONCE WHEN I WAS about ten, my mom took Ali and me down to Florida to see her aunt, who'd just moved there. She lived in a trailer park for senior citizens that sat on the edge of an orange grove. I remembered stepping out onto her deck and taking a deep breath of the tantalizing aroma of orange blossoms.

That was exactly how Meghan smelled as I picked her up and carried her toward the truck. I made it up the bank before I stopped at a tree and let her slide down me. Taking her face in my hands, I covered her lips with mine, kissing her with such thoroughness that our hearts were pounding when I broke away.

"Wait here." I touched the tip of her nose. "I need to do one more thing."

She nodded, leaning back against the trunk of the tree. I saw her touch her lips with the tip of one finger, and it was all I could do to scramble back to the truck. I pulled off the tarp and tossed it to the ground, and then I lowered the tailgate and climbed into the truck bed. I pulled out the bag that was tucked in the corner and found the candles and matches. Carefully, I lit each one and placed them around the edge of the truck.

The last thing I did was dig my phone out of my pocket and plug it into the blaster I'd stolen from her that afternoon. I queued up the play list that I'd put together last night and hit play. Country music at just the right volume filled the air.

I jumped off the back and went back to Meghan. "Okay, come on now. We're all set up."

She smiled and followed me without asking questions. I liked that about her; she trusted me and wasn't going to insist on knowing everything I was doing. When she saw the truck bed, piled in quilts and pillows, with the candles giving off a soft glow, her mouth dropped and her hand went to her heart.

"Sam. Oh my God. This is ... it's beautiful. It's perfect." She turned to look up at me, her eyes shining. "You got this all ready for us? When?"

I slid my arm around her side. "I have my ways. Here, let me boost you up." I held her by the waist and lifted until she was crawling up toward the pillows.

"What's this?" Meghan poked at the bag on the side.

"Supplies." I climbed up and joined her. "Bug spray." I held it up. "Because I don't want you getting bitten up by anything but me."

She giggled and reached for it. "Okay, good thinking. What else you got?"

"Protection." I tossed the strip of condoms onto the pillow.

Meghan raised her eyebrow. "Someone's optimistic."

"Hey, preparation is important." I reached back into the bag. "And I stole Ali's favorite wine, too. Remind me to replace it, please, or there'll be hell to pay."

"Got it. Did you bring cups?"

I shook my head. "No, we're going old school tonight and drinking it straight from the bottle."

I loved that she didn't blink. "Excellent." She lay back, falling onto the pillows with a soft thud. "Sam, this is amazing. Wine, protections from all the elements, blankets, candlelight, music ..." She looked over at the blaster. "Hey, isn't that mine?"

"Yeah, I had to liberate it from your room. Sorry." I lay down next to her.

"That's okay, it was for a good cause. Though I think this is the first time it's ever had country music played on it."

"Then it must be a really happy blaster. Since this is clearly the best music ever."

Meghan snorted. "Oh, please. Twangy, whining cowboys? Give me my rock bad boys any day."

"Hey." I rolled and held myself over her, bracing on my forearms. "Don't diss my music. Have you ever made love to country?"

Her eyes grew soft, and she sucked in her bottom lip. "I can't say that I have."

"Then you're in for a world-shattering experience." I lowered my hips until they rested on hers. "Because the songs I put on this play list were chosen just for you. For tonight."

I let my lips stroke over her mouth, teasing and tempting. She was pliant and eager as her arms reached around my neck. I moved over her lips, waiting until she arched against me before I nudged her to open to my tongue. Stroking the inside of her mouth, I framed her face with my hands and caressed her cheek.

Meghan slipped her hands beneath my shirt and traced the muscles on my back. "Do you know how much I love to touch you? When I watch you work and see your strength ... it just makes me want you."

I pushed up to my knees and stripped off my shirt. "Now that you've told me that, I'm never going to wear a shirt again."

She ran her hands up my ribs, brushing her palms over my nipples. At her touch, pure lust ran down to my already-stiff cock. I bit her bottom lip softly and sucked it into my mouth before kissing down her neck, stopping at the pulsing vein near the base of her throat to circle my tongue there.

"God, Sam, you feel good." Meghan lowered her hands to my ass, trying to get me closer to her.

I kissed and licked my way back up to her ear. "I want you naked and screaming under me. I thought we could take this slow, but there's something about you ... I feel like I'm going to die if I can't be inside you."

She moaned, and I fumbled for the hem of her shirt. "Lift up a little, so I can get this off you."

Meghan crunched up, raising her arms to help me. I almost swallowed my tongue when I saw the bra she was wearing. It was black lace, plunging low, and the pale pink peaks of her nipples pushed against the material. As though I couldn't help it, I lowered my mouth to catch one of them between my teeth, worrying it without biting down too hard.

She cried out, but I knew it was from pleasure, not pain. I balanced on one arm and covered her other breast with my hand, palming it and feathering my thumb over the nipple.

Meghan writhed beneath me. I pulled down one cup of her bra and covered the rosy peak with my mouth, sucking and pressing it to the roof of my mouth. Her hands clawed at my back, and she moaned my name.

"What do you want, Meghan?" I already knew, because it was the same thing that I needed, but I had to hear her say it.

"I want—more. I want you. I need you inside me."

Reaching behind her back, I unhooked the bra and threw it to the side. I pushed her breasts together, kissing them and then moving lower, down her stomach. My fingers played under the waistband of her jeans before I unbuttoned them and tugged down the zipper.

"Sam." Her hands threaded into my hair, and I knew she was coaxing me on.

"Yeah, I know, babe. I'm getting there." I pulled off her jeans and inhaled fast when I saw the tiny piece of lace between her legs. "Oh my God, Meghan. Are you trying to give me a heart attack?" I touched her, letting one finger tip trail over the panties, dipping down to where the black cloth was soaked. I added just enough pressure to feel the hard nub of nerves beneath.

"Sam—please." Meghan grasped my hand, pushing it against herself.

"Shhh. I'm going to make it better. Much, much better." I hooked my fingers into each side of the panties, pulling them down her legs and over her feet. My mouth was level with the juncture of her legs. I parted her, slow and tender, and kissed within them, circling her clit with my tongue as my fingers explored.

She let out a strangled cry. "So close. Oh, God, Sam. Don't stop."

"Not planning on it." I sucked the bundle of nerves at the same time that I plunged two fingers inside her. Meghan rocked her hips, trying to get closer to my mouth. She gripped my hair and her whole body spasmed as she ground out my name. I could feel her pulsing around my fingers and twitching beneath my tongue.

When she collapsed onto the quilts with a heave of breath, I kissed down to her feet and then back up, letting my lips cover every bit of the silken skin on her legs as I moved. She hummed a little, and when I reached her face again, she opened her eyes enough to offer me a lazy smile.

"Hi." She reached out to draw me closer and kiss me, this time with sensual slowness, as though we could lie here forever enjoying each other.

"Hi." I ran my hands over her breasts again, loving the feeling of their weight and fullness in my hands. "You're incredible, did you know that?"

"I know you make me feel incredible." She laced her hands together behind my neck. "When you touch me, it's like you set me on fire. And I burn for you, until I think I'll end up cinders."

She kissed me again, pulling me tighter to her as her tongue tangled with mine. Her fingers danced over my chest again, trailed down my stomach and skated beneath my jeans. I sucked in my breath to give her room, and when her small palm closed over my throbbing cock, I groaned.

"I think you're way too dressed." Meghan sat up on her knees, her hair falling in a silken curtain around her shoulders. She unbuttoned my pants and tugged at them. "But I also think you're going to have to help me get them off." She smirked at me. "You get them off and I'll get you off."

I shook my head in mock outrage and sat up to help her maneuver the jeans off. My boxers caught on the button, so I took them off too and discarded them in the corner with Meghan's clothes.

"Much better." She swung one leg over me, straddling my hips so that her hands were on my shoulders and my dick jutted out behind her. Laying there looking at her, with her red hair spread around her face and her body glorious with the globes of her breasts, I thought I'd never seen anyone so beautiful, so perfect. I knew this vision would haunt my memory for a long time.

"I like this." I lifted her boobs, using one finger to draw a circle around a nipple. "Are you going to ride me?"

"Maybe." She flashed that sassy smile that used to annoy the hell out of me. Now it only made me want more. "But first I'm going to taste you."

She slithered down my body, and I thought I was going to lose it when her boobs ran over my cock. But in a few seconds, Meghan's hand was on me, stroking and pumping, pausing now and then to cup my balls or to circle the head with her thumb. Just when I wasn't sure I was going to live and didn't care if I died, she surrounded me with the burning silk of her mouth, sinking over me, taking in each inch.

She gave that same little hum that I'd come to associate with her pleasure, and the vibration ran out of her mouth and into my dick, making my hips buck up to meet her lips.

"Shhh." She glanced up at my face through her lashes, and

the sight of her there between my legs, taking me into her mouth, hair cascading over us both as her breasts brushed my legs was my undoing. I reached for her shoulders.

"Now. I need to be inside you now." I tried to drag her up to me, desperate to have her on top of me. Or under me. I didn't really care, as long as it ended the same way.

I heard the sound of her soft laughter as she crawled her way toward me. She leaned to the side of my head and picked up the strip of condoms from the pillow next to me. All of my senses were overwhelmed: the scent of oranges wafting from her skin, the feel of her legs alongside mine and her weight on my thighs, the taste of her still on my lips, and the crinkle of paper as she tore open the little packet were only heightened by the sight of her rolling latex over my pulsing cock.

She raised herself over me, holding me just at her entrance. She teased a little, rubbing me up and down her wet sex, before she sank down.

And then we were both frantic. I held her hips and thrust my own upward, needing to meet her rocking pelvis. Meghan's mouth was slightly opened, her eyes closed, as she threw back her head and touched her own breasts, finding the perfect rhythm that made us both moan.

"Oh, God, Meghan—I'm going to come—" I didn't recognize my own voice, hoarse with desire and strain.

"Yes, now—now." She arched her body, and I felt her pulsing around me. It pushed me over the edge into madness, an insanity where I shouted her name again and again as all the stars in the sky fell over both of us.

Meghan collapsed onto me, both of us slick with sweat and breathing hard. I managed enough energy to lift my hand and stroke down her back. She murmured something against my chest, but I wasn't sure what it was. It didn't matter, because I didn't think my brain had enough blood running through it to make sense of anything, and the pounding of my heart drowned out the rest of the world.

After a few minutes, she lifted her head and smiled at me. "I'm hot." She peeled herself away from me and lay down with her head on the other pillow.

I touched the side of her face, pulling a few strands of hair away from her damp cheek. "Me, too. You have that effect on me."

One side of her mouth lifted in a half-smile. "I thought I drove you crazy. And not in a good way."

I chuckled. "Well, you did. But turns out this was the crazy you were driving me to. So I guess it's okay."

"Just okay?" She raised one eyebrow.

I rolled to my side, facing her. "Much more than okay. I think I died for a minute there." I sat up and felt a trickle sweat roll down my spine. "Hey, I have an idea. Want to cool off?"

Meghan pushed herself up. "How?"

"Swim in the river. C'mon."

But she didn't move. "Sam, aren't there snakes in the river? And it's really cold."

"Babe, the only thing that might bite you in there is me." I leaned across her and sank my teeth gently into the slope of her breast, then ran my tongue over to soothe it. "And cold is the point." I swiped something from the pillow and then jumped off the tailgate and offered her my hand.

She was still reluctant, I could tell, but she crawled down toward me anyway. I caught her waist and swung her down to the ground with me.

"You trust me, right?" I gazed down at her, at the moonlight reflecting on her skin. She turned luminous green eyes to me, considering for a minute before she nodded.

"Yes, I trust you, Sam."

It felt like we were both talking about more than just a dip in the water, but neither of us acknowledged that. Instead I pulled her toward the riverbank, lacing our fingers together as we picked our way through the dark, the feel of each other's hand the only sure thing in the night.

Chapter FIFTEEN

Meghan

"THAT WATER WAS FRIGID."

I sat in the back of the truck again shivering as Sam wrapped me in a quilt and pulled me onto his lap.

"Yeah, it was, but I warmed you up, didn't I?"

I tried to bite back a grin, but it didn't work. "Yes, you might have raised the temperature of the river by a degree or two. And scared some fish, probably." I reached up to smooth his wet hair out of his eyes. "I'm very impressed you thought to bring the condoms with us."

"Hey, I'm nothing if not resourceful. And hopeful." He smiled as he leaned his forehead against mine.

"You know, you don't do that enough." I traced a finger around his lips. "Smile, I mean. You're so serious."

I felt rather than heard his sigh. "I haven't had much chance to be anything but in the last ten years."

"I get that. But I hope you'll try to smile more often. Play a little. There's this whole side of you that no one really sees. If you'd asked me when we met, I would've said you were a grump. And maybe a little bit of an asshole."

He laughed then, settling back on the pillows, and pulled me to lie against his chest, my legs still tangled with his. "Yeah, you had every right to think that. The day I walked into Boomer's and saw you there, it just knocked me off my feet. I don't know why, but being a jerk felt like the best way to deal with it."

"You did it well." I shifted so that my ear was against his heart. We were both silent for several moments, as the water evaporated from our chilled skin and a breeze stirred the leaves above our heads.

"Thank you for tonight." I traced a line down the middle of his stomach. "This is the best date I've ever had, in my entire life."

His arms tightened around me. "I'm glad. And me, too." I felt him draw in a deep breath. "I've never brought anyone else to this spot. Ever."

My heart stuttered, and I swallowed hard. "You haven't?"

"No. My dad first brought me here when I was about twelve. He said as I was getting older, he knew there were going to be times I needed to be alone, to think, and fishing was the best way to do that. We had other spots he and my grandfather had taken me to fish when I was little, but this was secret, and special. He told me I was only the second person he'd taken to this spot."

"Who was the first?" I snuggled my body even closer to Sam's.

"My mom. He brought her here on their first date. I, uh, assume they didn't enjoy it in quite the same way we did, seeing as it *was* the first date, but he told me there was nothing like fishing with a woman to really get to know her."

I laughed. "I think I would've liked your dad."

"Oh, yeah, you would've. And he would've gotten a kick out of you. He liked feisty girls."

"That doesn't surprise me. I mean, look at Ali."

"True."

I hoisted myself above him and moved my mouth up his neck to his lips, where I nibbled and licked until I covered him, drawing out a long kiss. "Thank you, even more. It makes tonight special to know that."

Sam held my face in his hands. "Not over yet. I think we still have three condoms yet."

I smiled. "Wow. You really are ambitious. But it's got to be getting late, and you have to work tomorrow. I mean, I do, too, but I don't have to be up at the crack of dawn."

"I don't care. I can deal with a few yawns tomorrow. This is a night when we're not looking at clocks." He rolled over, pinning me down beneath him. "And I have so much more I want to do with you."

I ran my hands down his back and gripped that solid rear. "And when I can't walk tomorrow?"

He grinned into my eyes, a wolfish gleam in his. "Well, you can always teach sitting down."

DAWN WAS PAINTING THE sky when Sam and I finally climbed back into the cab of the truck. I'd helped him fold up the quilts and pile them along with the pillows in under the tarp, and we'd gathered the fishing supplies, blown out the candles and put away the bug spray.

"You know, we still have one of these left." I waved the last tiny square of paper as Sam got into the driver's seat.

"Yeah, I know. I did that on purpose." He winked at me. "I figured it was an incentive to do this again. Soon."

"I don't think I need an incentive." I slipped my hand into his. "This was the most perfect night I've ever had, Sam. But the porch is going to seem awfully tame after tonight."

"That's okay." He eased the truck over the road, and I

grabbed the door with my free hand, trying to stay on the seat. "You need some porch time to balance out the nights when we can get away. You know? Like a tease. Coming attraction, and all that."

"True." I laid my head back, closing my eyes with a huge yawn. "God, what time is it?" We'd dozed a little throughout the night, but I felt heavy with sleepiness.

"I think about four. You can catch a few hours before you need to get ready for work."

"What about you?" I rubbed my thumb on his palm, between our hands.

He shrugged. "I'll probably just grab a shower and head out to the fields. If I start feeling bad, I can always come home and catch a nap mid-day. The house is empty, and it's quiet."

I smiled. "Something to remember. You know, when the house is empty ... I do have an hour-long lunch break between my morning and afternoon classes."

"Aw, don't tell me that. I'll start scheming."

"I'm counting on it." I thought of how I could justify a trip back to the farm at lunch, and then it hit me, with a painful weight, that I only had four more weeks in Burton. At the beginning of the summer, two months had felt endless, but now ... I wished I could freeze time, or at least slow it down. I wasn't ready to let go of whatever this was between Sam and me. I knew its limitations, but as long as summer went on, so could we.

The farm was silent as Sam parked the truck. We closed our doors as quietly as we could and snuck through the kitchen door. Sam whispered to me that he would take care of emptying the truck out later, after everyone was gone.

I turned to go toward my room, but Sam caught my arm, pulling me tight to his body. "One more kiss." He wrapped his arms around me and covered my lips.

I opened my mouth to deepen the kiss, and our tongues twined lazily around each other. Sam ran his hands down my sides, pausing to tease my breasts, and I felt him harden against me.

"We still have one more rubber, you know." He murmured the words with his mouth on my neck, making me squirm.

"And so you're going to come join me in Grandma's bed?" I whispered.

He blanched. "Okay, you got me. But I have to admit, for a minute there, I was tempted."

I pulled his head down and put my mouth next to his ear. "Then you better not think about the fact that I'm going to go into my room, strip off all my clothes and crawl naked between the sheets. I bet the blanket will brush up against my boobs and make my nipples go hard ... and while I'm falling asleep, I'll still feel you there, between my legs. Your mouth ... your hands ... and ... hmmmm." I twisted out of his arms, tip-toed to kiss his cheek and whispered, "Good night, Sam. Thank you for tonight. See you later today."

As I slipped away toward my waiting bed, I thought I heard him laughing softly as he said, "Damn it, Meghan."

"MEGHAN—ARE YOU UP?"

A knocking at my door made me sit up straight in bed, disoriented and sleepy. Ali leaned in and her mouth dropped open when she spotted me.

"Sheesh, Meghan! I'm leaving for the stand, and I saw you hadn't had coffee yet. It's nine o'clock."

"Shit. Damn. Hell." I clutched the sheet to my chest. "Get out of here and let me get dressed, please. I can't believe I overslept."

Ali turned around in the doorway but didn't leave. "Late night, I guess?"

I jumped out of bed and grabbed my robe, shoving my arms

into the sleeves. "More like an early morning. You can turn around." I opened a drawer and began pulling out clothes. "Can you call someone, let them know I'm running late? Have one of the parents stay with the kids 'til I get there?"

"Yeah, don't worry, I'll take care of it." Ali grinned at me. "But don't think you've heard the last of this."

I made it into school before ten by some miracle of time bending. The mother who was watching the class smiled at me sympathetically. "Ali said you weren't feeling well. You okay?"

"Oh ... yes. Thanks. Just something I ate, I guess. Thanks for covering for me. I'm so sorry."

"Not a problem. You've been working so hard for us, and we all appreciate it. I know it must not be much fun for a college kid like you, stuck in a backwater town like Burton. Not really anything to do."

An image of Sam standing with me in the river last night, water streaming from his hair down his perfect chest flashed into my mind. I coughed and shook my head. "Oh, not really. I love the town. Everyone here has been so welcoming. And teaching has been so much fun. I'm not much of a party girl, so this has been a perfect summer."

And after she left me with my little group of budding artists, I realized that I had spoken the truth.

I struggled through the rest of the morning, trying to keep my yawning to a minimum until the first class left. As the last student's voice echoed down the hallway, I laid my head on the desk.

"Looks like teacher had a long night."

I jerked up my head, my heart thumping in surprise. Sam stood in the classroom doorway, leaning against the jam.

"God, you scared me to death. Again. What are you doing here?" A tiny thread of trepidation circled my heart, remembering the last time he'd shown up at the school, after he'd kissed me. Was this a replay? Was he going to tell me last night had been a mistake?

"I thought you might need a little pick-me-up about now." He held up a brown paper bag. "And I remembered you said you had an hour for lunch."

"Oh, God bless you. I overslept this morning, didn't get here until almost an hour after I was supposed to, and I didn't bring anything for lunch."

Sam walked into the room and dropped the bag onto the desk. A delicious aroma floated from it, and my mouth began to water. He reached in and pulled out two foil-wrapped packages.

"I wasn't sure what you liked, so I got you the same thing I eat." He peeled back the wrapping, revealing a seed-covered bun. "Pulled pork with cole slaw on top. And there's extra barbecue sauce, too."

"It smells so good. That's perfect, exactly how I like it."

He pulled two bottles of water out of the bag, unscrewing the lid on mine before handing it to me along with a bunch of napkins, and then opened a foam container filled with French fries and little tubs of ketchup. As I picked up my sandwich, he dragged over a chair and sat down across from me.

"So how're you feeling? You overslept, huh?" A mischievous smile, almost cocky, spread over his face.

I swallowed my bite of sandwich and stuck out my tongue at him. "Yes, I did. Proud of yourself, are you? If Ali hadn't come in to wake me up, I'd probably still be asleep."

He tried to tamp down the smile. "Why would that make me proud? Oh, you mean because I kept you awake all night?" He lowered his voice, leaning toward me. "Because I made you come, like, seven times?"

My face heated. "Were you counting?"

He shrugged. "Maybe."

"Well, you missed one then." I picked up a fry and dipped it into ketchup before popping it into my mouth.

Sam's eyes widened. "Really? Eight? Wow, I'm even better than I thought." He caught my hand and brought it to his mouth, kissing the knuckles before releasing it. "You know I'm just playing, right? I mean, yeah, I'm glad you enjoyed yourself last night, but I'm not that kind of guy."

"The kind who goes around bragging about his conquests? Nah, I didn't think you were." I wiped my face with a napkin. "But after last night, you'd have the right."

"Maybe, but so would you. And that's why I wanted to bring you lunch. Just to tell you ... last night was incredible. I've never had anything like that, ever."

"I haven't, either." I covered his hand with mine. "And thank you for lunch. It's going to get me through the afternoon."

"Like I said, I aim to please." He finished his sandwich, balled up the wrapper and tossed it into the trashcan.

"I was kind of surprised to see you here, though. I have to admit, for a minute I thought you might be here to tell me it was a mistake. That you hadn't meant for it to happen."

His face grew serious. "No, I'd never say that. Not about last night. A kiss, yeah ... and I felt so guilty that day. I'd been telling myself to stay away from you, so when the kiss happened, it felt like I'd done something wrong."

"Do you still think I'm too young for you?"

He glanced up, and I caught a fleeting expression of vulnerability. "Probably. But I'm tired of finding reasons not to touch you. Tired of spending all day building walls, just for you to knock them down the minute I see you."

"I'm glad." I stood up and walked around the desk. Taking his face between my hands, I kissed his lips, swiping my tongue into his mouth and when it opened for me, I tasted barbecue sauce. I'd only meant for it to be a quick kiss, a thank you, but when he snaked his arms around me to rub his hands over my ass, I pulled him tighter and deepened it.

"Oh, I'm sorry." We jumped apart at the sound of a voice in the door. Maureen Evans stood there, holding her nephew's hand. He was staring at Sam and me, his eyes bright and mouth open.

Sam recovered first. "Hey, Reenie. Hi, there, Graham." He

stood up and held out his hand for the boy to give him a fist bump.

"I'm so sorry," Maureen repeated. "We're early, but I told Mom I'd drop Graham off on my way to the office. I thought he could just sit and draw until the other kids got here." She flashed me a smile. "No sugar today. Mom learned her lesson."

"That's okay." I managed a smile. "Sam just brought me some lunch. Wasn't that nice of him?" I was rambling, but Maureen took pity on me.

"Is that Smoky Joe's I smell? God, I didn't realize how hungry I am. Might have to swing by and get some to-go."

"Well, I better get back to work." Sam stood by the door. He looked at me, indecision on his face.

"Thanks again for bringing me lunch. It was delicious."

He glanced at Maureen, who had gotten over her embarrassment at interrupting us and was watching back and forth as we spoke. And then, as though he had finally made up his mind, Sam strode back over to me, tilted my face up to his and kissed me. "See you at home."

He left the room without looking back. I stood gaping after him, my fingers on my lips as though I could hold his kiss there.

"Oh. My. God." Maureen came the rest of the way in. "Graham, get some paper and crayons and sit down." She walked up to the desk and swatted my arm. "Get the hell out. You and Sam?"

"Um." It was the most I could manage at the moment.

"I mean, everyone knows Sam's a catch, but he's never let himself get caught, you know? There's rumors about him ah, visiting certain women." She cast a look at her nephew, but he was busy coloring. "But he doesn't date. This is huge."

"Maureen." I managed to find my voice. "Please don't make a big deal over this. Don't tell anyone. It's not what you think. We're not really dating, we're just ... you know. Just a summer fling, okay? I'm leaving to go back to Savannah, but Sam'll still be here, and I don't want him to have to deal with people asking him what happened. Please."

Her face was inscrutable, but she nodded. "Yeah, sure." She cocked her head. "But are you sure this is just a fling? It didn't look casual to me. The electricity in this room—good God. It crackled. It felt like more than a fling to me."

"No, really. Sam has the farm and his family. I have another year of college. We're just enjoying each other right now."

Maureen sighed. "Whatever you say. You don't have to worry about me telling anyone. I don't gossip." She took her phone out of her jeans pocket and checked the time. "Oh, shit, I've got to go. I have an appointment in fifteen minutes." She turned to Graham. "Listen, kid, behave yourself, and Granny will see you after class." She sketched a wave at me and took off down the hall.

I collapsed back into my chair and put my hands to my cheeks. This casual summer affair was getting more complicated by the minute.

SAM DIDN'T SAY ANYTHING to me about our encounter with Maureen when he came home that evening. I was helping Ali with dinner and working with Bridget on perspective when I saw his truck pull alongside the barn. He glanced up at the kitchen window, and I waved, sighing a little without even thinking about it.

Ali looked over my shoulder. "Aha, I see why you're going mushy." She shoved at my arm. "Go on, get out there and greet him."

I looked at Bridget, her small face focused on the pencil and paper. "Not in front of the munchkin. I promised Sam."

She rolled her eyes. "I'm just saying, don't worry about it on my account."

The screen door squealed open, and Sam came in, his eyes

on me right away. He halted in front of the laundry room, paused and then took the extra steps toward me. Leaning down, he gripped the back of my neck, pulled me close and kissed me, open-mouthed and deep. I breathed in his scent of soil, sweat and man.

"Hi." Straightening up again, he rubbed his thumb over my cheek. "Did you stay awake this afternoon?"

"Just barely." I realized I was staring up at him, probably looking like a lovesick girl with stars in my eyes. I turned back toward the sink and dried my hands. "How about you? Good afternoon?"

"Yep."

I watched out of the corner of my eye as he pulled a clean shirt on. I wanted to beg him not to cover up his chest, but it might have been a little too much, I decided. Bridget might pick up on that.

We fell into our normal rhythm of dinner, talk and clean up. While Ali supervised Bridget's bath and bedtime ritual, Sam helped me with the dishes. He was playful, blowing bubbles into my face and splashing water until my shirt was soaked.

"Look at this." I peeled the cotton away from my stomach. "See what you did?"

"Oh, don't worry, I'm looking." He chucked the dishtowel onto the counter and grasping the bottom of my tee, pulled upward. "You don't want to keep wet clothes on, you know. You'll get pneumonia. Least that's what my grandma used to say."

I let him tug it over my head, smiling when his eyes widened upon seeing my white eyelet bra. "I should go get a dry shirt."

"Nah, just come with me." He took my hand and led me through the living room and onto the front porch. "See, you can dry off here in the fresh air."

It was twilight, and I glanced around, uncertain. "What if someone comes up the drive and sees me here without a shirt?"

Sam frowned at me for a minute, and then he threw back his head and laughed, long and hard.

"What?" I crossed my arms over my chest. "It could happen."

"No." He shook his head, still chuckling. "I'm laughing because here you were with me on the side of the road, naked in the cab of my truck, and you weren't worried about anyone catching us. But now you're on the front porch in your bra, and you're scared someone might see. Here, at our farm, out in the middle of nowhere."

I shook my head at him. "I was a little distracted when we were in the truck on the side of the road." I turned around. "But if you're going to make fun of me, I can just go into my room ..."

Sam caught me by the arm. "Nope. Can't do that." He swung me close and tightened his arm around my lower back, pressing me against him so that I could feel his desire. "You need body heat to help dry you, and since I'm the one who made you wet, I need to provide the warmth."

I traced a line down his cheek to the side of his mouth. "Yeah, you make me wet. Really, really wet."

He nuzzled my neck. "My pleasure, Babe. Believe me ... it's my pleasure."

RAIN MOVED IN A few days later, making the days gray and damp. Our evenings on the porch felt even more intimate with the sound of the rain in the eves and the fall of it around us.

Sam came home the second night of the storm, shaking water off his hair. "What a mess." He kissed me as he passed, almost absently. "I was going to run over to town and pick up the new blade for the tractor, but I ran out of time before dinner. Want to take a ride with me after we eat?"

I nearly dropped the plate of sliced tomatoes I was carrying. "Really? You want to take me with you? Aren't you afraid ..." I slid my eyes to Bridget. "You know. That people will talk?"

189

He grinned at me. "Nope. Let them talk. Who cares, right? After all, once Reenie saw us, I figure that ship's sailed."

"I don't think she'll say anything." I glanced at Ali. "She seems like the kind of person who'll keep her word, and she told me she wouldn't."

"We'll see." Sam sat down. "Do you want to go or not?"

Of course I did. And so right after dinner, I was sitting next to him in the truck, bouncing down the road. He had one hand on the steering wheel and the other around me, pulling me tight enough against him that I could lean my head on his shoulder. On the radio, a country singer was talking about checking some girl for ticks.

"I can't believe you listen to this." I watched him lean forward to turn up the volume. The windshield wipers competed with the radio as the rain picked up again.

"Of course I do. This is real music." He rested his elbow on the door by the closed window. "It's about real people, like me. What's not to love?"

"Hmmm." I linked my hand with his, as it hung by my neck. "But ticks? Really?"

Sam laughed. "Yeah, ticks. What, you don't think it would be romantic for me to check you for ticks? I bet I can prove it to you."

"I bet you could, too," I mused. The song changed to something slower, dreamier ... two people, a man and a woman, singing about how her love just did something to him. Sam tightened his arm around me and kissed the side of my head, and I think right there, I fell a little bit in love with country music.

We pulled up in front of the hardware store, and I slid out Sam's door behind him. He took my hand and led me inside through a door with a tinkling bell. The man behind the counter was leaning on a wall, shooting the breeze with an older guy in a one-piece coverall. When they caught sight of us, both men stared.

"Hey, Larry." Sam grinned at him. "Billy. Y'all got that

blade I called about?"

Larry regained his voice first. "Uh, yeah, sure, Sam. It's just in the back."

We all stood still for a minute, and then Sam cleared his throat. "You want me to get it myself?"

"No, no. I'll get it." His eyes lingered on me, darting down to our joined hands.

"You gonna introduce us to the lady, boy, or you gonna give your mama a bad name by not using the manners she beat into you?" The other man cuffed Sam on the arm.

Sam shook his head. "Wondered how long you could hold back your mouth. Meghan, this is Larry. He owns the store. Billy works down at the grange. Y'all, this is Meghan. She's teaching art at the school this summer."

Both men offered me their hands and mumbled something that sounded as though they were pleased to meet me. I tried to smile and not let the awkwardness make me shuffle my feet like a kid.

When Larry went in the back for the blade, Billy turned to me. "So what's a pretty lady like you doing with this sorry son of a—uh, gun? If you're lookin' for a date around here, I can set you up."

Sam's fingers gripped my hand a little harder. "Mind your own damn business, Billy."

"Hey, Sam." Larry stuck his head out of the storeroom. "Can you come back here for a minute? I want to make sure I pull the right blade."

Releasing my hand, Sam ducked behind the counter and disappeared into the back. Billy turned to me, lowering his voice.

"Let me tell you something, missy. That boy there? He's the genuine article. Not a better man in this town. Lots of boys would have sold out and left after what happened to his parents, but he didn't. I've never known a harder worker in all my years, and that's the truth."

Sam and Larry came back up front, Sam glancing suspiciously at Billy. "What kind of tall tales are you spinning for Meghan?"

He shook his head. "Never you mind. Just givin' your girl the real deal on things around here."

"Yeah, I'm sure." He slanted me a look. "Don't believe a word he says."

Sam paid, and we left, darting through the rain. As I climbed back into the truck, he caught me around the waist and turned me back to face him, perched on the edge of the seat, protected from the weather.

"What did Billy say to you?"

I cast my eyes up as though trying to remember. "Oh, he said you're a horrible flirt, and you have a new girl in town with you every week."

"Yeah?" He leaned into me, his body between my knees. "And did you buy his stories?"

"I don't know. You seem pretty smooth."

Sam snorted. "Okay." He kissed me. "Whatever you say." I scooted over to the middle of the seat. As we drove out of town, I snuggled closer to him. A part of my brain was screaming for me to remember that this was temporary. It couldn't last.

I ignored that voice. I planned to enjoy this man and whatever was between us for as long as I could.

Chapter SIXTEEN

Sam

OUR FARM HAD BEEN in the family for more generations than I knew, and over the years, there'd been some
changes in how we did things. We didn't use a horse
to pull the plow anymore, much to my niece's disappointment.
We'd gone from not using any fertilizers or insecticides in the
nineteenth century to using all of them in the twentieth to switching over to only natural help in the twenty-first century. I used
the same almanac to tell me when to plant and when to harvest,
but mine wasn't a paperback book; it was on my cell phone.

But over a hundred and fifty years later, one thing hadn't
changed. We were still completely at the mercy of the weather
and unable to do a damn thing to change it.

Two nights after Meghan and I had our night down at the
river, a front came up along the Florida coast, a hurricane that
never developed, and it stalled over eastern Georgia. We had
days and days of torrential rain. I was stuck in the house most

of the time; I went over to the stand each day, but business was slow there, since only the most stalwart souls ventured out in this weather to buy fruit and vegetables from a stand instead of a grocery store. I spent more of my time planning for harvest and for next year's crops.

"I don't mind a day or two of rain, but this is ridiculous." I sat on the porch with Meghan after dinner. The steady patter on the roof had been cozy the first few nights, but now it just pissed me off.

"I know. I was supposed to take the kids out to a few places around town to do sketches, and we have to keep putting it off. They're all restless during class, too. I can't imagine how you're holding it together."

I raised an eyebrow. "What's that supposed to mean?"

She smiled at me, unfazed. "It means you're a man who needs to be outside. You thrive on walking in those fields and being with your plants. You're kind of like a caged lion when you have to be inside for too long."

"Hmm." I folded my arms over my chest. "I like the lion part, but I'm not sure about the rest."

"You can be not sure, but it's true." She laid down her drawing tablet and pencil and scooted closer to me on the wicker love seat. "Are you missing anything else, maybe?"

"What else would I be missing?" I played dumb, mostly because she was right that I was being antsy inside, and I wasn't sure how I felt about her knowing me that well.

"Oh, I don't know. Maybe something like this." She leaned closer, kissing my ear lobe as her hand ventured to my zipper. "No alone time." She licked the side of my neck. "Other than the porch, I mean."

"I've gone longer than a week without sex. As you know." Still, I took her hand from the front of my pants and laced our fingers together. "But yeah, it is kind of messing with any plans to go back to the river."

"And I've thought about driving home during

194

lunch a few times, but with the stand not being busy, I know Ali doesn't always stay there all day." "Yeah, and she left Bridge with me today. That would've been frustrating, to have you come home and not be able to do anything."

"It's got to stop raining soon." Meghan wrapped both of her arms around one of mine, her boobs pressing into my side making me ache. "And then we'll make up for lost time."

Of course, she was right. Three days later, I awoke to clear skies, with no rain in the forecast. I spent the day out walking the fields, checking for any damage almost two solid weeks of wet might have done to the crops still out there. When I finally drove the farm truck back to the house, all I could think about was kidnapping Meghan back out to the river and keeping her up all night—again.

Her car was in the driveway when I got out to get cleaned up. I turned on the faucet, pulled off my dirty shirt with one hand and cupped water in the other. I had just made the first swipe with the rag when I felt arms slip around my waist.

"Now see, this is how things were meant to be." Meghan's lips touched my back and her fingers crept up to tease my nipples.

I turned in her arms, a swell of something that scared the shit of me rising in my chest. It felt so right, so perfect, to have her greet me at the end of a hard day of work, her pretty curls dancing around her shoulders, her eyes bright and full of life. Like I could do this every day and never get tired of it.

Not knowing what to do with that thought, I tugged her closer and kissed her until the lips under mine were the only things I could think about.

"Hi." I lifted my mouth just long enough to speak. "Ali and Bridget?"

She smiled. "Still at the stand for another hour. Cassie sprained her ankle, and Ali's expecting a delivery, so she has to wait there. And Bridget went home with her friend Kate to spend the night."

Something new was rising now, and it was not anything I dreaded. "We're alone here? For at least an hour?"

"We are." She pulled at my arm and began walking backward toward the kitchen. "Your room?"

"Oh, yeah."

We made it into the kitchen before I had to kiss her again, backing her into the counter where I lifted her up and stood between her knees, my hands gripping her rear and my mouth on her neck, heading south.

When I heard a knocking, I decided it had to be my heart. Or something we were shaking in the kitchen. Or maybe even a lost group of Jehovah's Witnesses who had wandered to my front door and would just go the hell away if ignored.

"Sam." Meghan lifted her head from my lips. "Someone's at the door."

"Uh-huh. They'll go away. Shhhh, just be quiet, they'll think no one's at home."

"What if it's important?"

"Babe, nothing's more important than what we're doing right here."

"But what if it's something with Ali or Bridget?"

I sucked on the pulse in her throat. "Someone would call."

"Unless they didn't have your number, just the address."

I blew out a breath of frustration and dug my fingers through my hair. "Fine. I'll get the fucking door and then—" I pointed at her. "Then you—me—upstairs, naked. Lots of naked."

She giggled and pushed at my shoulder. "Go, and then the nakedness."

I stomped to the front door, cursing anyone who was stupid enough to come by my house at this moment and already making up reasons to send them away. The plague, maybe, forcing us to be quarantined. Or a rabid dog on the premises. Something really believable.

I threw open the door, and I must have been wearing my

frustration on my face for all the world to see, because the guy standing on the other side took an instinctive step backward. It was to his advantage that I had no idea who he was—just a man younger than me, with black hair that reached almost to his shoulder. He was thin and not quite as tall as me.

"I'm sorry, I'm not sure I'm at the right house," he began, and my hopes soared. He had the wrong address, and I could send him on his way without resorting to violence.

"Who're you looking for?" I opened the door a little wider and put one hand on my hip.

"I'm—" He started to speak again, and then he looked over my shoulder, and his eyes brightened. "Hey, Megs!"

I looked over my shoulder at Meghan, who stood frozen a few feet behind me. Her eyes were round and her mouth had dropped open.

The guy smiled at me. "I came to see Meghan. I had the address, but I wasn't sure if this was the place."

"Owen." Meghan's voice was flat, and when she said his name, it dashed my hopes that this dude was her brother, whose name I knew was Joseph.

"Surprise!" Whoever he was, this Owen didn't know how to read Meghan at all. He was still going on as though this was a big happy pop-up visit, when I could see in her face that she wasn't happy. Well, join the club, because I wasn't either. Matter of fact, I was damned pissed.

"Owen, what are you doing here?" Her tone bordered on hostile. Hell, it more than bordered. It actually set up camp there. That made me just a little happier.

He was beginning to get the picture, and the shit-eating grin on his face faltered. "I was just ... I got back to town, after being away all summer. Remember, I went to Europe with Dr. Edgars?"

If Meghan remembered this, she wasn't copping to it. She lifted her shoulder in a little no-but-keep-going gesture.

"Yeah, well, I got back to Savannah, and I went by to see

you, and the girl who's staying in your apartment told me you were here. I mean, she gave me your address."

I raised one eyebrow and looked at Meghan. She rolled her eyes. "Laura and I sub-let our apartment to one of Laura's friends who was doing summer session. I don't know why she'd give out my address, though."

A sense of warmth spread through me when Meghan called my house her address. I wanted to rub it in this idiot Owen's face, that my farm was where she belonged.

"And I really don't know why you'd haul your ass all the way out here to see me, Owen. Without calling. What the hell?"

"I figured you were bored out here in the sticks, and I was going to come and take you to dinner. Some place nice, back in the city. Give you a little break." He glanced at me. "I thought you could use it by now. You're not a prisoner here, you know."

"Owen." Meghan's tone said clearly that she'd had enough. "You have no idea ..." And then she stopped and dropped her head into her hand, sighing. She looked up at me, her eyes pleading for something. I wasn't sure what it was. "Sam, would you give me just a minute with Owen? We'll sit out on the porch. And then I'll be right back in." She walked past me, not giving me the chance to say no. Her hand trailed over my chest as she stepped over the threshold.

There was nothing for me to do but close the door behind her. I didn't slam it, which I thought spoke well of my maturity, and I didn't hover in the living room, on the other side of the front windows, like my dad used to do when I began dating and brought girls home to sit on the porch. I stalked back into the kitchen, pulled out a kitchen chair and sat down.

I had no idea who this Owen was, but he was obviously someone she knew from school. He'd mentioned going on a trip. Europe, with a doctor somebody, probably one of their professors, I thought. I wondered if Meghan would regret that instead of spending her months off partying through foreign countries and checking out all the art she'd studied, she'd been stuck here on a farm in Georgia, teaching sticky little kids how to draw and hanging out with a guy old enough—well, older. Grumpy, that was what she'd called me.

I'd let myself forget for a little while how different we were. When it was just us, out here on the farm, it was easy to see what we had in common and how well Meghan meshed with my life. But that wasn't reality. Reality was her apartment in the city with Laura, classes and parties and the college world. It wasn't meeting me at the end of the day, fishing by the river all night or sitting with me out on the porch. She'd told me from the beginning that this was just a fling. Just something temporary between two people who didn't want strings attached. If I was hurt now, I had no one to blame but myself.

"Sam." She leaned against the doorway to the kitchen, and she looked ... drained. Her eyes were tired, but she tried a smile that I knew was for my benefit only. "Sorry about that."

I didn't answer. I wasn't sure I could speak without saying something I'd regret. Something that might be close to begging.

She crossed to sit in a chair across the table from me. "That was Owen. Well, you probably figured that out. Sorry I didn't introduce you, but I was really shocked to see him. As you could probably tell."

I swallowed over the lump in my throat. "You're welcome to have friends come out here to visit you, Meghan. You know that. Or I hope you do."

"Owen's not really a friend. Or maybe ... well, I don't know. Laura's really my only friend at school. I know other people, but there's no one I'd want to come out here. No one I care about. And Laura's in North Carolina, you remember that."

I nodded. Meghan mentioned Laura frequently, and I knew the two talked via cell quite a bit.

She took a deep breath. "I met Owen in freshman year, and I knew from the beginning that he had a crush on me. He was the one who always came by our dorm room or made sure he was at the same parties we went to. Laura always teased me that all I had to do was crook my finger and Owen would propose."

When I nodded again, I felt like an idiot. But I knew there was nothing I needed to say here.

"I made sure we were just friends. I never encouraged him in any way or flirted. I didn't want to hurt him. When he finally started dating someone else, I was thrilled. But then one night he got drunk and came to my apartment, and he told me the girl he was dating was just a substitute for me, that when I was ready, he'd drop her for me. I felt horrible. I didn't know what to do. So for the longest time, I didn't do anything.

"Then my dad got sick and I was back and forth to Florida all the time. When Daddy—died, I was there, and I stayed until the funeral, but then I had to go back to school. Joseph was staying with Mom, but I had exams. So I came back, and I was hurting so bad. I just wanted it to stop. I wanted anything that would make the pain go away. I went out that night, and I got drunk. I mean, really, really wasted. I drank until I couldn't remember my own name ... and you can probably guess what happened next. Owen was there, and he found me crying in a corner. He took me home, and we ..." She dropped her forehead onto her arm so that her voice was muffled when she finished. "We had sex."

I closed my eyes. I remembered that pain. I had done some fairly reprehensible things in the name of making it go away. I imagined Meghan, hurting and needing comfort, and I couldn't blame her for what had happened.

"Honestly, I didn't even remember it. I woke up with him looking down at me like we'd just had our wedding night. I couldn't get away from him fast enough, and I tried to explain what had happened, but nothing's ever gotten through to him. He keeps hanging around, no matter how many other guys I sleep with." Her eyes flashed to me, worried. "He thinks in the end we're going to end up together, so he's willing to wait me out."

"What did you tell him just now?" I understood this guy was hung up on her, but someone had to tell him to get lost. If

Meghan couldn't do it, I was happy to volunteer.

"I sat him down and told him that I was never going to be with him again. I told him that what had happened between us once was a huge mistake and that I couldn't even remember it at all. I said he didn't mean anything to me, that I only let him hang around me because I felt sorry for him." She raised eyes to me that were brimming with misery. "I was cruel, and that's the one thing I've always sworn I wouldn't be. But I didn't know what else to do."

I couldn't sit still anymore. I went around the table and knelt in front of her chair, pulling her to me. "You had to tell him. The guy's living his life based on a lie, on the chance that you might someday change your mind. What you did was the kindest choice." I stroked her hair. "Don't beat yourself up. It's going to be better in the long run."

She shook against my shoulder, and I realized she was sobbing. "I'm a terrible person, Sam. You were right that day. I'm irresponsible and immature and I'm a bad friend."

"Meghan, no." I lifted her up, sat down in the chair and held her on my lap. "I was stupid. You're one of the kindest, most mature people I know. Plus, you're so full of joy and life, you make everyone around you happier. Hell, you even made me smile, right?"

She sniffed, loudly. "He was so upset when he left, Sam. What if he gets in an accident? What if—" She shuddered. "He wouldn't do anything to himself, would he? Oh, God. I need to call Ziggy. He used to be his roommate. He needs to know." She reached into her back pocket and pulled out her cell. I held her while she scrolled her contacts and hit a name. She spoke to the guy who answered for a few minutes, choking a few times as she explained what had happened.

After a short conversation, she hung up. "Ziggy's going to text me when Owen gets back, and he won't leave him alone until he seems okay. Those guys are idiots, but they're good friends. I know Ziggy'll watch out for him."

I kissed the top of her head. "I'm sorry you had to do that."

Meghan craned her neck around to look at me. "I'm sorry Owen ruined our hour alone. Ali should be here any minute now."

I touched her cheek. "That's okay. You couldn't help it. And when Ali gets home, I think I'll take the two of you over to Kenny's for dinner, so you don't have to cook or clean up."

She narrowed her eyes. "You're being awfully understanding. I thought you were going to be mad about missing out on the naked."

"I might have been, except that I just remembered that Bridget is going to be gone all night. My sister's a big girl. She can handle the idea of you being in my room with me." I turned her face and kissed her. "We might not have had our hour, but we'll have all night."

Chapter SEVENTEEN

Meghan

ONCE THE WEATHER CLEARED up, it hit me that I only had two more weeks with my students. I planned several field trips, taking them to the park, to a few special places in town and even out to our neighbor Fred's farm to draw horses. They loved it, and I enjoyed watching their eyes light up when a new concept clicked in their minds.

I was moving between the kids when I caught sight of someone heading our way. Fred had given us permission to be in the field, and I realized the man was a little taller and a little slimmer than the farmer. As he grew nearer, I recognized the artfully-mussed hair.

Alex put on a stern face. "Hey, what're all you guys doing in my pasture?"

They all laughed. Apparently, even though he only returned to Burton a few times a year, Alex was popular among the elementary school set. Either that or these kids weren't easily scared.

He smiled at me. "Hello, pretty girl. Are you responsible for these hooligans?"

"Guilty as charged." I leaned up to give him a quick hug. "The bigger question is, what're you doing here? I thought you went back to Atlanta weeks ago."

"I did." He swatted at the back of his neck, where a mosquito had landed. "I've got a meeting in Savannah tomorrow, so I decided to stop off and visit the old homestead for the night."

"Bet your mom and dad were glad to see you." I knew Fred and his wife Ellen missed their only son.

"Of course they were. I'm kidnapping Mom into the city with me tomorrow, so she can have a little fun while I'm at my meeting. She's tickled." He ran his eyes up and down me, with one brow raised. "So, things are going well with Sam the Man? You two crazy kids setting a date yet?"

I shook my head. "You know the score. We're just enjoying ourselves. Nothing serious." I kept my eyes on the black horse grazing at the edge of the field. "And I leave next week."

"And how does Sammy boy feel about your imminent departure?"

"I'm sure he's fine with it."

"But he hasn't said anything."

I shrugged. "Not really. We don't talk about the future. He's got a life here, and I've got mine—elsewhere. That's why we keep things casual."

"Hmmm." Alex smirked. "Funny thing. I ran into Reenie Evans when I stopped for gas on my way to the farm last night. She seemed to think what you and Sam have going on is pretty intense."

My eyes flashed up to his face. "She wasn't supposed to— she promised not to say anything to anyone."

"And she probably wouldn't have, except I brought it up and pushed her about it. And Reenie doesn't consider me just anyone. She and I were best friends with Ali coming up through school. She wasn't gossiping."

I pressed my lips together. "Still, it's nobody's business. After I leave, I don't want people giving Sam a hard time and pestering him." I leveled a look at him. "Got it?"

Alex held up his hands. "Whoa, sister, don't look at me. Atlanta, remember? I'm the least of your worries."

Ali's car pulled up along the far side of the field, interrupting any reply I might have made. I'd asked the parents to pick up their offspring right from the farm so that I didn't have to drive back into town, and Ali had decided to take Bridget right to the stand with her. She sauntered over, her face lighting up as she spied Alex.

"Miss Meghan, I can't get his ears right." Jared, one of my third graders, stood up and tugged at my hand.

"That's my cue to exit, stage left." Alex snuck a quick kiss to my cheek. "I'm going to get the skinny on all things Burton with my pal over there. See you later, lovely."

I crouched down to check out Jared's work, but I was all too aware of Alex and Ali, whispering and glancing at me. That could only spell trouble.

Once all the children had been collected, I headed back to our farm. *Our* farm. I wasn't sure just when I'd begun thinking of it that way, but it was true. The smell of the soil, the worn buildings and the vivid green of the fields had woven their way into my heart. I didn't want to think about how much the man who worked the land played into those feelings of belonging.

Since I was seldom home this early in the day, I took advantage of the opportunity to grab my easel, paints and music and go into the woods. There were pictures in my head begging to be given life, and I was eager to spend some time pouring them onto the canvas.

I set up, turned on my favorite play list and began working on a scene that had been in my mind for the last few weeks. The forest was silent except for the chirp of bugs and the chattering of squirrels, and I enjoyed having the time to hear myself think. I'd loved teaching this summer, and I knew for sure it was what

I wanted to do after graduation. But there was something to be said for a little break now and then.

Something had shifted between Sam and me since the day Owen had made his unexpected visit. He was by turns more tender and yet somehow almost aloof. I wasn't sure how that could be true, but it was. When we made love—and that was doubtless what we were doing; it had moved beyond sex after that first night—he seemed desperate, not only to bring us both pleasure, but to connect in some way. But when I brought it up, he joked about our friends-with-benefits arrangements. I couldn't be angry; it was exactly what I had wanted, and I had gotten it.

Absorbed in both my work and my thoughts, I was working on the background, making the trees come to life, when a shadow fell across the canvas. I didn't startle as I might have, because I could smell Sam's unique aroma. Instead I smiled.

"Are you here for a lesson?" I kept moving my brush over the canvas.

"I might be." He didn't touch me, not wanting to disturb my work, but he stood so near that I could feel him against my skin. I breathed deep, inhaling his scent. Laying down my brush, I turned.

"Okay." I stood up and pointed to my small artist's stool, the collapsible one I used when I was working outside. "Sit down."

He looked down at me, considering. His brown eyes were filled with that inscrutable something that I'd been noticing for the last few weeks. He hadn't shaved this morning, and soft blond scruff covered his jaw and cheeks, tempting my fingers.

"All right. It's about time I get a lesson, considering I've been feeding and housing the teacher for the last two months. Not to mention giving her the best sex of her life."

I laughed, surprised by his teasing. "The best, huh? Someone's full of himself this afternoon."

He spread his hands in front of him. "I only speak the truth. Now, are you going to teach me or not?" He sat down on the chair, looking faintly uncomfortable and more than a little incongruous; it was obviously not designed for a man of his size.

I bit back a smile. "Pick up the brush, and we'll work on some stroke work." My brush looked tiny in his large hands. I found another one to use myself, to demonstrate what to do.

He was surprisingly adept, and after a few minutes, he was painting passable leaves. I worked on a few other techniques with him, leaning over his shoulder so I could help.

"No, not quite like that. Here, let me show you." I covered his hand holding the brush with mine and brought it to the canvas. "See? Just a light touch at the top and then a little more as you move down—yes. Just like that."

He grinned up at me. "Am I natural, or do you make all your students feel good about themselves? Or are you just trying to get into my pants?"

I laughed. "All of the above. Yes, you're actually good. And I do try to make my students feel good about what they can do." I swung a leg over his lap, facing him while I straddled his hips. "And I definitely want to get into your pants."

"Oh, you do?" He laid my brush on the tray and used both hands to hold me by my ribs. "Isn't there some rule against that?"

"Not if the student is a really sexy guy who is more than happy to put out to his teacher." I thought about what I'd just said. "Well, and assuming both are above the age of consent. Which we both are."

"Hmm. If you decide you want to teach, you might want to brush up on those pesky little details." He threaded his fingers through my hair. "But this student is more than a little hot for teacher."

I hummed a little, feeling the thrill of desire shoot straight to my core. "Is it safe out here? I mean, will anyone find us?"

Sam shook his head. "I don't think so. Ali's going to be at the stand for another few hours, and I guess Bridge is with her." When I nodded, he grinned. "Sounds like I'm at your mercy."

"Your bad luck, then. Because I don't plan to show you any mercy." I crossed my arms and grabbed the hem of my shirt, pulling up until it was over my head. The cooler air in the forest made me shiver, and my nipple puckered within my red lace bra.

"Oh, Meghan." Sam ran his hands over the lace. "Another new one. And red this time."

"What, this old thing?" I pretended ignorance. "I just put it on this morning when I was thinking about this really hot guy I was hoping might see it. When I put it on, I touched myself like this ..." I covered my nipples with my fingers, caressing, and let my eyes drift shut.

Sam growled and his mouth pushed my hands away from my breasts. He sucked hard at one nipple through the lace, while his fingers rolled the other one. I moaned, moving so that he could take more into his mouth. I could feel his erection pushing against my sensitive sex, and I wriggled.

"I'm not going to last long if you keep that up." He spoke without taking my nipple from his mouth.

"Maybe I want fast and hard today." I fumbled with the button of his jeans, wanting them out of the way.

"Shit." Sam leaned back, his eyes closed. "I don't have a condom."

"Mr. Prepared came out here without latex?" I continued undoing his pants while I teased him.

"I was cutting through the woods. I didn't expect to find you here."

"It's okay." I slid my hand under his jeans and boxers. "I'm on the pill, and I'm clean and healthy. I've been checked out."

He grunted as I took him in my hand. "I've never had sex without a condom. I'm clean."

"Then we're okay." I patted his hip. "Lift up so I can get to you."

He acquiesced, and I wriggled both jeans and boxers out of the way. His cock was stiff, and I fisted my hand around it, sliding up and down, starting slow but picking up speed. Sam groaned.

"Have I told you I like your skirt?" He pushed it up to my

hips so that it hung behind me like a cape around my middle. His fingers sought me through my panties, stroking up and down over my wetness. "These damn things are in my way." He held my eyes as he closed his hand over the piece of fabric and ripped.

"Did you notice those panties matched my bra?" I rubbed my thumb in a circle over the head of his cock, and he jerked upwards.

"No. I'll buy you new ones. Come here." He gathered me to him and stood up.

"Where are we going?" I ran my fingers over his hair and down his jaw. "Hmmm ... your beard is so soft."

"Soft is not a word we want to use right now." He spoke wryly, and I laughed. "And not far." He stopped a few feet away, beneath the trees, and laid me down on a patch of soft green grass.

"We could have stayed over there." I watched him kick off his pants.

"That damned chair thing of yours wouldn't have stood up to hard and fast." He pushed my skirt out of the way again and parted my legs. "And that's what you said you wanted."

Without giving me a moment to respond, he lifted my hips and sank into me. I arched to meet him and wound my legs around his waist, hooking my heels together as he moved within me, skin to skin for the first time, pounding a rhythm that had me panting along with him.

Delicious pressure built low in my abdomen, making me want more. I gripped Sam's back with one hand, and with the other I reached between us, touching my clit and then moving lower to where we were joined. Sam gritted his teeth, pumping faster, and I screamed his name as I fell apart. He followed almost right away, his entire body one tensed muscle as he climaxed.

Sam rolled to the side, pulling him with me and holding me to his chest as we both struggled to catch our breath.

"I like art lessons." He wound my hair around his hand and

held it up, away from my neck, so that my skin could cool. I loved that he thought of that, that he considered my comfort.

"That's convenient, because I love teaching." I kissed his neck. After a few moments, he draped my hair to the side, smoothing it down so that it lay on the grass. His lips grazed my forehead, and I felt his sigh.

"It's a beautiful afternoon." I raked my nails lightly over his forearm. "God, you have great arms. You know, when you hold yourself over me, and your arms are tensed, that's the sexiest thing." I twisted, bringing my lips to just under his chin. "And sometimes when you're wearing a long-sleeved shirt, like last week when you went to the Guild meeting, and you roll up the cuffs to just above your wrists, it makes me so horny. I just want to lick up your arms and feel your muscles tense under my lips."

His chest moved up and down beneath me as he laughed. "Meghan, I think you're the only woman I've ever met who thinks forearms are sexy."

"You're obviously not hanging around with the right women. You should make that part of your criteria for future girlfriends."

He stilled, and I knew I'd come close to breaking our unspoken rule, the one that had hung over us with increasing heaviness the last few weeks. We didn't talk about what would happen when I left or what the future might hold for each of us after our summer fling had ended.

"You leave next week." Sam's voice was neutral, carefully so. I felt the tension in his body.

"Yes."

His chest rose and fell in even breaths. "I thought maybe before you go, we could go back to the river. Spend the night."

To say good-bye. He didn't speak the words, but we both felt them. I waited until I was certain I could speak without my voice breaking.

"That would be wonderful."

"Okay." He rubbed my shoulder. "Then we'll do it. I think

Ali and Bridget are planning a special dinner for you that night, so after we eat ..."

"I'll meet you at the truck."

"Yes." He gathered me closer, the only obvious sign that he might be dreading me going. "When does Laura come back?"

The shift in topic made me frown. "Ah, not until the end of the month. When classes begin. She wants to spend every minute with Brian. I'm not going back to Savannah right away, either. I'm going home, to the Cove."

"You are?" Surprise tinged his voice.

"Yeah, for a little while. It'll make my mom and Logan happy, and I'd like to see my nephew. He's growing up so fast. I don't want to be an absentee auntie."

"Are you looking forward to hanging out with your old friends from home?" Again, there was neither encouragement nor condemnation, as though he wanted my answer without any influence from his own feelings.

"No, most of them are gone. They left to go to college or get jobs, and I don't think any of them are in the Cove now. I didn't stay in touch with most of the people who graduated with me."

"So you'll just spend time with family?"

I nodded, my ear rubbing against his chest. "Yeah, family and friends. My parents' friends, I mean. And the people who work at the Tide are like family, too. My mom's so excited about me coming down that she's throwing a big party at the restaurant after closing on Sunday."

"That sounds wonderful. You'll get to have a little vacation after all your hard work here." His words would've been perfect, if he were in fact just the guy who had hosted me for the summer and not the guy who was lying naked in the forest with me.

I wanted to say, *I don't have to go.* I wanted him to ask me not to leave, or at least to care that I was. I wasn't sure when it had happened, but my summer fling had turned into something real, without doubt the most real relationship I'd ever had. And yet here we lay, talking about its ending in emotionless tones, as though we were discussing the ending of a movie or a book. Come to think of it, I was a lot more passionate about both of those.

But these were our terms. I'd both insisted on them and agreed to them, and there was no going back now. Sam had the farm, and I knew from our talks that this had been one of their most successful summers ever. He was pretty sure they could take back another parcel of leased land next spring, if he were careful and planned just right. And Ali had told me that she thought they'd be able to swing art lessons for Bridget, too, which I knew was gratifying to both Sam and her.

"It must be such a relief to you and Ali, to know you're safe-guarding your family's legacy. That you both brought it back from the brink of losing it, and you'll be able to pass it on to the next generation."

Sam pushed up on his arms into a sitting position. "What brought that up?"

"I don't know." I lifted my shoulder. "I was just thinking ... I understand how much it means to you. I get it. After being here all summer, I can't imagine how you could ever give it up. You should be proud of what you've done."

He held my chin, staring into my eyes. I willed him to say something, anything, but he only kissed me, one quick light peck on my lips.

"We'd better get dressed. It's almost supper time, and I don't think I could come up with a good explanation if Bridge finds us out here naked."

AS THE END OF my time in Burton came closer, a lump of dread took up residence in my stomach and grew every day. Ali didn't help, as she took to pointing out what I'd be missing when I left.

"I drove by Myrtle Cantor's orchards today. Apples are going to be good this year. Oh, sorry, Meghan, you'll be gone by the time they come in."

"I heard they've set the date for the harvest dance. Too bad you'll miss that, Meghan."

"No, Bridge, Meghan won't be here on your first day of school."

Each time Ali mentioned something about me leaving, Sam's mouth tightened and his face shuttered. Most of the time he found an excuse to leave the room.

Our after-supper sessions on the front porch had taken on a slightly desperate edge, too. Sam became more daring, and I wasn't objecting. More often than not, whatever bra I was wearing ended up on the floor.

"I think Ali knows better than to come out here after dark, and Bridge is sleeping." I knelt on the floor in front of Sam, who was sprawled in the rocking chair. Walking my fingers up his leg, I teased toward the zipper of his jeans.

He grabbed my hand. "You may be right, but you know when you have your mouth on me, I can't keep quiet. I won't be able to look my sister in the eye if she hears me yelling your name while you suck me off."

I sighed. He wasn't wrong, but I found I couldn't get enough of him. I may have pouted, just a little.

"Hey, come on up here." Sam lifted me onto his lap. "We'll be out at the river tomorrow night, and my body'll be yours."

Mine, but for only one more night. Mine, but only temporarily. And that fact made the lump in my stomach ache even more.

On my last day of classes, the parents and students surprised me with a little party in the afternoon. They presented me with a framed collage that all the kids had contributed to making and a homemade card each of them had signed. There were cookies and punch, and I cried when they presented the gifts to me.

"Miss Meghan, when are you coming back?" Rachel, who

was just going into first grade, slipped her little hand into mine as I nibbled on cookies.

"Oh, sweetie, I was just here for the summer. But I think there's a good chance your school will be able to hire a full-time art teacher pretty soon, and then you won't even miss me."

"We'll definitely miss you, Meghan." Rachel's mother smiled. "You've taught these kids so much. I can't imagine a better teacher."

"I couldn't, either." Ali met my eyes. "I think lots of people are going to miss Meghan."

"Luckily for you, I'm only going to be about forty-five minutes away in Savannah, and you can visit me when you come into the city. I'll take you to my favorite galleries, and I can even show you around the college." I patted Rachel's shoulder.

An older woman with gray bouffant hair stepped closer, and Ali introduced us. "Meghan, this is Mrs. Abbott. She's on the school board, and her granddaughter Nicole was one of your students."

"Of course. Nicole is a very talented painter." I shook the woman's hand.

"I've heard nothing but praise for you and your classes, Miss Hawthorne." Mrs. Abbott's voice held all the music of the south, a refined accent that went beyond a drawl.

"Thank you. I've enjoyed teaching this summer. I appreciate Burton—and ArtCorps, of course—for giving me the opportunity."

"I'm happy to hear that. As I understand it, you'll be entering your senior year of college in Savannah this fall. Is that correct?"

This lady made me want to stand up straighter and fold my hands. "Yes, ma'am, it is."

"Aha. Well, as you might know, we've been without a formal art program in the school for a few years now. It's a cut I always regretted that we had to make, but there's been an anonymous donation to the home and school association." Her lips twitched, and there was no doubt in my mind who'd contributed that money. "So we'll be able to reinstate art in our schools this year. I've spoken with the rest of the board, and we'd like you to consider the position."

I frowned. "I'm sorry, I'm not sure I follow you. I'm not a teacher yet, just a volunteer."

"I do understand that. What we had in mind was a part-time job for the first year, while you're still at school, and then moving into something full-time after graduation. Even if you could give us a day or two a week to begin, we could run the class as we've done this summer. We can smooth out details later, but I wanted to extend the offer before you left town."

I opened my mouth to explain all the reasons I couldn't possibly take the job. A few months ago, the idea of burying myself in a little backwater town like Burton would've been horrifying. But now, the possibility was bittersweet. I couldn't imagine agreeing to come back when it felt like Sam didn't want me here. If he did, he would've asked me not to leave, and he hadn't said anything. The idea of being in Burton and not being with Sam was unthinkable.

Before I could speak, though, Ali put her arm around my shoulders. "That is so exciting, Mrs. Abbott. Meghan's leaving tomorrow to go spend a few weeks with her family in Florida, and I'm sure she'll use that time to think it all over."

Mrs. Abbott didn't seem put off that Ali was answering for me. She beamed at us. "Why, that's just fine. I'm sure Alison here has your contact information, and we'll call you after your little vacation, just to see where everyone stands."

When she had walked away, I turned on Ali with wide eyes. "Are your freaking crazy? Why would you say that to her?"

"What?" Ali was all innocence. "I just didn't think you should say no right now. What if something happens and you decide you want to spend more time around here? Wouldn't it be great to already have a job in place?"

"Nothing is going to happen. I'm leaving tomorrow morning, and that's it. I'm not coming back here." I kept my voice down and a pleasant expression on my face.

Ali rolled her eyes. "You're being ridiculous." She smiled at someone across the room, but I heard the frustration in her tone.

"No, I'm being realistic. We told you from the beginning that this thing between Sam and me is just temporary."

"Then why wouldn't you consider coming back here, if Sam doesn't mean anything to you?"

"I never said that he doesn't mean anything to me." My voice rose and a few people near us turned to look at me. I closed my eyes. "Let's talk about this later."

"Fine. But don't burn any bridges yet. Promise me that?"

I shook my head. "All right. I promise. Nothing hasty. I'll wait until after I come back from Florida to tell them I'm not taking the job."

I STOOD AT THE kitchen window, watching as Sam went through his ritual of washing up. I couldn't go out to show my appreciation as I would have liked, since Ali and Bridge were both in the room with me. But no way was I missing this show tonight. Not when it was the final performance for me.

"Meghan, the lasagna is ready." Bridge took my hand. "Just like the night you got here."

I picked her up and gave her a smacking kiss on her cheek. "You are the best, Miss Bridget. I'm so excited to see how you do with your art lessons. You'll send me pictures, right?"

"Yes." She played with my necklace. "But why won't you come back and see them yourself?"

"Honey, leave Meghan be and go wash your hands."

I slid the little girl down and watched her dash out of the kitchen. Ali smiled apologetically. "Sorry about that. I swear I didn't put her up to it. And I tried to get her to go upstairs so you could ogle my brother in peace."

I flushed. "Ogling was accomplished. I might need you to video that and send it to me. You know, just to keep it fresh in my mind."

Ali made a face. "I don't think so. Making a B-grade porn of my own brother is not high on my to-do list."

The screen door opened, and Sam stepped in. He nodded to both of us before getting a clean shirt from the laundry room. A lump rose in my throat. Another last. The day had been full of them.

Dinner was an odd affair, with Bridget chattering away while Ali, Sam and I made vain attempts to act as though nothing were wrong. I ate mechanically, and more than once I looked up to find Sam staring at me, his eyes unreadable.

When the food was eaten and the dishes were done, Ali took Bridget upstairs to get her ready for bed. She flashed me a sympathetic look before she left the room.

Sam stood up and went to the window. "Are you ready to go now? I thought maybe if we got an early start, you could get a decent night's sleep. After we come back to the house, I mean."

The last thing I wanted to do tonight was sleep, but I pushed back my chair. "Sure. That sounds like a good idea."

He offered me a hand, and when I took it, he lifted mine to brush his lips across the knuckles before entwining our fingers. "Come on. The fish are waiting."

We held hands all during the drive to the river, and when Sam stopped the truck, he pulled me closer to him. The kiss he gave me made my heart pound, and for a minute, I thought we might skip fishing altogether. But then Sam pulled back, smiled at me and let go of my hand.

We settled down to our fishing, both of us silent. Sam caught a catfish early on, but he threw him right back.

"I don't feel like fussing with it tonight." He glanced at me sideways. "Catfish is delicious, but sometimes it feels like too much work for just that one meal."

I sensed he was talking about more than just fish. "Yeah,

I understand what you mean. I guess if you were going to be able to enjoy catfish every day for the rest of your life, the work might not seem so bad."

"But who wants to eat catfish every day forever?" Sam's lips twitched.

"If you found the right catfish, it might be all you ever wanted." I was really belaboring this analogy.

"How would you know if you found the right one? If you're fishing a lot, you're going to catch a lot of catfish. Hard to tell which one would be good enough to only eat that fish."

"You'd know. If you were willing to look and spend some time on it, you could tell when you found the right—catfish."

Sam stretched an arm to wrap around me. "I think I'm tired of talking about catfish. And I'm definitely ready to stop fishing."

I reeled in my line. "If we don't fish, whatever will we do now?" I blinked up at him.

"I think I can figure out something." He took my rod with his and leaned them against the cab of the truck. When he returned to the riverbank, he pulled me to my feet and tugged me close for a kiss.

His lips teased, first only touching the corners of my mouth and then sucking at my bottom lip. When I tried to angle my mouth to his, he framed my face with his hands and ran his tongue against the seam of my lips. I opened willingly, but he didn't plunge his tongue as I expected. Instead he stroked the inside of my mouth, touching and then withdrawing until I was ready to cry with frustration.

He stopped abruptly and bent down. Before I could question him, he'd scooped me into his arms, holding me against his chest as we walked to the truck.

"The first night I saw you, I carried you from my truck to that loaner car. You'd been passed out the whole ride into town, but when I held you like this, you opened your eyes and looked up at me. I thought you might panic, but you only smiled, whispered something and touched my face."

"I remember that, a little. I woke up the next morning with the hangover from hell, and when Laura told me what had happened, I had just a quick flash of memory—of your eyes." I reached up to trace the lines of his cheek. "What did I say to you that night?"

Sam's eyes shifted away from mine. "I don't know. It was just something you mumbled." He set me on the tailgate of the truck, and I scooted backwards while he climbed up to join me.

"Thank you for saving us that night." I leaned over to kiss his cheek. "I don't think I ever said that."

Sam shook his head. "I think you did that day at Boomer's, but I was being too much of an asshole to tell you that it was my pleasure." He laid one finger on my lips and then ran it down in a straight line to my cleavage. He used that finger to tug one side of the neck of my shirt down, exposing a bra made of purple lace.

"Oh, baby. Where do you get these? Do you have one in every color?"

I giggled. "I guess you'll have to keep checking to find out." I said it without thinking, and then reality hit me hard; tonight was the last time Sam would be enjoying my bra and what it held. He frowned, and I thought he might say something, but instead he brought his lips to the stiff peak beneath the lace.

I loved the way Sam looked at my breasts and especially how he touched them. His eyes held reverence as he palmed them, lifting each one. And his fingers on my nipples drove me to the point of frenzy. He took his time, sucking and licking, using his teeth with just enough pressure to send shots of need right down to my center, making me crave more. More of everything.

"I love your breasts." As though he'd read my mind, Sam spoke, watching his fingers bring my nipples to hard nubs. "Your eyes go hazy when I do this." He lowered his mouth again and sucked before he caught the nipple between his teeth and rolled it. "And when I do that, it's like your body can't be still. You start wriggling like if I don't take you now, you're going to explode."

"That's exactly how it feels." I took his other hand in both of mine and placed it on the breast his mouth wasn't laving. "I think I could almost come just from watching you suck on my boobs. It makes me crazy."

Sam made a low sound deep in his throat. "I never want to stop. I want to take you so hard tonight, so fast, but at the same time, I want to make every single touch last forever. Does that make sense?"

"Yes." I lay back onto the pillows. "I feel the same way. I want you now, but I don't want it to end."

He pushed up onto his hands, staring down at me. I wanted him to tell me that it didn't have to end, but he only brushed the hair out of my face. "I'll make it last as long as I can. I promise." He skimmed his fingers to my waist and rolled my shirt up. "But first, I want you naked under me."

I sat up and peeled off my top and then reached behind my back to unhook the purple bra. Sam leaned back to watch me, his eyes hooded.

Sitting in just my skirt, I paused to let him take me in. Slowly, I brought my hands to my breasts, lifting and squeezing them. I ran my fingers over my nipples, still damp from Sam's mouth. Pinching them, I whispered his name. "I can still feel you here. Mmmmm."

"You're killing me." His voice was husky. "Take off your skirt now."

"This?" I picked up the cloth that covered my legs. "I think I can do that." I rose onto my knees, unbuttoned the waistband of the long cotton skirt and let it fall in a pool of material on the quilts. When Sam saw the string and lace that passed for my underwear, I thought his eyes might roll back in his head.

Holding his gaze, I slipped one hand between my legs, first touching myself over the lace and then pulling the underwear aside. Sam's mouth dropped open, and his tongue darted out to wet his lips. I wriggled the panties down to my knees, but before I could get them completely off, he had me on my back.

"I'll finish this." I wasn't sure what he meant, but I trusted him to do it well. He slipped the underwear over my feet and tossed the panties over his shoulder.

"Sam!" I giggled. "I think you threw them into the trees."

He shrugged as he crawled over me. "I did. And when I find them someday, I know I'll get hard, just remembering how god-damn sexy you look, lying here naked and wet, ready for me."

As if to make his point, he reached his hand between my legs and parted my folds with one finger. I let my knees drop to the side and arched my neck, moaning. Sam brought his mouth to my sex and circled the small bundle of nerves that craved his attention, adding more pressure with each swipe. He teased my entrance without slipping his fingers within, driving me into a frenzy of need as he brought his lips to my ear.

"Come for me now, babe. I want to make you come so many times, you can't move. Do it now."

He twisted his hand so that his thumb covered my clit while he finally plunged two fingers inside me. Shrieking, I bucked against his hand as pleasure burst through me, spiraling upwards, and my body pulsed around his fingers. Before I could begin to recover, Sam replaced his fingers with his mouth, but there was nothing gentle here. He speared his tongue into me, over and over, and then moved up to suck on my sensitive nub, his lips relentless. His tongue stiffened to lick me, and my body moved without my control, clutching at his hair and crying out again as another climax, more powerful than the first, gripped me.

My chest was heaving as my breath came in short pants. "God, Sam." I fisted his shirt in my hand and pulled him up to me. "You're wearing way too many clothes. Get rid of them."

"Your wish." He pulled off his shirt, and before it hit the truck bed, I had my mouth on his skin. If this was the last time I was going to be able to enjoy him, I was going to make every second count. I paused only long enough to let him shuck off his jeans.

In the moonlight, he was the most beautiful thing I'd ever seen. His skin gleamed beneath the sprinkling of soft hair on his chest, the line tapering down to his stiff cock. His legs were roped with strong muscles from years of hard farm work, and his eyes were filled with hunger.

I wanted it all, and I wanted it now.

Chapter EIGHTEEN

Sam

MEGHAN'S EYES WERE LIQUID green as she stared at me. She was soft and pliant after coming twice, but I could almost feel her desire growing again. Her hand closed on my cock, stroking up and down. She squeezed the head, and I moaned, my control slipping away with every movement of her fingers.

And when she took me into her mouth, my vision tunneled.

She watched me watching her as she lowered her lips around the shaft, taking me inch by inch until I hit the back of her throat. Her tongue circled, and then she sucked hard as she withdrew. Her eyes never left my face, and my entire world shrunk to her mouth on my skin.

"I'm not going to last long with you doing that."

"Mmmhmmm." The vibration of her voice added a new dimension to Meghan's brand of delectable torture. She lifted her mouth and stroked me with her fingers. "Why is that? Because it feels good?"

A groan was all I could manage. "You have no idea."

"Does it make you crazy? Because that's what I want. I want this to be the only thing you can think about. I want this to be why you live and breathe." She brought her mouth to my cock again and moving faster, pumped her mouth up and down. "I want every part of you to burn for me. Only me."

"I do. I am." I dug my fingers into her thick hair. "And now I want to be inside you."

Meghan swirled her tongue over me one more time before she raised her head and slid up to my face. "That's good, because I need you inside me now."

I flipped her over and brought my knees between her thighs as she parted her legs again. "You're going to come again, and I'm going to feel it with my cock buried in you."

Her eyes dilated until they were nearly black. "I'll be happy to help you with that." She guided me to her entrance as I lowered myself. Rubbing the head of my dick over her slick and swollen folds, she raised up to take me.

I didn't need a second invitation. I slid within the tight sheath that was still pulsing from her last orgasm. "Meghan, you feel so good. So perfect." I stroked within her, finding the spot that made her writhe even more. Balancing on one arm, I took both of her wrists in my other hand and pinioned them above her head, then brought my mouth to one tempting nipple, sucking hard.

Meghan gave a strangled cry, and her frantic movements drove me ever closer to the edge of my own release, and I plunged faster, sure and strong.

"Sam." I opened my eyes, looking down at Meghan's face. Tears ran down her cheeks, and she was biting her lip. "Don't stop, please. Don't stop. Sam—" Her voice rose, and the sound of my name on her lips, the sight of her tears, drove me to come as she rocked her hips up one more time. As my body tensed, I dropped my lips to her ear, whispering her name over and over.

It took several moments before my vision cleared and my breath came back. I fell to Meghan's side, dropping one arm over my eyes. I wanted to hold her closer, stroke her hair, murmur little meaningless words to her. But her departure was a tangible thing, lying between us, making it harder for me to reach out, knowing that soon she wouldn't be here.

Tonight we could connect, over and over, until the sun came up. Tonight we could play and giggle, pretend that this time would last forever. We could ignore the rest of the world and make this small clearing on the river our only reality. But it couldn't last. When tomorrow came, as it inevitably would, she was leaving, and I'd never see her again.

Meghan's mind must have been following the same paths as mine, because she rolled over to me, slipping one arm across my stomach and laying her head on my chest. Her face was still wet with tears, and without looking at her, I brought my hand to her cheek and swiped at the wet there.

"The first time I saw you here, at Boomer's, I thought I'd never see you again. Which sounded like a good thing, because I was so mad. But I was wrong."

I smiled, knowing she couldn't see my face. "That night on the side of the road—" I began.

"Wait, which night? With Laura, or the night we ..." Her hand drifted lower to caress me.

"With Laura. When I first saw you. Even though you were passed out, and we only had that one moment when your eyes opened, there was something that made me ..." I wasn't sure how to say it. I was a farmer with a business degree, not a poet. I struggled to find the right words. "Something that drew me to you. I wanted to hold you in my arms longer. But I told myself that was crazy, and you were a college kid, and we'd never have anything in common. And when I drove away, I thought it was okay, because I'd never see you again."

"And then we ran into each other at Boomer's, and you realized you were wrong." She kissed my chest, and my heart sped up.

"Yeah, and I handled it like a champ." I shook my head. "When I walked into my living room and saw you there back in June, I think part of me decided the third time had to be the charm."

She nuzzled into my neck again. "Are you sorry, Sam? That we had this summer? Do you wish you'd talked me out of it?"

I brought my arms down to draw her closer. "Never. I know we got off to a rough start, but these few months—" I swallowed and tried to ignore the stinging in my eyes. I hadn't cried since my parents' accident. Hell if I was going to start now. "They've been good. Fun. I'm glad we could be friends."

"Friends. Yes." She echoed my words, but I couldn't decipher her tone. "I'm glad, too."

Silence surrounded us. I ran my fingers up and down her arm as the frogs chirped and the crickets sang. Meghan was quiet for so long that I thought she might have fallen asleep until she turned over, propping her chin on my sternum. "I'm hot."

"Yeah, baby, you are." I brushed the back of my knuckles over her cheek.

"Goof." She swatted at my hand. "I want to go for a swim."

I raised my eyebrows. "You do? I thought you were afraid of snakes and frigid water."

She pushed herself up. "No, not tonight. I want to do everything. I want to swim with you, and I want you to take me hard in the water. And then I want to come back here and lick all the water off your body and take our time to make love, take it so slow we think we're going to die from waiting."

I studied her eyes, bright with unshed tears, desperate to forget that tomorrow would come. Touching her lips, I smiled.

"Then that's what we'll do."

WE DRESSED IN THE early morning, both of us sated and sleepy. My stomach clenched as I watched Meghan lean over to pick up her shirt, her boobs swinging. I didn't know how she could make me hard again after the night we'd just shared, but she did.

As if by silent agreement, we hadn't talked about anything serious for the rest of the evening. Meghan cried again the last time I sank between her legs, and I'd kissed away her tears, but I didn't ask her why she wept and she didn't bring it up.

The truck rocked us up and down over the potholed road, and I reached to hold her hand. Her fingers squeezed mine, painfully, as she stared out the window.

I pulled into my normal spot alongside the barn. A stream of sunlight broke through the dim glow of dawn, and for a moment I watched the beam dance on the sparse grass of the path that led to the fields.

Neither of us moved. This was the last minute, and once I opened my door and went around to help her out of the truck, the spell would be broken. Summer—at least, my summer with Meghan—would be officially over.

I wasn't ready. I knew it with certainty, but knowing it didn't change the facts. And the facts said that Meghan still had another year of college, and by her own admission, she wasn't looking for anything long-term or permanent. She was recovering from her dad's death, and she was struggling to figure out who she was. I had a hunch that the series of short-term hookups and boyfriends were over; there was still pain in her heart over what had happened with Owen, and that wasn't going to go away any time soon.

I didn't know what I was going to say until the words spilled out of my mouth. "I was wrong in what I said to you at Boomer's that day, and what I said the night we had sex the first time. The night alongside the road, that is." I shot her a grin and gripped her hand tighter. "When we met, I only saw your immaturity. It was what I wanted to see, because setting you up like that let me keep you at a distance." I stared out the windshield. "But what I didn't see then, and what wouldn't let me keep you at arms' length, was your heart."

She drew a long, shuddering breath, but she didn't respond.

"Meghan, your heart is beautiful. It's kind and loving and compassionate. I've seen you with Bridget, and with the rest of the kids in your class, and I've seen you with people in town. You ... you draw them in. And that's because of the person you are."

She shook her head, full out sobbing now.

"You're going to have any future you want. It's all bright and shiny, you know? The world is open to you. I hope you take it and run. I hope you shock the hell out of anyone stupid enough to underestimate you. And I hope that sometimes, you think back on this summer, and me, and you smile. I hope you remember me ... well. Not the raving lunatic, but maybe the guy who took you fishing."

I couldn't say anything else. I reached for the handle that opened my door, but before I could move out of the cab, Meghan grabbed my arm. "Sam. I don't want to leave. I don't want this summer to be over. I don't want *us* to be over. It hurts, and I can't stand it."

I pulled her close to me, my arms tight around her shoulders. "Shhh, babe. I know. But it'll get better. Leaving is hard, but you know you don't belong here. This little town can't hold the future you have. You'll go down to Florida and be with your family, and by the time you're back in Savannah for school, it won't hurt anymore. You have so much to look forward to." I forced myself to try to make the words believable. "And so do I. A lot of work, yeah, but I'm going to have time for fun now, too. You've reminded me of that. So thank you."

I kissed the top of her head and opened my door. "Come on. You need to get a little sleep before you leave. I don't want you nodding off on the road."

I closed my door and struggled to get myself under control

as I walked around the truck. When I reached the passenger's side, Meghan gave me her hand and let me help her out.

I wrapped her into my arms, holding her one last time. I could feel the pounding of her heart against mine, her breasts crushed to my chest. Her tears wet my shirt, and her curls tickled my chin. When her sobs slowed, I leaned back, and gripping her chin, I kissed her with slow surety, pouring everything I'd felt this summer into one last shared touch.

I stepped back, rubbing her upper arms. "Go on inside now. Go to bed and get some sleep." I dared to lift my fingers to her cheek one last time. "Sleep well."

"Sam, I—" She tried to speak, but she was crying too hard. I turned her toward the house, led her up the steps and opened the door. With one last glance, she stepped into the kitchen. I closed the screen, and for a second, she stood there, her hands against the door. And then she turned and vanished into the shadows of the house.

I stalked away, and climbing into the farm truck, I gunned the engine, breaking the silence of the dawn. I didn't stop until I reached the fields farthest from the house. When I got out of the truck, I squatted by the tender shoots of collards and spinach that were just beginning to appear, part of our fall crop. Fingering the leaves, I sat there for a long time, waiting for the smell of the soil and the green fields to give me the comfort it always did.

Today, it didn't work.

Meghan

I HADN'T CRIED THIS hard since Daddy died. I lay in the room which wasn't really mine any longer—after I left, I knew it would go back to being Grandma's—and I wept until I fell asleep. Even then, my dreams were troubled and tumultuous.

Sunlight across my face woke me a few hours later. I rubbed at my swollen, gritty eyes and stumbled out into the kitchen, disoriented. Ali sat at the table, a cup of coffee in front of her.

"Hey." She didn't tease me this morning or even try to make me smile. Instead she stood up and retrieved a mug from the cabinet. She poured my coffee, added milk and sugar and set it down on the table. "Sit."

I obeyed, and she gave me a few minutes to come to life as I drank.

"Thank you." When I could trust myself to speak, I offered her a forced smile. "This is perfect." I took another sip. "Why aren't you at the stand?"

"I told Cassie that I wouldn't be in until later. Bridge and I wanted to see you off." Her eyes were sad, but I saw understanding there, too. Resignation. "I wasn't sure what time you were leaving."

I shrugged. "I guess any time. Everything's pretty much packed."

Ali toyed with the handle of her mug. "Are you waiting for Sam to come home?"

"No." I shook my head. "We already said good-bye. This morning. I can't do that again." I didn't know how I could have any tears left, but they trickled down my face anyway.

Ali laid her hand over mine on the table. "Okay." She hesitated, and I knew she was trying to decide what to say. "Meghan, are you sure about this? I know you and Sam have this no-strings policy, whatever that is, but it doesn't look like it's making you happy. He's been walking around for days like someone shot his dog, and your eyes are so puffy, I can tell you've been doing some hard crying. Something that hurts this much might not be the right decision."

I swallowed back a sob that threatened to break loose. "This is what we both need, Ali. Sam told me this morning. He wants me to leave, and you know, he's right. This is what we agreed to, and changing the rules just because someone changed her mind isn't fair." I met her eyes. "I have to finish school. I have a life waiting for me, outside of Burton."

"I know that, but where is it written that you have to give up one to have the other? Meghan, you go to school forty-five minutes away. That's not exactly a long-distance relationship. And it's only until you graduate. Then you could take up Mrs. Abbott's offer and come back here for good. Did you even tell Sam what she said?"

I gripped Ali's hand. "No, and don't you, either. I won't stay here and hang around like some pathetic little girl when he wants to move on. If he wanted me to stay, he would've told me. You know Sam. There's no beating around the bush."

"Maybe not, but he's still a guy. And sometimes guys speak in a language that we don't always understand. He might not have said the words, Meghan, but I know my brother. He wants you to stay. Or at least not leave for good. He's in love with you, Meghan. It's plain to everyone, except maybe you."

I stared at her, and this time I couldn't fight the tears. "No, he's not. He pushed me away this morning. He told me I had a lot to look forward to, and so did he. He says he's going to have fun now because I reminded him about that. And if that's the only good thing to come out of this summer, then I'm glad." I dropped my forehead onto my hand. "Don't let him crawl back into his hole, Ali. Make him take you out to do stuff. And make him go on real dates, not just skulking around town with whatever woman he's banging at the time."

Ali rolled her eyes. "You're both so blind. I could just smack you. And if you think I can make Sam do anything, maybe you don't know my brother as well as I think you do."

I pushed back my chair. Suddenly, I needed to leave, to make the break, as fast as I could. If I sat here talking with Ali, she'd wear me down, and I'd end up doing something I regretted. Like begging Sam not to let me go.

"I'm going to get a shower and then grab my bags. If I get on the road pretty soon, I can be to the Cove before dark."

I HATED GOOD-BYES. Each time my parents drove me to college, even though I loved being there, I cried when they left. When I'd taken Laura to the train station back in May for her trip to North Carolina, I'd sobbed so much that she said I was never allowed to drop her off for any trip ever again.

Standing in the yard outside the kitchen, with my car loaded up, I tried really hard not to break down when Bridget barreled herself into my legs. "Meghan, I'm going to miss you so much. But I'll send you lots of drawings. I promise."

"Make sure you do." I swept her into my arms, hugged her tight, kissed her round cheek and then set her on the ground. Ali stood next to her daughter, hands tucked into the front pockets of her jeans.

"It's been so much fun, Ali." The tears would not be stopped. "Thank you for being such a good friend to me this summer. Thanks for bringing me to Burton. And for letting me stay here, and feeding me all the good food ..."

"Oh, come here, you crazy girl." She held me tight, rocking a little as I'd seen her do with Bridge. "You know we love you, right? And any time you need a place to go, this is your home, too. For as long as you need it, forever. You hear?"

I nodded. "Thank you. I couldn't imagine a better place to call home." It was true, I realized. The old buildings, the land and every other integral part of this farm had seeped into my veins, and become a part of me. It felt as comfortable as the Tide or the beach.

"You just remember that. And text me when you get to Florida, because I'll be worrying until I hear from you."

"I will." I climbed into the driver's seat and put down the window. Drawing a deep breath, I glanced down the path to the fields, almost willing Sam to appear in the rattletrap old farm truck. When he didn't, I threw the car into reverse.

Ali leaned in the window. "I'm only going to say this one more time. You don't get an unlimited number of chances in life, and I don't want to see you screw this up. If you get down to Florida and realize you've left something essential up here, something like your heart, you hightail it back. Don't let anything stand in your way."

I gazed up at her, and in her eyes, I saw the lingering pain of her own heartbreak. "If you had to do it again, Ali, what would you do different?"

I expected her to say she wouldn't have changed a thing. Instead she gave me a small, tremulous smile. "I'd go with him. I'd leave that day, with just the clothes on my back, knowing that nothing else mattered." She patted my hand where it rested on the door. "There's not a day goes by that I don't regret telling him to leave without me."

She stepped away from the car. I eased up on the brake, letting it roll back and then shifted to drive. With a final wave to both Ali and Bridget, I drove down the driveway and out of their lives.

Chapter
NINETEEN

Sam

I STAYED OUT IN the field until it was nearly dark, just to make sure I didn't run into her again. I didn't know how long she'd slept after I'd left her that morning, and it was possible Ali had talked her into staying later. I couldn't say good-bye again. I'd end up breaking down and begging her to stay.

But when I finally pulled back into the yard, the little blue Honda was gone. I sat for a minute, absorbing it, before I jumped out and went on with my regular routine.

Ali was sitting at the kitchen table when I walked in. I stopped in the laundry room to toss my dirty tee in the basket, but I didn't bother with a clean one.

"I kept some dinner for you." My sister pointed to the foil-covered plate on the counter. "Figured you might be hungry after not eating all day."

I shook my head. "Nope. But thanks. I'm just going to get a shower and go to sleep. It was a long day."

I expected her to fight me on the eating, but she only nodded. "Okay, I'll put it in the fridge in case you want it tomorrow. Sleep well." I turned and was nearly through the doorway when she added, "Meghan just texted me, right before you came in. She made it home safely."

I fisted my hand against the wave of pain. "Good. Thanks for telling me." I climbed the steps and walked down the hallway, passing Bridget's room. She was on her stomach on the floor, drawing with the special pencil and pad Meghan had given her.

"Hi." She waved to me, her small face serious.

"Hi." As tired as I was, I couldn't help stepping into her room to tousle her hair. I looked down at her paper. "Wow, Bridge. That's really good. It's your mama's herb garden, isn't it?"

She grinned. "Yup. Meghan taught me about drawing plants." She glanced back down at the pad. "She's gone. I'm going to miss her so much, Uncle Sammy. It was like having a big sister or something. Like another mom, maybe, but one who didn't make me do stuff."

I reached down to muss her hair. "I know, peanut. But it's okay. School will be starting soon, and then you won't miss her so much." I turned to head for my own bedroom and was two steps down the hall when she called to me again.

"Do you miss her, too?"

I paused but didn't look back. "Yeah, squirt. I do."

Inside my room, the bed looked so inviting that I decided to skip the shower. I'd get one in the morning, and it wasn't like I had to be sweet-smelling for anyone tonight. I took off my pants, leaving them on the floor where they dropped, and crawled between the sheets. Within minutes, I'd fallen into a heavy sleep.

ALI DIDN'T FUSS AT me for anything in the first week after Meghan left. I was so preoccupied that it didn't sink in right away, but then one night I got up from dinner and left my plate on the table. She picked it up and carried it to the sink without a word. I watched her, frowning.

"I left my plate on the table."

She glanced at me over her shoulder, but there was no irritation on her face. "Yeah, you did. It's okay, I got it."

"Why didn't you yell at me? You always yell when I forget to clear my place."

She lifted her shoulders. "It's not a big deal."

"You've been letting a lot of stuff slide the last few days. What's up?"

"What do you mean?"

"I mean, you're letting me get away with shit. I want to know why. Am I dying or something?"

She rolled her eyes. "And how would I know that, Sam? You haven't been to a doctor in years, and I'm no fortune teller."

"Then what's up?"

Ali dropped a bunch of silverware into the dishwasher and slammed the door shut. "You want to know what's up? Okay, fine. I'm trying not to get on your back about anything, because I'm afraid if I do, I'll lose it. I'll go off on you, and I'll say things I shouldn't instead of just minding my own damn business."

I sat back down at the table. "When has that ever stopped you?"

She threw up her hands. "I'm trying to be a different person, Sam. You know, like, growth and improvement? Don't you get that?"

I nodded. "So what do you want to yell at me about?"

"I don't know where to start. Well, let's begin with the fact that you've missed dinner five out of the last six days. You work until it's dark and then you come home and fall into bed. And when you are here, like tonight, thanks to the rain, you're not actually here. You don't talk to Bridge or me, not really. You answer like a robot. And I have it on good authority that you missed a Guild meeting this week for the first time since we lost Mom and Dad."

I frowned. "Yeah, well, the farm's been demanding. I was too tired last Friday to drive all the way into town for the meeting. And I didn't want to sit there and hear them talk, either."

"Sam, you are such an idiot." Ali slammed her hand down on the table. "Everyone sees it but you. Or let me correct that: you see it, but you choose to pretend it's not true."

"What is it that I choose not to see?" I knew, but the roiling in my gut wouldn't let me acknowledge it.

"Meghan. You miss her."

I sighed. "Okay, yes, I miss her. But why is that such a big deal? You miss her, too. So does Bridge. Cassie told me she does, too. Any number of people in town miss Meghan. Why am I an idiot?"

"Because you're the one in love with her, you ass." Ali pulled out a chair and sat down across from me. "You're burying yourself in the farm again, like you did when Mom and Dad died, just to keep from having to think about her. Is it working, Sam? Are you forgetting about Meghan?"

I raked my fingers through my hair. "No, dammit. If you have to hear it, then no. I still see her all over the farm, everywhere we've been. I still expect her to greet me at the sink when I get home from the fields. Want to sit on the porch with her after supper. See her painting in the yard at dawn. But she's gone, Ali. And she's not coming back. We knew that from the beginning, so I need to just get over her and get on with my life."

Ali blew out a breath. "This is why you're an idiot, brother. Because she would've stayed. She didn't have to be gone, not for good. If you'd told her how you felt, she wouldn't have left. Or she would've made you go with her."

I stared at my sister. "I couldn't do that. What if I did tell her, and then she felt sorry for me and stayed out of pity? Or what if she thought she loved me, stayed in Burton, then hated me in a few years for taking that choice away from her? That would kill me, Ali."

I waited for her to argue back, but she only laughed. "Oh, you two are a pair. Do you know what Meghan told me the morning she left, Sam? She said she wouldn't stay here, no matter how much she cares for you, because you didn't want her. I'm not supposed to tell you this, but the school board offered her a job here, part-time during her last year of school and then full time after graduation. She didn't take it because she thought it would be awkward for you to have her around when you're trying to get on with your life."

"She turned them down?" My heart was flipping over in my chest, a glimmer of hope battling with the heaviness that had weighed me down the last week.

"No, she didn't tell them anything definite yet. But only because I stalled her. She won't come back here if she thinks you don't want her." Ali looked at me steadily. "So what are you going to do with that information? You going to sit here and brood until it's too late, and she's out of reach completely? Or are you going to do something for yourself for once in your damn life?"

I rubbed my face. "Ali. . yes, I'm in love with her. But it doesn't change the fact that the farm is here and needs me, and so do you. I have to think about that, too."

My sister gazed down at her hands, fingers twisting. "Sam, do you remember the night Flynn left?"

I drew my brows together in surprise at this abrupt change of subject. "Sure. It was the day after you graduated from high school."

She nodded. "And that night, the night of graduation ... he and I had a huge fight. We were parked down by the lake—oh, don't give me that look. It was eight years ago, and you can't do anything about it now." She made a face at me. "Anyway. Flynn had been talking for months about leaving. Getting out of town after graduation, just the two of us. He'd been working hard to save money, and we were going to travel, to see the world together. But that morning, before graduation, you told me about all your plans for the farm, how well things were going, and how if the two of us worked together, we could save it. We could keep it in the family, just like we'd been hoping."

"Oh, God, no, Ali. Is that why you and Flynn fought? Why you didn't go with him?"

She turned a miserable face toward me. "I couldn't leave you here by yourself. I couldn't abandon you and the farm. I thought—I really thought he'd come back. Or give in. Compromise. I would've traveled with him that summer if he'd promised we'd come back to Burton. But we both said things we didn't mean, and then the next day he was gone."

I reached across to take her hand. "Ali, I'm so sorry. I had no idea."

She smiled at me, but one tear ran down her cheek. "It's old news, Sam. Over and done, and too much time has passed to wonder what might have been. But I don't want you to make the same mistake. Meghan will never give you a her-or-us ultimatum. This isn't the same thing as Flynn and me, because she's willing to become part of your life here. You *can* have both. All you have to do is reach out and take that chance. Don't fuck this up, big brother. Please."

I stood up and pushed my chair in. Ali watched me, curious. "So what's it going to be?"

I grinned down at her. "I think it's time I checked out the beaches in Florida. I hear they're perfect this time of year."

Chapter TWENTY

Meghan

"WHO'S THE CUTEST BOY on the beach? Who's making all the girls check him out?" I bounced DJ on my hip, tickling him under the chin.

"Please, don't remind me." Lindsay, my sister-in-law, ruffled her son's dark hair. "I know he's just a year old, but I see these guys on the beach with the girls making eyes at them, and I think ... if they were looking at DJ like that, I'd want to scratch their eyes out."

I laughed. "You've got some time. But yeah, I think this boy's definitely going to be a chick magnet in about fifteen years." I nuzzled his plump neck. "Don't worry, sweetie. Auntie Megs will keep all the nasty girls away."

"Hey, are you two planning to crimp my son's style?" Joseph came out onto the deck of the restaurant, where Lindsay and I were playing with the baby. He stood behind his wife, wrapping his arms around her middle and pulling her back against him. He growled into her ear, and she giggled, blushing. A pang of loss and longing hit my chest, and I had to focus on standing still, forcing myself to smile again.

"We're looking out for his welfare. We can't have him getting tangled up with some skank." I winked at my brother.

Joseph took the baby from my arms. "Don't worry, kiddo, Dad's got your back. I'll keep the womenfolk in line when you need to check out hot babes on the beach."

Lindsay shook her head. "You're a bad influence, Joseph Hawthorne. Now give me my baby so I can go upstairs and put him down for a nap before the lunch rush begins." She scooped up DJ and headed inside.

"You need any help?" I pulled out a chair, scraping it against the wood of the deck, and sat down.

"Nah, we got this. You don't have to work on your vacation." He laid a hand on my shoulder and squeezed. "You okay, sis? You've been sort of quiet since you got home. Mom's worried."

I rolled my eyes. "Mom worries if we breathe the wrong way. I'm surprised she notices much, though. She's so wrapped up with Uncle Logan."

Joseph leaned against the deck railing. "Yeah, she is. But don't think she doesn't see everything going on." He paused, gazing out over the ocean. "Does it still really bother you? Mom and Logan, I mean?"

I shrugged. "No, not really. I guess it's always kind of a shock, though, you know? While I'm away, I don't have to think about them. Then I get home, and we're in the kitchen at his house, which is now her house, too, and I walk in on the two of them making out in the kitchen, with Mom on the counter."

Joseph winced. "Yeah, that's not a visual I need. But I guess because I'm around them all the time, I'm getting used to it." He ran a hand through his hair. "She's so happy, Meggie. And he would walk across fire for her. His eyes never leave her, and he's always trying to do things to bring her joy. I'm glad about that."

"I guess so." We were quiet for a minute, listening to the

waves break on the shore and the sound of the tourists on the beach.

"But you didn't answer me. What's going on? Did something happen at school? Or this summer?"

I reached behind my back to tie the top of my bikini tighter. "No, nothing happened." I stifled a sigh. "Okay, well, something did happen, but it's nothing. It's over, and I just need some time to move on."

"Aha. And was this something that happened named Sam?"

My eyes flashed to his. "How did you know that?"

Joseph chuckled. "Meghan, I'm not stupid. None of us are. You talk about everyone from Burton, but whenever you say his name, you get this look on your face. This careful, blank look. It's your tell. You did that when you talked about Dad, too, after he died. Like you could control how much you felt."

I crossed my arms on the table and dropped my head into them. "I made a mess, Joseph. I forced him into a no-ties, friends-with-benefits-only summer affair, and then I was stupid enough to go and fall in love with him. And now it hurts, and I miss him, and it feels like nothing will ever be good again."

My brother scooted his chair closer to me and put his arm around my shaking shoulders. "Aw, Meggie, don't cry. It can't be that bad. Did you tell him how you felt?"

I shook my head. "He made it clear from the beginning. He has obligations there, the farm and his sister. He didn't want to get involved with me, but I pushed. And so I got what I deserved."

He stroked my hair, and for one moment, it felt as though my father was standing there. Joseph was so much like him, and the sharp pain of loss struck me all over again.

"I don't think you can know that until you're honest with him about your feelings, Meggie. Wouldn't you rather know than just assume he doesn't feel the same way?"

I sniffled. "If he did, why wouldn't he tell me?"

Joseph rolled his eyes. "If you do, why wouldn't you tell

him? Logic, woman, logic. If the two of you feel the same way, but no one's admitting it, you're both going to be sorry."

I pulled a few paper napkins from the dispenser on the table. "And just how did you get to be so smart about this kind of stuff? Weren't you the one coming to me just a few years ago, crying about girls and love?"

He winked at me. "One, I have a wife. Two, I have a son." His face grew serious, and he added, "And I almost screwed that all up. Every single day of my life, I'm grateful that Lindsay gave me a second chance, after I left her alone and pregnant."

"You didn't know she was," I reminded him.

"No, but that's not an excuse. Everything could've been bad, and it would've been no one's fault but mine. Instead, I have a beautiful wife, the cutest son in the world, and a life that I absolutely love. So I may not be smart about a lot of things, but I know one thing. Love doesn't always give you more than one chance to get it right. You've got to grab it and hold on tight." He looked over my shoulder. "Okay, Sadie's in the window, glowering. Must be getting busy in there." He leaned over and dropped a kiss on my head. "Want me to bring you anything?"

"No, thanks." I shook my head. "I think I'll go lay on the sand for a little bit. Maybe go in the water. See what this vacation business is all about."

Joseph laughed. "Okay, sis. Have fun."

I picked up my beach bag and went down the three steps that led from the deck to the beach. The sand was hot, and I ran toward the water to cool off my feet. The ocean was just the right temperature this time of year: not too cold to swim, and not too hot to enjoy it after being in the sun.

I played in the waves for a few minutes, going in as far as my hips. My first week in the Cove had flown by in a flurry of family get-togethers and catching up with everyone in town. I realized that while I hadn't been lying to Sam about not having friends from high school here, I did have a town full of people who loved me, who cared about how I was doing. It had been fun to hear about everything that had happened this summer and plans for the rest of the year, and to tell them all about teaching in Burton and how much I'd loved it.

I hadn't heard anything from Sam. Not that I'd expected to. I'd sent Ali a text telling her I was home, and she'd responded by telling me that they all missed me already. That had been it. And maybe it was better this way, making a clean break from everyone once and for all.

After floating for a few minutes, I let the surf carry me back to the shore. Shaking water from my hair, I twisted it up and clipped it off my neck, then dried off with the towel I'd laid out in the sun. When I'd stopped dripping, I spread the towel again and laid down on my stomach, letting the sun bake my back.

I was nearly dozing when I felt the cool of a shadow blocking the sun from my legs. I stayed still, hoping whoever was standing next to me would go away.

"So this is the beach."

I scrambled to sit up, trying to get my Wayfarers back in place over my eyes so I could squint into the brightness.

"Sam?" If Santa Claus himself had appeared on the Crystal Cove beach, I wouldn't have been more shocked, but there he stood.

He was wearing shorts, something I'd never seen him in before. They had that crisp, new look, as though he'd just bought them. He stood with his hands on his hips, staring down at me, the same serious expression on his face that I'd grown to love so much.

"Hey, Meghan." He crouched next to me. "Can I share your towel? Ali made me go out and buy shorts and flip-flops, but she didn't think to get me a beach towel."

"Oh—uh, yeah, of course." I moved over, and he sat down next to me, his scent filling my head as his hip bumped against mine.

"This is pretty." He gestured over the ocean and the sand. "I can see why you love it here. I wouldn't want to leave, either."

I licked my lips, nervous. "It's a place, Sam. I love the people here, and yeah, it's beautiful, but then so is Georgia. Especially certain parts of Georgia."

"Yeah." I saw his Adam's apple bob up and down as he swallowed. "And sometimes even the most beautiful places don't mean much without the right people there."

I nodded. "Did you drive all the way to Crystal Cove to discuss scenery, Sam? Or was there something else you had in mind?"

He looked down at me and with one finger, dragged my sunglasses down my nose. "I can't talk to you while I can't see your eyes, Meghan."

I tilted my head. "How come?"

He smiled, and the finger moved from my glasses to my cheek. "Because your eyes tell me everything I need to know. If I'm smart enough to look."

"So what are they telling you now?"

The smile faded from his face. "That you're sad. That maybe you're a little wary about why I'm here."

"I have been sad." I shoved my sunglasses to the top of my head and looked out over the waves. "But I'm not wary, exactly. I'm just ... curious."

He drew in a deep breath. "I drove down here because Ali says I'm an idiot. She says everyone can tell that I'm in love with you, but I'm the only one who can act on it. Who can tell you." He stared into my eyes. "So that's why I'm here. To tell you ... I love you, Meghan. I don't want you to leave. Or more accurately, I want you to come back. I've been miserable without you."

Tears pooled in my eyes. "Did Ali make you come down?"

He shook his head. "No. She only pointed out to me how unfair it was that I hadn't been honest with you." He shifted on the towel, and I could tell he was nervous. "I don't want to pressure you. I just wanted you to know. So you can make an informed decision."

I bit back the surge of joy that was rising in my chest. "Interestingly, I just had a conversation with my brother, during which time he informed me that I needed to tell you how I feel. He says I can't be mad at you for not being open with me if I'm not telling you about my own feelings." I glanced at Sam sideways. "Word is I haven't been the happiest person since I got back here, either."

A smile spread over Sam's face. "I am always in favor of sisters listening to their brother's advice. So you should probably tell me everything."

I swallowed. "I broke our rule, Sam. I didn't mean to, but I did. I fell in love with you, and I don't want to leave you."

Before the last word left my lips, Sam was on top of me, pressing me into the towel. His mouth angled over mine, and his tongue thrust between my lips. I hummed in pleasure as I matched his movements with my own, slipping my hands under his shirt to revel in those muscles I loved to touch.

"Don't ever leave me again, okay?" He kissed down my neck, between my breasts. "And God, Meghan, look at this bathing suit." He glanced up and down the beach. "What if guys saw you in this?"

I giggled, threading my hands through the hair in the back of his head. "Pretty sure they have. This is a beach, Sam. This is what we wear here."

"Nope." He shook his head and covered the exposed slope of my boob with his mouth. "These are for me only. Mine." He held my chin between two fingers. "You understand? You're mine. For always."

I covered his hands with my own. "As long as you understand that it goes both ways." I slid my hands down his body to grip his backside. "Mine. For always."

Sam dropped his head against my shoulder and sighed into my hair. "It's a deal." He pushed up again and looked down at me, brushing a strand of hair from my cheek. "When can I take you home?"

I smiled. *Home*. I realized it didn't matter where that was, because as long as Sam was there, I'd be content.

"I'd like you to meet my mom and Logan. Joseph ... oh, did you meet him already?"

Sam nodded. "Yeah, and his wife, too. Nice people." He wrapped me in his arms, dragging me onto his lap. "And I'll meet anyone you want, but I want to get you alone, too. If we sit out here like this too long, I'm going to embarrass you. Everything shows in these shorts."

I trailed one hand down his stomach. "Everything? I like that idea. You can't hide anything from me."

"Never will." He framed my face. "Meghan, I love you. I want forever with you. I hope forever can be on the farm in Georgia, but if that doesn't work for you, I'll figure out something else. But you come first. Before the farm, before Ali and Bridget. It's you and me."

I leaned in to kiss his lips. "You are my forever, Sam. I can't imagine living anywhere else but on the farm, with your sister and Bridge, but like you said, the where doesn't matter. It's you." I smiled and laced our fingers together. "You're the catch I won't toss back."

He growled low in his throat. "Better not. Because I'll come back for you every time."

I looked up into his face, so filled with love, and I stroked his jaw. "I think I knew from the first time I opened my eyes and looked up at you. It felt like coming home."

He grinned down at me. "I didn't tell you the whole truth, you know. About that first night. I did hear what you said. You looked at me, touched my face and said, 'Oh, it's you.' Like you already knew me."

I held him tight and whispered into his ear. "It *is* you, Sam. It'll always be you."

The End

If you've enjoyed Meghan and Sam's story, don't miss THE POSSE. Spend some time in Crystal Cove and get to know Meghan's family as well as the men who woo her mother in this beach romance.

One woman, three men, and a beach romance as unpredictable as the riptide ...

Being a widow at the age of forty-four was never in Jude Hawthorne's plans. After her husband's death, she's left with her family's beach restaurant and two nearly-grown children. The last thing she's looking for is another chance at love.

However, if her husband's best friends, the Posse, have anything to say about it, love is just what she's going to get. The Posse is determined to take care of Jude, and when they decide the best way to do that is for one of them to sweep her off her feet, three begin to vie for her affections. But only one can reach her heart.

In a story of friendship, loss and second chances, Jude will learn her life is far from being over.

Want to check out Tawdra's other books and keep up-to-date on new releases? You can follow her on Facebook here (https://www.facebook.com/AuthorTawdraKandle), Twitter (@tawdra) and on her website, http://tawdrakandle.com. And the best way to get all the news is by subscribing to her newsletter, (http://bit.ly/ZNrpD9).

Coming in the spring of 2015:

THE FIRST ONE (The One Trilogy, Book 2)

ALI AND FLYNN WERE HIGH school sweethearts. For four years, they'd planned their escape from the small Georgia town where they'd always lived. They wanted to see the world, leaving behind all the sadness and responsibility back at home.

But on graduation day, only one of them hit the road.

Eight years down that road, Flynn is ready to come home. He's a big-shot writer, and he's made most of his plans reality. But he's done it alone. Now he's heading back to Georgia to find out if one last dream can still come true.

Ali's spent those years working hard, raising a daughter and helping her brother keep their family farm alive. Thinking about Flynn and what might have been is a pain she tries to avoid ... even when it's impossible.

Flynn's return brings back feelings Ali thought were long dead and hopes she'd abandoned. Finding their way back to each other will change them forever, opening old wounds and stirring up memories.

Can the first love be the one?

The Ultimate Play List

The *Last* ONE

Man! I Feel Like A Woman! Shania Twain
T-R-O-U-B-L-E Travis Tritt
Chicken Fried Zac Brown Band
Trouble Is Charlie Worsham
Red High Heels Kellie Pickler
Burn Jo Dee Messina
Fishin' In The Dark Nitty Gritty Dirt Band
A Little Mud on the Tires Brad Paisley
Ticks Brad Paisley
It's Your Love Tim MacGraw and Faith Hill
Beat This Summer Brad Paisley

Acknowledgements

This has been a crazy year. Between book events, releases, getting ready to move and not knowing where, all of my friends and book supporters have had to work extra hard just to keep up. I appreciate it so much.

What a thrill and an honor it's been to meet so many readers this year! Whether we've hung out in Daytona, Charleston, Atlanta, New Orleans, Pennsylvania, New Jersey, Orlando or Tampa, I've loved visiting with you all. Thanks for coming out and supporting me.

I'm grateful to the usual suspects for making Meghan and Sam's book possible: Stacey, now of Champagne Formatting, who makes everything so pretty even when I'm flakey about dates; Mandie, who advises, shares, arranges promo and tells me I can do it; and Jen and everyone at PBT who just say yes when I ask for almost anything.

Amanda Long has been my de facto editor for some time now. She is insightful, wicked funny and ruthless; it's the best combination ever in any editor. I am, I think, a better writer and a better storyteller thanks, to Amanda. And I've made her cry twice now, which I count as a win.

A special thank you to my sweet friend Olivia Hardin, whose books I adore, and who has been there to keep me sane. Under the rock is the coolest place to hang.

This gorgeous cover is courtesy of LP Hidalgo of Book-Fabulous Designs. When Stephanie and I decided to try something new, she recommended BookFabulous, and it was a terrific choice. I'm happy to have a few talented artists on my side!

I sometimes thank total strangers for their unwitting help in making a book possible, and for Meghan and Sam's story, I send out a huge thanks to Brad Paisley and Charlie Worsham, whose songs crystallized everything for me. Country music played a big role in the writing of this book. Like Sam says, it's real music about real people. See the play list at the end. And go listen to that music.

On the opposite end of the spectrum from total strangers is my wonderful family, who put up with what I do, with me being away from home and preoccupied with imaginary people when I am at home. I love you all, and I'm excited about our next adventure!

I really do have the best readers ever, and their enthusiasm and encouragement keep me writing. I love the messages, the notes, reviews and posts ... you all rock my world, daily.

About the Author

Photo: Marilyn Bellinger

Tawdra Thompson Kandle lives in central Florida with her husband, children, cats and dog. She loves homeschooling, cooking, traveling and reading, not necessarily in that order. And yes, she has purple hair.

You can follow Tawdra here …
Facebook:https://www.facebook.com/AuthorTawdraKandle
Twitter:https://twitter.com/tawdra
Website: tawdrakandle.com
Newsletter: http://bit.ly/ZNrpD9

Other Books by the Author

The King Series
Fearless
Breathless
Restless
Endless

THE *Posse*

The Perfect Dish Duo
Best Served Cold
Just Desserts

The Seredipity Duet
UNDENIABLE
UNQUENCHABLE

ROMANTIC EDGE BOOKS

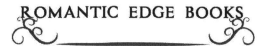

Meet the authors of Romantic Edge Books: Eight Authors Writing Romance with an Edge

If you have enjoyed **The Last One** by Tawdra Kandle, here are some other authors you may enjoy:

Oliva Hardin
Liz Schulte
C.G. Powell
Stephanie Nelson
Melissa Lummis

Other Books from Hayson Publishing

Through the Valley Love Endures by Eddie David Santiago

All for Hope by Olivia Hardin

The King Series by Tawdra Kandle
Fearless
Breathless
Restless
Endless
The Posse by Tawdra Kandle
Best Served Cold by Tawdra Kandle
Undeniable by Tawdra Kandle
Unquenchable by Tawdra Kandle

Imperfection by Phaedra Seabolt

Annie Crow Knoll: Sunrise by Gail Priest
Annie Crow Knoll: Sunset by Gail Priest

Tough Love by Marcie A. Bridges

Haunted U by Jessica Gibson

Made in the USA
Columbia, SC
03 July 2020

13232909R00143